love your library

Buckinghamshire Libraries
0845 230 3232
www.buckscc.gov.uk/libraries

24 hour renewal line
0303 123 0035

		Withdrawn

This book is published by
Grosvenor House Publishing Ltd
28-30 High Street, Guildford, Surrey, GU1 3EL.
www.grosvenorhousepublishing.co.uk

A CIP record for this book
is available from the British Library

ISBN 978-1-78148-505-7

*This book is dedicated
to my wife Ann for her invaluable input.*

My thanks to Ronnie, Keith, Katerina
for editorial, creative and visual effects,
my son Andrew for web page design and daughter
Paula for promotions, a true team effort.

A Message from the Author

I never thought that Book 1 would receive so many excellent comments from children, who took time to e-mail me with such positive feedback, many of whom requested to know, what happens to the infamous Dragon Black.

My grandchildren, the principal characters of Book 1 were invited to develop the adventure and with their input, 'Dragon Black's Revenge' evolved.

Will there be a third book? Only the readers will decide, for the adventure I consider, is now theirs.

Each and Every reader has the opportunity of visiting www.draegonia.com to leave comments and suggestions as to how they believe the adventure may progress and finally end.

Who knows the adventure may well continue into Book 3.

Michael W Libra

Introduction

Dragons of Draegonia Book 1 introduced the Dragons and the Island of Draegonia. An island that undetected can appear or disappear at will, in any part of the World's oceans or seas, never appearing in the same place twice. Draegonia is a mysterious magical island, home to some very special, unusual and unique dragons.

Draegonian Dragons each have their own distinctive colour matching their individual disposition, attitude, role or position. For example Dragon Gold is Mayor, Dragon Blue responsible for law, and Dragon Red in charge of preventing 'Flame Outs'. There are many dragons on the island, but none feared more than the infamous Dragon Black who was finally brought to account for the disappearance and death of more than 170 dragons.

It was only through the skill, strength and determination of four shipwrecked children, who after a terrible storm had been washed up on the island, that led to Black's arrest, trial and subsequent banishment, to face a slow, painful death. (Book 1 The Story Begins)

Dragon Black was ordered to return the four, who were instrumental in bringing him to justice, safely back to their homes. To ensure he did not renege or attempt to do away with them, an explosive anti tamper collar was tightly fitted around his neck. The collar's inbuilt electronic triggering device would detonate its explosive charge should any unauthorised attempt of removal be attempted.

In addition, a specially made chair designed to transport the four was also affixed to Dragon Black's back. The chair, also armed with an explosive charge, could be detonated by a transmitter in the possession of the children.

Dragon Black had no choice but to return them safely home and departing immediately afterwards, searching for a cure to his 'Flame Out', that if not found, would result in his slow and painful death. Black's last snarled words were. "IF THEY THINK THIS IS THE END, WELL IT'S NOT!!"

Chapters

CHAPTER 1

Memories and a Gift.

George was celebrating his fourteenth birthday in style. His cousins Grace, also approaching 14, Joel 12 and Zach soon to be 10, stood looking at the pile of cards and parcels sprawled on the table where a late tea of fish cakes and chips followed by chocolate cake had just been served up. "Wow, look at that lot," Zach cried out as he tucked into a second helping of chocolate cake. "You're getting crumbs everywhere, and don't talk with your mouth full." His sister demanded. "How come he has seconds?" Joel moaned, grabbing the one remaining cut slice left on the plate. George was staring at an envelope that was different from all the rest of his cards. This one was multi coloured and on a type of paper that only the four knew of its significance. "What's that?" Grace wanted to know, as she moved closer, pointing to the rectangular stiff envelope. Her two brothers' stopped eating and stared as George turned the envelope round to reveal no stamp but on its reverse side, a gold seal across its flap. Not containing his enthusiasm any more Zach sidled up to his hero George and in a large voice bellowed "Well open it then."

As George, using a letter opener, unsealed the flap and started to remove the one and only thick piece of parchment from within, he recalled those exciting and death defying moments experienced some years earlier.

George had flashbacks to when the four had not weathered a ferocious storm very well. Their little craft, 'Princess' had

1

floundered and sank in very rough seas, their lives only saved by the boat's life raft that eventually was washed up on the southern sandy shores of the Island of Draegonia.

It was on that island they first met Dragon White, who frightened by the appearance of the four children, had tried to scare them off, but in doing so was shot in the mouth with a safety flare that led to her and all other dragons losing their ability to spit flames.

The memories flooded back as George and his three companions stared hard at the card in front of them. On the green thick parchment, engraved in gold, was a dragon design. The card displayed highly embellished silver words;

Dragons of Draegonia wish George Slayer

A Very Happy Birthday

And by virtue of our powers give to you

One Birthday Wish'.

George flipped the card over and on its rear spotted a number of instructions all related to how his wish may be used. He was about to read out loud just as Joel shouted. "That's fantastic, what are you going to wish for?"

"We need to think about this carefully guys, let's not waste something that obviously is very valuable." George said, hastily replacing the card back in the envelope. "Oh come on, make a wish, I would like a mountain bike," Zach chanted as his sister looked on rather annoyed.

"Zach, its George's gift and it is for George to use, mind you if he wants help making his wish I am sure we could all help hlm." Grace smiled for she knew that when it came to sharing, her cousin would not let them down.

George, eagle eyed, glanced at the three who were now all in deep conversation with each other, making out their wish lists. With a friendly smile and chuckle and pointing to the card, George spoke in a soft voice. "I'm not going to do anything with this, well certainly not today, not until we all agree what would be the right and proper thing for us to wish for." "Oh don't be so boring George," grunted Joel. Zach, listening to the conversation agreed entirely with his sentiments. Grace pointed towards the window where their four rather worn, old bikes were standing against their neighbour's wall. "So let's wish for new bikes, that'll be good eh!" She said with a grin, but not entirely meaning it.

George shook his head, placed the dragon's 'Wish Card' into his inside jacket pocket. "I'll keep this safe for the time being and will let you know what I decide, once I have had chance to think. In the meantime, let's get some music on, our mates will be here soon." Joel needed no more prompting and turned his I-Pod volume up to full blast. The room resonated with the sounds of the latest tracks downloaded from ITunes just as the first of George's friends started to arrive.

CHAPTER 2

Whatever happened
to Dragon Black?

Two Years earlier Dragon Black had dropped off George, the last of the four children transported under duress from Draegonia. He headed eastwards finally turning north into the night's stormy sky. It had started to rain as Black soared high into the air, particles of ice forming on his scaly black armour plated skin, thickening with every 300 meters as he climbed. The four-seater chair strapped to his back became more of a drag as ice rapidly formed all around it. Higher and higher Black flew until it became too cold for any more ice to develop.

Some dragon weeks earlier Black had been sentenced to hard labour moving enormous rocks into the rough seas surrounding the northern rocky beaches of Draegonia, to form breakwaters for a new purpose built lagoon. His 18 hour day on the meanest of dragon rations had made him leaner and much fitter, but without his 'Dragon Flame' and the ability to breathe out life-supporting fire, the icy cold conditions he was now experiencing, were taking their toll.

Gasping for breath he flew higher still, hoping to break into clean, sunlit, warmer air. As he flew higher he felt the explosive collar contracting as a result of the severe cold. The higher he climbed the tighter it became around his very swollen throbbing neck, causing him to occasionally choke. Dragon Black knew his days were numbered. He could not remove the collar, as unlike the chair, it had a self detonation device fitted that could only be released electronically. Black growled, his evil eyes glinting as he recalled it was four children who had designed and fitted both the chair and the life threatening collar contraption.

A struggling Dragon Black flew higher and higher still and reaching a height of seven and a half thousand meters (nearly four miles high) temperatures fell to minus 30C. He now found breathing difficult, almost impossible and every flap of his powerful muscular wings more painful than the last.

All of a sudden, he heard a metallic **clang** that sounded just like the noise made when metal is banged on metal. This was followed by an almost inconspicuous click of an old metal lock parting. **Crack**, a different sound, but this time the sound was followed by a ferocious piercing stab in his belly as one of the metal straps holding the four seater chair broke cleanly away from its locking device. There was another loud crack and a second metal strap broke and with it, the burdensome chair slowly slid, almost in slow motion, to his side. Gaining speed, it fell, tumbling over and over as it hurtled towards the turbulent ocean below, plunging into oblivion.

Black was for a brief moment overjoyed. He could manoeuvre far better, he could fly even higher and the heavy weight of his burden, that caused him so much pain, was gone. If only, he could rid himself of the life threatening collar. But, this would take some ingenuity, as well as luck, if he was to avoid his head being blown off.

The immense cold was still continuing to take its toll as Dragon Black tried to maintain his height above the thickening deep grey and black storm clouds rising upwards towards him. He was tired, cold and exhausted and in order to increase his speed without additional effort, commenced a shallow descent and in a steady glide, headed towards the abyss below.

Descending more slowly through the intense freezing rain, Dragon Black's skin appeared to change from its usual metallic jet coal black colour, to a reflective silvery grey, as sheet ice started to form once more all over his body. It was at this point Black decided he could go no further and dived headlong towards the surface. Suddenly, he broke through the low wet clouds within a hundred meters from the raging seas beneath, when he saw for the very first time, a slow, pulsating, bright flashing light and headed for it.

The light was coming from the top of a tall white concrete structure situated on the highest point of several groups of formidable jagged rocks protruding from the very rough seas. Surrounding what obviously was some form of lighthouse, were numerous, more sem-submerged rocks, broken from view by huge waves whipped up by the winds, cascading all over them. Black headed for a small clearing close to the tall white tower and as he got closer could see the lashing of waves climbing high into the sky before crashing down into foaming white froth below.

Dragon Black had finally found a place to rest, an automated lighthouse far out to sea, requiring little attendance and no lighthouse keeper. Black hugged the slimy, cold and very wet structure, wrapping one large wing around it. This lonely bleak outpost, designed to warn off any approaching vessels from the dangers surrounding it, was for the time being at least the new home of the most fearful dragon of all times.

Black surveyed all about him. He had food, well at least an abundance of fresh fish. Rain water could be obtained from the numerous crevices of the lighthouse, affording some fresh drinking water.

Dragon Black could survive, well for the time being at least. He had found a place to rest, but his thoughts were not for his own wellbeing. They were centred on making plans to get even. Dragon Black settled down for the remainder of the stormy night, howling winds and driving rain making it impossible for any chance of sleeping. Black thought to himself how he would return to Draegonia specifically to wreak havoc on those who had crossed him. But first, how was he to rid himself of the deadly explosive collar? He knew that those on Draegonia held a device that should he appear, could be used to detonate it.

Black's anger continued to fuel his evil thoughts; he knew it would only be a matter of time before he found the island and The Dragons of Draegonia. The time would come when they would no longer need to ask "Whatever happened to Dragon Black?"

CHAPTER 3

A Ruling Overturned

On the Island of Draegonia, time had moved on since the departure of four children perched high on the back of the banished Dragon Black. Elections had taken place and there was now a new Council of Dragons headed up by Dragon Gold.

Dragons White and Cream were still employed to maintain the South and North Beaches, keeping them free of all washed-up debris. Often they would find items they considered to be treasure trove and worth keeping. These were usually washed ashore from ship wrecks or broken containers lost over board from cargo and other commercial vessels. All items were given to the Chief of Police who meticulously kept a log. He then arranged for the treasure trove to be either stored or where appropriate, destroyed those he considered to be of no practical use.

Draegonia was alive with the hustle and bustle of dragons going about their business. Dragon Chez Rainbow, one of Draegonia's leading restaurants had dragons going in and out of the restaurant's main arched doorway, being greeted by a rainbow coloured dragon who growled softly in a French accent.

Dragon Pink, who had been instrumental in returning to all the dragons their ability to shoot flames, was busy assisting Dragon Blue, the Chief of Police, as his clerical administrator.

Dragon Red, the Fire Officer in charge of ensuring dragons had their all-important flames and responsible for re-ignition if lost, was polishing his red fire truck when Dragon Grey appeared. "How is your back today, Dragon Red?" "Much better thank you, those tablets worked a treat, but what brings you here? I am sure it's not to enquire just about my back" Dragon Red quizzically asked. "No, you're right Red; I have been looking at the results of the tests we have made in the laboratories on the virus that resulted in us dragons losing our flames. Apparently the virus was created from heating up a special kind of seaweed that starts a cold like infection, the sneezes of which transmit the disease very rapidly." Dragon Red stopped what he was doing and stood up to his full height and turning to face Dragon Grey asked. "What's the point of doing the research; we found a cure and have eradicated the disease?" Dragon Grey lowered his voice and looked in all directions, ensuring no other dragon close by could over hear, whispered. "We have mutated, you know changed the structure of the virus so that it can be injected or fired in the form of a dart into an enemy, in fact we have developed a true chemical weapon that could be used to defend ourselves with." Red blinked, shook his head and knowingly nodded as he spoke. "Look Dragon Grey, we had real problems last time when the accident occurred and the dangers of such a chemical or biological weapon being manufactured is dangerous and really unthinkable. Who authorised its development?" Grey, once more looked round and moving his head closer still to Dragon Red's spoke in a whisper. "Dragon Brown authorised it with the full knowledge of Dragon Gold. Apparently it is part of the defence strategy agreed by the Council of Dragons last month when both you and Dragon Blue were unfortunately unable to attend." Dragon Red shook his head in disbelief and told Dragon Grey that such an order should not have been approved without all the members of the Council being present and that he would take the matter up with Dragon Blue. Dragon Red packing away his dusters and polish, thanked Grey for providing such important information, assuring that he would not divulge where he had obtained it. Dragon Red finally closed his work shop door and with great haste charged off towards Draegonia's Police Station.

Dragon Pink was finalising her entries, in the 'Beach Combers Property Book' of the washed up items found on the beaches by Dragons White and Cream that morning;

1 Life Belt Ring with the name Princess.
2 Two fire extinguishers.
3 11 Plastic bottles that used to contain water.
4 10 assorted aluminium cans (contents unknown).
5 1 Plastic bucket. And clear thick plastic tubing.
6 1 Sealed and locked water proofed packing case with a half peeled label depicting incomplete words of, orks display unit, p dry.
7 3 Short lengths of rope.
8 2 Very large blue crystallised glass bottles, empty.
9 4 Reels containing heavy duty nylon and waxed cord fishing lines.
10 Packets of assorted hooks.
11 Wooden Box marked 'Ophthalmic', containing an assortment of optical lenses and mirrors.

"The rubbish that gets washed up these days, it's a pity that humans don't take more care of the environment." She stated out aloud so that Dragon Blue could hear. "Quite right Pink, but without all the flotsam and jetsam that arrives on our beaches, we would not be able to make those little luxuries we are used to and at least we can recycle most of the items, so there really is little wasted." Pink nodded, closed the book and gave a warm smile to Dragon Red who a little out of breath, entered.

"Blue, did you know about the 'Chemical Warfare' weapon that the Council of Dragons authorised to be researched and developed at the Draegonia Hospital Laboratory?" Red breathlessly garbled out. Dragon Blue somewhat calmer than

Dragon Red came from behind his desk and beckoned Dragon Red to have a crouch (dragons very rarely sit). "There must be some mistake." Blue retorted. "Why would we be developing such a weapon, who or what would it be used against and ....." Blue was hastily interrupted by Dragon Red. "I have no idea," he said, "but it has been developed, it was ordered by the Council of Dragons and neither you nor I were consulted about it." A somewhat annoyed Dragon Blue picked up the 'Dragon Communicator' and blew into it. 'Dragon Communicators' consisted of an ear piece and a hand-held air phone, each with tubes attached that directly entered into the cave wall connecting to the 'Dragon Communications Exchange'. A gruff growl could be heard asking Dragon Blue who he would like to speak with. "Get me Dragon Gold, and be quick about it," Blue demanded.

Following a short pause and lots of wheezes and blowing noises, Dragon Gold's voice was heard to announce. "Mayor Gold here, how can I help, Dragon Blue?" Dragon Blue restated what he had learnt without indicating who or where he had obtained the information from. "So," Blue summed up. "Have I got the facts right and if so who is going to be responsible for the safe keeping of such a dangerous weapon?" Dragon Gold was heard to cough, nervously realising that perhaps the Council of Dragons had sanctioned a ruling without full attendance, a serious error of protocol. "I can only apologise" Gold said. "You are quite right both you and Dragon Red should have been counselled but as it would have been a majority decision in any event, your non-attendance did not seem important at the time." Blue, with a throat curdling growl retorted quite angrily. "That's no defence Gold; the Council has overstepped their authority. If Dragon Red and I had been at the meeting I am sure we would have demonstrated the foolishness of developing weapons that could be used against us." Dragon Blue, now quite irate, continued. "And I wish to call an urgent meeting with all Council members to discuss this matter in more detail, before we allow any more catastrophes, how soon can we meet?" Blue, listened for a few moments then wishing Dragon Gold a good day, replaced the 'Dragon Communicator' and turned to Dragon Red. "He has confirmed and agreed a time and date, the Council of Dragons will meet in two dragon days at ten in the morning." Dragon Red acknowledged the information and without further discussion nodded his head and saying farewell to both Dragons Blue and Pink returned back to the Fire Station.

The Council of Dragons had always held their meetings within the Hall of Dragons, Draegonia's centre of administration overlooking the main square. Accessed by several steps between two very tall ornate columns the main entrance led through to a labyrinth of corridors and tunnels feeding from the centre, the largest of all caves, the Great Hall.

The Great Hall was once overseen by the infamous Dragon Black who used to perch high on the centre plinth, growling out orders, sending frightened dragons in all directions to do his bidding. Today, the Great Hall had some serenity about it. It was no longer dark but illuminated by several huge glass chandeliers made from washed up glass bottles that had been treated with dragon heat making them look very much like crystal glass. In each of the slim crystal glass mouths were small cuts of rope, their ends floating and sucking up 'Dragon Flower Oil'. The flames from the makeshift candles burnt brightly, giving off little smoke but sweet smelling aromas of the island's multitude of varied scented flowers.

Crouched around the oval stone table beneath the tall plinth were the seven appointed dragons who made up the Council of Dragons. Situated at the far end next to Dragons Mauve and Purple was Dragon Gold who, acting as Chair Dragon, quickly brought the meeting to order.

"This is a special meeting, convened at the request of Dragon Blue, but before we commence with the business at hand, I would like to offer my and the Council's apologies for passing legislation concerning the 'Flame Out' chemical, without either Dragon Blue or Dragon Red being in attendance." Dragon Red said nothing but frowned and shook his head in annoyance. Blue, stern faced, stood up. "The apologies are accepted but let's get down to the important issue at hand. I understand from my investigations that this chemical has already been perfected. I also am given to believe that it has been specifically engineered to be administered in the form of a dart. Is that correct?"

Dragon Gold, in some embarrassment, nodded. Dragon Red, containing himself no longer, jumped up in support of his close friend and demanded. "So where is this chemical weapon right now? Who is responsible for its safety and how much of it has been made?"

"Enough, crouch down both of you." An authoritative voice bellowed. It was Dragon Brown who had raised himself up to his full height to speak. "Let me answer those questions Dragon Red. Firstly the chemical that has been developed is still held under secure guard at the Draegonia Hospital Laboratory. The chemical has a virus base and has only been cultivated to produce no more than 100 darts, the tips of which are still under development as they have not performed well under test conditions. These, when ready, will be transported to the military camp for future safe keeping."

Dragon Red on hearing this immediately banged the table with a clenched claw, once more stood up and growled furiously. "This is wrong; we have made a weapon of considerable consequence and are willing to pass it over to the military for **their** safe keeping." He paused then added, "**And** for their obvious use." Brown in angry response also banged furiously on the table and raised his voice for all to hear whilst focussing a steely gaze on Dragon Red. "Dragon Red, you're implying that I, who represent Draegonia's military, have a hidden agenda, that I cannot be trusted and am unable to guard or keep our weapons safe?"

Gesturing for Dragon Brown to return to his crouched position, Dragon Blue stood up once more and moved closer in support of Dragon Red and roared. "Before we all get too heated to see common sense, let me make a suggestion. We have several cells that must be considered the most secure places within Draegonia. We could make the deepest cell into a containment area thus providing safe and secure storage. Access will be through one door only and this to be secured by three independent locks. Each lock would have a different key each to be held by three council approved appointees."

The six dragons listened intently as Blue continued. "I suggest one key should be held by Dragon Brown on behalf of the Military. The key for the second lock could be held by Dragon Gold on behalf of the Council of Dragons. The key for the last remaining lock would be held by me on behalf of Draegonia's Police force."

Dragon Gold, who wanted the issues to be dealt with speedily and without dissension, quickly passed his eyes over the attending dragons and quietly but with some authority brought the meeting to order. "Excellent solutions Dragon Blue, all in favour raise your paws." Five dragons were quick to raise their paws followed by a more hesitant Dragon Brown. Recognising that a unanimous vote had been successfully achieved, Dragon Gold thrashed his glittering gold tail three times. The flicks of his tail made loud cracks; the echoes reverberated through the many corridors and tunnels leading from the Great Hall. Dragon Gold had in traditional manner signified both the approval of the proposal and the end to the extraordinary meeting.

The six dragons swiftly returned to their individual caves, not realising the significance or future consequences of their actions.

CHAPTER 4

A Birthday Gift

Time passed, with the Island of Draegonia appearing, disappearing and reappearing several times in different oceans and high seas of the world.

Dragon Pink, who had been the only Dragon of Draegonia not to have had her wings clipped having reached the age of flying maturity was, at last, beginning to make small flights, her wings strengthening by each dragon day.

Pink was fortunate. No dragon other than the banished Dragon Black had been allowed or able to fly and the skills necessary had unfortunately been lost over centuries. But today, she was being trained and assisted by Dragon White, who every time Pink crash landed, would offer encouragement and advice.

Pink's flight distances improved the more she practiced. "You know," White exclaimed, "It won't be too long before you will be able to fly nonstop, completely round the Island." Pink just grinned, nodded and with a friendly soft growl, flapped her small wings and said, "Yes, but with my sense of direction where would I end up, most probably burning my tail on top of that Volcano?" Both Dragons looked towards the centre of Draegonia where soft greyish white plumes of smoke, interspersed with the occasional flash of orange heat, were drifting skywards from the volcano's impressive mouth. Both dragons thought back to an earlier time, recalling someone special, who with his three cousins had evaded volcanic death and had made Draegonia a safer place to live, was in a few days, going to be celebrating a 14th Birthday.

Turning to Pink, Dragon White cocking her head to one side said. "Before you say anything, I know it's George's birthday in a few days time. Have you sent a gift or a card Dragon Pink?" Pink looked uneasy and placing a claw-like hand to her mouth replied. "Oh dear, I nearly forgot and after what he and his friends did for us." Pink thought for a moment then with a sparkle in her eyes cried out. "I'll make it up to him as we do have a little time." "What are you going to send and how are you going to get it to him?" White asked. Pink gave a wry smile and in a soft secretive voice retorted. "I have something that has been in my family for a very, very long time. It is a magical gift, that by writing the name of the recipient on it, will find its way to them." White listened knowingly, then with some excitement asked. "So what's the gift is it what I think it is?" Pink nodded excitedly. "Yes, the *'Wish Card'* which has been in my family for centuries and as you're aware, is only one of its kind." Pink continued. "It is so special that only those with good hearts and true thoughts can make use of it." White listened on. "The 'Wish Card' allows only for one wish and once made the wish cannot be changed. Also the 'Wish Card' cannot be used for evil or harm and I know that George is the right person to receive it." White nodded, her eyes sparkling in agreement, "You know Pink you have a good heart yourself, there are few Dragons who would give away such a valuable magical gift." Pink just grinned, she knew that the gift she was bestowing would be used for good and although she may never see her friends George, Grace, Joel and Zach again, still knew they would all benefit.

On returning to her pink cave embedded in the lower side of the mountainous volcano, she opened up a concealed compartment from within her cave wall and removed a special card-like material and envelope. As she carried both items to her desk, brightly coloured pinpricks of light seemed to dance around them, the edges of the card glowing red then orange, blue, yellow and silver. With her razor edged claw she carefully engraved a message on its rear and on the front inscribed;

Dragons of Draegonia wish George Slayer

A Very Happy Birthday

And by virtue of Dragon Magic give to you

One Birthday Wish'.

Pink lit a small oil based lamp and took from the compartment a wedge of gold wax like material. She placed the 'Wish Card' in the envelope, stuck the flap down, heated the wax stick and allowed the hot gold gel to slowly fall, sealing the bottom edges of the flap with a perfectly thick round layer of the dragon seal. Pink closed her eyes and placing the tip of her needle pointed claw in the centre of the now hardened seal, spoke a few words that only dragons knew their significance. When she had finished, a blue glow started to emanate from the seal, turning white and pink as it grew larger, then it seemed to sparkle throwing small yellow star shapes all around the envelope. The envelope, unaided, began to rise up from the table, where Pink had placed it. For a brief moment it just hovered then, in a blinding flash, disappeared. An undaunted Dragon Pink blew out the light used to melt the magic wax and quickly exited back onto the main street of Draegonia. Pink looked towards the East and in a quiet, softly-spoken voice said, "Good luck George, Happy Birthday and use your wish well."

CHAPTER 5

Freedom at Last

A number of human months had now passed AND Dragon Black was still using the seclusion and cover of the numerous rocks and lonely lighthouse outpost as his temporary home. Black had three dilemmas. The collar round his neck held a high explosive charge that if opened without the correct electronic device emitting the right radio frequency, his evil looking head, would be blown right off. He shuddered at the thought. His second more urgent concern was the fact that he had been without his 'Dragon Flame' for nearly two years and that dragons invariably never survived more than five years after such a loss. Then there was his third dilemma, how was he to locate The Island of Draegonia? These problems fuelled Black's ever growing hatred, driving him on each day to search for answers. The collar was a problem he could not address as he had no idea how he was going to safely remove it. However, the more urgent matter and a problem he could address, was the preventing or at least the slowing down of his inevitable death, as a result of losing his 'Dragon Flame'.

Dragon Black knew that 'Dragon Flames' fuelled their bodies giving them energy, much like the heat required by a hot water boiler. The hotter the flame the more energy produced to heat the water. But allow the flame to die, the water would soon turn icy cold, much like Dragon Black's blood. For without the energy from his nonexistent flame his body would eventually die. His one aim was to survive and his plan was clever if simple.

During the day, in the heat of the sun, Dragon Black lay outstretched, motionless, apart from the movement of his head as he caught the unsuspecting flying fish passing by his veracious mouth. Dragon Black blended in well with the spiky coal-like blackness of the jagged rocks, his jet black skin difficult to differentiate from a distance. The heat from the sun was absorbed through his skin fuelling his body for the night's work that lay ahead.

As dusk approached, Dragon Black rose up, stretching his body and powering up his gigantic wings. Every night he soared high into the air searching for the Island of Draegonia and those who had sentenced him to a life of misery. Each night Black flew in a different direction, extending his range to the limits of his endurance thinking how he would get even with those who had caused him so much pain and suffering. Black's thoughts centred on how one day he would locate Draegonia, how he would get even with all the dragons and how once more he would regain his rightful role of leader. He smiled as the thoughts of having all dragons bowing down to him as his slaves were pictured in his mind's eye.

The island was of course difficult to find. It would only appear in one location once and even then it would be shrouded in a magical mist making it impossible to see except through dragon eyes and especially the piercing fiery eyes of Dragon Black, that were more than able to penetrate such mist.

Black had been searching for the island every night for almost two long years and knew that even with his method of absorbing the energy from the sun; he was only delaying the inevitable. Then, one evening, a series of events happened to change his luck. It started with a storm so ferocious that it reminded Black of a similar storm some years earlier that triggered events leading to his current predicament.

The seas were violently erupting; the dark clouds forming a black canopy across the sky broken only by the numerous flashes of forked lightening illuminating the hostile and deadly rocks that were reaching out of ferocious seas for their prey. As the howling winds increased their strength the waves became steeper and more violent, crashing hard against the rocks throwing large plumes of spray against the one and only refuge, the lighthouse with its concentrated beam of revolving white light desperately penetrating the enveloping blackness of night, now obscured by Black's presence.

Then it happened just as Dragon Black was about to hurl himself headlong into the hurricane force winds. Two very bright white lights appeared somewhere in the distance, followed by two explosive bangs. The white hot lights soared high into the ever lowering stormy sky disappearing into ever thickening clouds. Then, one by one the lights reappeared and as they did so their colour changed from the dazzling white, to a fiery red, then into a hot orange with grey smoke like tails trailing from behind as they sank towards the cauldron of the whipped-up sea.

Black's eyes narrowed, squinting because of the driving rain, it was difficult to see. What were these lights? Where were they coming from? Then it happened again, another flash as a third rocket propelled skywards exploding with a white flash disappearing into the Cumulus Nimbus (Thunder Storm Clouds). As it climbed higher it seemed to pause, then changed colour, a bright red.

Black expanded his huge wings and with one enormous flap shot skywards breaking into the wet cold and turbulent air towards the glow. Within minutes he could see that the orange light was descending slowly on what looked like a small umbrella. Little did he realise that this was a distress flare carried high into the sky by a rocket then lowered by a parachute to provide maximum time to be seen. Black was not impressed and with his left wing destroyed the distress flare with one swipe, hurling it at speed to the waters below.

Black followed and breaking through the cloud saw something being tossed by the huge 80 foot waves. It was a ship. A tanker that had obviously been driven in rough sees towards the rocks surrounding the lighthouse. Then again two more rockets shot into the sky illuminating the decks of the stricken ship that he believed had lost total engine power and was floundering in the rough seas.

None of my business, Black thought, let them get on with it. Black was just about to depart when he saw three small figures running across the washed decks heading for the life boats, one of which was being lowered. The figures were shouting and waving at each other frantically urging all to abandon ship. Some were using two way hand held radios linking them with the Captain who was still in the Wheel House (Bridge). Little did Dragon Black know how his luck was about to change.

Several things happened in succession, each contributing to the freeing of Dragon Black from his self imposed imprisonment on the rocks. The handheld VHF radio transmitters had revolving dials that altered their frequencies and when matched could communicate with each other user. In the emergency that was unfolding several frequencies were being used by different crew members. Some were talking on the aircraft distress frequency 121.5 MHZ sending out May Day messages of position, type of vessel, number on board and nature of the emergency. Others were on alternative VHF channels 16 (156.8MHz) for maritime use. Others were using different frequencies. Some were in contact advising the Captain of the damage others talking to the few remaining crew in the engine room who were trying to man the pumps to expel the ever increasing water level, flooding the ship. The combination of different frequencies being used and the proximity of Dragon Black made what seemed impossible, possible.

There was a tingle in Black's neck, followed by a sharp clicking noise as the collar round his neck unlocked. Black felt the collar loosen then with the clasp fully undone it slipped from his neck, hurtling towards the deck of the stricken tanker floundering below.

The collar struck the iron deck at a point close to the tanker's venting pipes used to release pressure within the oil filled compartments. As the collar collided with the active vent there was an explosion. Sheets of flame shot high into the sky, smoke enveloped all around. Black grinned, he had been set free. His good fortune was however yet to continue. The explosion from Black's collar had made a significant hole in the tanker's walkway with flaming oil gushing out, spreading mercilessly across the wide deck.

One life boat and been launched, the second still slung ready and waiting for the Captain and his two officers, who were both frantically running towards it.

As they covered the 100 metres to the safety of the life boat neither were aware that decks had been breached, releasing from its cargo hundreds of thousands of gallons of lethal oil.

Both officers, pointing emergency flare guns into the sky fired simultaneously letting off their ballistic charges just as Dragon Black appeared overhead, mouth wide open as he laughed at the commotion and distress of all on board.

His laughter was short lived. Both projectiles from the guns crashed into the roof of his open mouth just as a pressurised fountain of hot oil from the gaping hole of the tanker followed, filling Black's mouth fully with crude oil. The ballistic missiles then exploded, both at the same time. Black more by shock than injury, with open mouth, was propelled backwards away from the gushing oil, wings splayed out, stopping for a moment in mid air. Then he felt it. A searing white hot heat that made his mouth glow, his teeth becoming red hot his tongue swelling up to three times its normal size. Then losing all momentum of flight he tumbled over and over heading towards the stricken craft now devoid of crew and life crafts below.

Dragon Black crashed into the middle of the oil furnished blaze and gasped for breath as more flames from the deck's cavernous inferno entered his mouth. The pain was excruciating and letting out an almighty roar Dragon Black expelled a powerful brilliant red and white flame from his evil mouth, almost half the tanker's length. Black's flame, through a combination of coincidences, had been restored. The freak accident, the ship's handheld radios, the ballistic safety flares and the hot flaming oil from the cargo had all contributed to the removal of Black's collar and the restoration of his 'Dragon flame'.

Black stood up, shook himself, let out another burst of fire from his mouth watched from their life boats in amazement by 16 survivors of the stricken tanker that was now slowly sinking into raging seas. Dragon Black ignoring the small boats and their insignificant occupants soared skywards. He was back with a vengeance and with renewed energy his one and only objective was to find the Island of Draegonia and the dragons who he intended to get even with.

CHAPTER 6

A Big Mistake

"It's just not right," said Dragon Red as he handed Dragon Blue the petition for signing. Blue took the wad of signatures and thumbed through the pages. "It looks as though everyone has signed them then Dragon Red." "Yes." He replied "But it is still not right, why won't Dragon Gold just issue an order to destroy forever, those darned darts that could destroy us dragons?" Dragon Blue carefully put his signature to the list and shrugged his shoulders. "Look it's no good complaining. All we have to do is present this petition at the next Council of Dragons meeting and insist that all weapons designed to kill dragons are outlawed." Dragon Red nodded in agreement. "So when is the next meeting date planned for?" Blue thumbed his 'Dragon Diary' but before he could answer Dragon Pink piped up. "It is next Dragon Tuesday 1500 hours; I have already put it into your diary Dragon Blue." "Most efficient," Blue responded closing his diary and placing it upon his table that was covered in 'Dragon Parchments', keys, 'Dragon chains' and old files. "Now if you will kindly leave me to get on Dragon Red, I'll see you at the meeting."

Dragon Red grunted and with a wave of his bright red clawed hand trotted off towards his cave. He could do no more until the meeting except make sure that he had as many signatures as possible to demonstrate to the Council the importance of the destruction of the 100 darts locked away in the darkness of Dragon Blue's adapted but secure cell.

Dragon Tuesday arrived like any other day on Draegonia. Warm breezes rustled the leaves of trees; the sun casting shadows in the mid afternoon sun as seven senior Dragons once again took their positions around the table within the Great Hall. Calling the meeting to order Dragon Gold read out the minutes of the last meeting that called for the appointment of an assistant doctor, new dragon books for the dragon school, more help for the completion of the lagoon in the north of the island and the instruction to Dragon Red to elicit opinion regarding the recommendation that all chemical weapons aimed at killing or maiming dragons be destroyed. "Dragon Red," Gold looked directly into Red's eyes. "Have you completed the survey of opinion to the agreed question we directed you to ask?" Dragon Gold paused then looking at a copy of the questionnaire read out aloud.

"The Council of Dragons hereby decrees that every dragon residing on Draegonia be given the opportunity to provide their opinion and or answer to the following questions.

1) *Do you agree that weapons (chemical or other) that are designed to maim, kill or remove 'Dragon Flames' be developed specifically for the defence and security of Draegonia and its inhabitants, provided that such weapons are kept under strict control and made secure by the Council of Dragons?*

YES   *NO*

2) *If you do not agree to the above do you specifically wish to see such weapons banned from future development and the full destruction of any weapon produced and or stockpiled?*

YES   *NO*

Dragon Gold put the parchment down and asked Dragon Red to report the findings of the survey. Dragon Red slowly rose from his crouched position and picking up his report and supporting statistic sheet read out aloud.

"Draegonia has a population of 127 dragons, all of which have been individually approached by me and given the opportunity to answer the approved questions; I report the findings as follows."

Dragon Red removing the front page of his report, carefully placed it on the oval table, revealing the sheet of statistics beneath. Dragon Red continued,

"The results of our survey and independently verified by Dragon Blue is as follows. Out of the 127 dragons, 32 were under the dragon *age of *voting*.

Of the 95 dragons with votes 16 abstained from giving their opinion on the basis they considered they were not qualified to do so.

Of the 79 remaining 11 answered yes to question 1, with 68 answering No.

Of the 68 who answered no to question 1, 53 answered yes to question 2 with the remaining 15 answering NO."

Dragon Red paused for breath, but before anyone could raise a question continued;

"Of the 15 who answered No to question 2, the majority felt that some weapons should be developed but perhaps to their

---

*Dragons do not get the vote until they have reached 250 Dragon years.

design stage rather than their full manufacture or production, on the basis that perhaps one day Draegonia might have a need to be defended.

The conclusion is that the vast majority of the Dragons of Draegonia wish to see the existence of current chemical weapons fully destroyed and no further research work in their manufacture take place."

Dragon Red crouched down and waited for a response from the six other dragons that had become very silent. Dragon Blue was the first to speak.

"I think we owe a vote of thanks to Dragon Red for the time and effort he has put into the survey, indeed visiting every dragon...." Before Dragon Blue had time to continue his praise, Dragon Brown extended himself to his full height and angrily raised his voice. "This is ridiculous, you're all going to allow this island to be defenceless, something that as Commander in Chief of the Army I cannot condone." Dragon Onyx nodded in agreement with Brown's outburst, as he was one of the fifteen concerned about Draegonia having no weapons at all. "I agree," he said. Another voice interjected. "Please sit down Dragon Brown." Gold pointed to where Dragon Brown slowly sank to his crouched position but still looking very annoyed. "I understand," Dragon Gold continued. "Your frustration and concerns for the welfare of us all are fully appreciated, but we are a democratic island and having got rid of a ruler who dictated to us all what we could and couldn't do (he was referring to the banished Dragon Black) I have no desire to impose upon our island any dictates that the majority of dragons disagree with." Dragons' Mauve and Blue thumped the table. "Quite right" said Dragon Mauve. Blue in support interjected, "Yes the Dragons of Draegonia have made their wishes abundantly clear Brown and we should act accordingly."

A lengthy discussion ensued with all dragons attempting to sway Dragon Brown's views and opinions, when finally; Dragon Gold stood up and demanded silence. "Dragons of the Council, it is herby decreed that all weapons held in store, designed to kill, maim dragons or remove 'Dragon flames' be destroyed, please advise me your recommendation how this might be done in the most expedient and safest way." Dragon Gold waited for an answer. There was again silence, broken by a cough from Dragon Brown, who arose to his feet. "As much as I am against this order I believe it be sensible to ensure that the weapons we refer to, and let's be clear about this they are the 100 chemical darts designed to remove 'Dragon Flames', be destroyed by fire. I therefore recommend that in front of all Dragons of Draegonia, they be cast into the fiery furnace of our Volcano." Dragon Brown returned to his crouched position and waited for a response. Each dragon nodded their approval and after waiting for any other comment, Dragon Gold once more stood up and made the official announcement.

"This meeting is brought to order and the agreement is made and fully endorsed by the Council that on Dragon Saturday week at the fullness of the sun all Dragons of Draegonia will attend Volcano Peak to witness the destruction by fire of the chemical weapons currently stored in Draegonia's Police Head Quarters. I further declare that Dragon Blue and Dragon Brown will meet with me at 1100 Dragon Hours with their keys, in order that we might access the secure cell where these items are held. We shall then convey the weapons to Volcano Peak to be incinerated. All in agreement please signify."

The dragons all raised their tails and thumped the ground once followed by Dragon Gold who with his tail thumped the floor three times and in a loud voice proclaimed. "It is agreed and this meeting is now closed."

The next day the news of the Council of Dragons decision resounded round the Island with dragons all discussing the merits of the actions that had been agreed. To be informed that all dragons were commanded to attend the destruction by Volcanic Fire was a major event as in the past such actions were usually confined to some poor dragon being thrown into the volcano at the express command of Dragon Black. How things had changed and significantly changed for the better. No more executions, no more threats and soon no more weapons considered lethal against dragons. It was no wonder that all the dragons were smiling, happy and feeling good.

CHAPTER 7

The Return

Dragon Saturday came and with every dragon heading for the top of the Volcano's lofty peak, the track leading up to it became busy and congested. Some dragons had decided to make a celebration of the day and took with them hampers of food and dragon wine. Others had made special dark glasses to protect their eyes, from what they expected to be an explosive glare once the chemical weapons were tossed into the volcano's veracious mouth. Some were carrying 'Dragon Cameras,' devices that took images through complex lenses, painting them onto special paper.

During all the hustle and bustle and excitement three of the Council of Dragons, each with their special keys, approached the inner sanctum of the Police station and its cells. One cell in particular, the darkest and dampest of all, was situated at the end of a long dimly lit corridor, protected by its heavy iron gate, secured by three enormous locks that had been taken from washed up treasure chests of bygone years. The gate's huge rusty iron hinges were firmly embedded into the hardened rock wall. "Bring that light closer will you Dragon Blue, I can't see a thing." Dragon Gold was trying to find the lock that his key fitted but in the darkness was also finding it difficult to focus. "Here let me open the lock." Blue offered to help, taking Gold's key from him. Dragon Gold's lock was quickly released followed by Dragon Blue inserting his own key and undoing the second of the three locks. "Move aside Dragon Blue let Dragon Brown access the last and remaining third lock," Gold ordered. Brown turned the key and as he did so memories flooded back of the time he had been thrown into the very same cell on the orders of Dragon Black. "Come, come get a move on." Dragon Gold said, hurriedly pushing past the other two. "Where is it then" he continued, "I can't see much in this light, shine the lamp over there."

Dragon Gold was frantically searching the cell but could only make out a dragon bed and small dragon table and nothing else. Dragon Gold took a deep intake of breath then coughed as the stale and musty air hit his chest. "Oh goodness it's gone!" Dragon Blue just laughed at Gold's outburst. "Of course its not gone, we are the only ones who have the keys, this place is the most secure on the island and I know where I put the package." Dragon Blue moved out of the flickering light into the darkness of one of the corners and bent over, grabbing a paper bag that had become quite damp. Inside were the 100 darts loosely tied together in a bundle. "Ahh, here they are." Dragon Blue cried out swinging round to see the others staring at him. There was a feint squelching noise of damp and wet paper parting as several of the darts fell to the floor. "Oh do be careful," ordered Dragon Brown standing with an open casket made especially for the containment of the darts and their final journey to their destruction. Dragon Brown continued to bark out his orders, "Pick them up put them in here and be careful not to stab yourself, remember those darts are lethal! They will remove your flame instantaneously even with the slightest prick of your skin."

Dragon Blue gingerly felt round the floor, his claw hand shaking somewhat nervously at the thought of being scratched or pricked. "Here," he said passing the bulk of the contents of the broken bag to Dragon Brown. "You put them in that box of yours whilst I pick up those that have fallen on the floor." Dragon Blue counted each one, as he gingerly lifted each between two claw tips. Four, Five, SIX, that's all of them." Blue was just about to turn away from his task when he spied one like hand and with clenched claws, in one swift movement, sharply brought it down signifying for Dragon Blue to push the casket into the fiery furnace below. As the casket toppled into the mouth of the volcano, exploding with a resounding bang and flashes of brilliant red, orange and white hot flames, a tremendous cheer went up from the audience of dragons. Music was struck up by the Rainbow Quartet with a rendition of Dragon Hendrix's 'Fire'. Dragons continued to applaud, others chatting together with great gusto, the party was now in full swing. Dragon Gold climbed down from his seat of authority and was immediately surrounded by dragons patting him on the back. Dragon Blue was also engulfed by congratulating dragons, whilst Dragon Brown, was.......

Brown was staring high into the sky, a shiver running down his spine, his tail nervously vibrating not believing what was heading towards him. No it must be an optical illusion, he thought. A shadow created by the fiery greyish black smoke, wafting upwards into the late afternoon sky. But this was no shadow and it was growing larger by the second.

The sun was for a few more seconds blotted out as the shadow fleetingly passed in between it and the congregation of dragon onlookers. Brown did not have to think any more. He knew, as streams of terrifying flames shot out of an angry, ferocious, and snarling mouth, scattering dragons in all directions, creating absolute pandemonium that signified in no uncertain terms, that **Dragon Black had returned.**

CHAPTER 8

Black Threatens Pink

Black's fury and rage gave no quarter; he swooped and dived on all around him, blasting those who could not hide with fearsome flames. Dragons rushed forwards in an attempt to protect others but were no match for Dragon Black's fire power. None of the dragons could fly and could only scurry to and fro as Black circled time after time showering those beneath with his terrifying red and white scorching flames. Many dragons quivered in fear, others ran off to hide and those brave enough to stand their ground were clinically dealt with. Black showed no compassion, no mercy and with full force of his fire power turned his frightened unarmed pray into smouldering charcoal dragon statues.

Dragon Brown spat a couple of significant bursts of his own flame but as its fiery tip approached Dragon Black, he just flapped his enormous wings, soaring high into the sky out of harm's way, only to dive back down again hurling more torrents of powerful white, yellow and red hot flames.

Dragons Blue, Gold and Brown tried valiantly to protect those closest to them but could offer little resistance, they were just not in Black's frightening league. The time he had been away living off of fish and exercising every night searching for them had made him leaner, meaner and physically more powerful than before.

Of course, it was his ability to fly that gave him an enormous advantage over those in turmoil beneath him, but his overall fire power, shooting at great distance plumes of intense heat fiery flames, made him more awesome than when he was once the dictator of Draegonia.

Dragon Gold stared at the unfolding carnage. He could see many dragons were being killed and numerous others crawling away, severely injured. He now realised that it would only be a matter of time before Dragon Black significantly reduced Draegonia dragon numbers and that most survivors would end up his slaves. Oh, why had Dragon Black not arrived earlier when they had a weapon to deal with him? Why had he been convinced to destroy those darts? Why had he not listened to Dragon Brown, who was so gallantly trying to defend them?

Dragon Gold reached down to the ground and picked up a white cloth that had been used as a picnic napkin. He tied it to Dragon Blue's staff that had fallen from his hands earlier and hoisting the staff skywards pointed it towards Dragon Black. Black saw the sign of surrender and firing one final blast of his powerful flames engulfed the few remaining dragons below him, singeing both them and the edges of the flag of surrender. Black, making his wings form powerful arcs acting as air brakes, hovered, surveying the holocaust he had so meticulously engineered.

Numerous dragons had taken to their heels, some less fortunate now formed charcoal images of their former selves, but here below Dragon Black were three dragons that he decided, he would spare their lives. Not because he cared, far from it. Dragon Black was going to make the lives of Dragons Gold, Blue and Dragon Brown miserable. He was going to wreak his vengeance of being humiliated, banished and placed in a position of almost certain death.

Black's anger raged within, his eyes glinting, teeth glistening, he slowly glided down to earth, the crushing force of his enormous powerful feet making visible indentations as he landed on the rocky dusty volcano floor. Cracks splintered out of the indentations, creeping silently in all directions, with each step he took. Dragon Black snorted, plumes of white smoke came from his nostrils, smaller flames from his mouth and in a rumbling growl commanded.

"Kneel before me," he pointed with his razor sharp claws to the ground in front of him. Dragon Brown shook his head saying that under no circumstances would he kneel before a murderer. His protestations were however short lived as Dragon Black cracked his tail bringing it crashing down on Brown's shoulders, forcing him to the floor. "When I tell you to kneel, you will kneel, when I tell you to bow, you will bow. I have returned and as your master, you and all of Draegonia will do my bidding, or else." Black immediately let out a mighty roar, flames spurting everywhere and grabbing Dragon Gold by his throat forced him onto the 3 o'clock positioned plinth overhanging the mouth of the volcano. "This is what I will do to anyone who disobeys me." Dragon Black was just about to send Gold to the fiery furnace below, when both Dragons' Blue and Brown shouted out in unison. "**NO**, we'll do what you want but spare him, please." Black looked at the two pleading for Gold's life and laughed. "You miserable dragons, you're not worth my energy" and with total contempt, tossed Dragon Gold on the ground in front of them. "You three will report to me, you're going to do exactly what I say, if you refuse or try anything funny." Black licked his lips, "I will terminate a dragon for each mistake you make. Do I make myself clear?" The three bedraggled Dragons reluctantly nodded in forced agreement. They were in no position to disagree and this was not the time to be a dead dragon hero.

Black reared his head, stood up to his full height and with outstretched wings could now be observed by those frightened dragons who had hurried to the city centre and safety of their caves. What were they to do, what was going to happen to them? How many more dragons would disappear? What new laws would be introduced? Every Dragon of Draegonia was now in fear of their lives, but none more, than those who had voted for the banishment of Dragon Black.

Dragon Black had allowed Dragons Blue, Gold and Brown to return to the city whilst Black, using the maze of tunnels and corridors within the volcanic mountain, strode purposely towards his seat of power, the Great Hall, where once again the infamous Dragon Black, would take charge of his throne. Passing a number of trembling dragon Guards, Black growled at them to smarten up, stand to attention and salute him. The guards did as they were commanded. They knew only too well not to try the patience of this dragon and that it would be better to be loyal rather than toasted.

Black entered The Great Hall situated in the heart of the Hall of Dragons, looked round and with one enormous fiery breath snuffed out half of the glowing lamps within the hanging chandeliers. "It's too bright in here" Black growled. He stomped round the Great Hall checking to make sure there were no hidden assassins; he was not going to trust anyone or anything. He was back and he was back to stay.

As the days passed the draconian rule of Dragon Black was felt by all. He imposed a curfew making it illegal for any dragon to be out after dusk. He imposed a new tax with every dragon having to give up more than half of their wealth. He shut the Dragon Times newspaper down and set up a daily meeting to be attended by all dragons, guaranteeing that they would learn firsthand of the new laws and imposed taxes. Dragon Black would appear in all his splendour outside the Hall of Dragons overlooking the main square. Perched high up on a purpose built black and cream marble plinth, Dragon Black would survey his subjects.

At the beginning of every meeting Black would undertake a dragon head count, ensuring none were missing. His priorities changed daily as his grip tightened. Initially he wanted to make sure that no one escaped the island to seek help. His method of containment was as usual based on fear. Black had decreed that any dragon attempting to escape would be caught and slain. To emphasise his tyranny and pecuniary punishments he also declared that the offending dragon's family would also face a tortuous death. Dragon Black enjoyed the fear he was bestowing. He would often smile to himself as his promise of making the Dragons of Draegonia pay had finally come to fruition.

Black was once more overseeing his daily Draegonia meeting. This particular day and this particular meeting was to be different as Dragon Black planned to strengthen his position and importantly his own security by building a private army of dragons loyal only to him. Looking down on the gathering, Black spoke. "I am looking for volunteers to be part of my Draegonian Elite Guard who will be responsible for my personal security and welfare. I will be appointing 30 dragons, who of course, will be given some very special privileges. They will have extra food; they will be paid and will not have to pay any taxes. They will be trained and will have the power of arrest as they replace Dragon Blue's redundant police force."

Gasps and murmurs were heard circulating from the gathering of all Draegonia's Dragons. Who would be foolish enough to volunteer? Who would be silly enough to believe Dragon Black, who on earth would trust him? None of the dragons moved or spoke. They just glared at Dragon Black. Some stared in horror, some with confusion, others with anger and hatred in their fearful eyes.

"Well, who will step forward?" Black growled in considerable anger and frustration, a characteristic he was well known for. Only a few of Black's junior guards moved and forming a line, stood in front of him. Black scowled, screwing his mouth into a sneer "Is that all," he challenged. "Are there none of you who would wish for the favours and luxury I can bestow?" Dragon Black continued to eye up each and every dragon. As his steely eyes gazed round, piercing all dragons within his stare, individual dragons slunk further back trying to hide themselves within groups of others. Afraid and weary, all dragons crowded together for support and protection, none volunteering to join Black's army.

"**Well,**" Black snarled. "So be it, you were all given an opportunity to join with me." Black pointed to his Guards. "**They** will have full authority and be in charge of law and order; **you will obey their commands** as though they were my own." Black lowered his head and snarling even more said in a thunderous and threatening tone, flames spilling from his saliva-dripping mouth. "**Anyone defying me will be charged with treason, is that clear?**" Dragon Black then in customary fashion thumped his gigantic tail on the ground three times, jumped down from his marble plinth and headed for the inner sanctum of the Hall of Dragons, The Great Hall.

As soon as Black disappeared from view, his Elite Guards unceremoniously pushed and prodded the onlookers, quickly dispersing them, leaving the square once again empty and eerily quiet.

Dragon Gold had departed with Dragon Blue and now, well out of sight of the guards, they huddled together slowly walking whilst discussing the events that had taken place.

"I hear Black has sent about several of our fittest dragons to the north of the Island in chains." "That's right Blue and I fear that is only the beginning." Gold stroked his chin and continued in a low voice for fear of being overheard. "Dragon Black is dividing our community. He obviously is fearful that some might be brave enough to oppose him, so the strongest of Draegonia's Dragons are being forced to work in chains and he threatens all others and their families with their lives. I fear none will ever stand up to him." Dragon Blue was considering every word. "You know," he said. "If we don't try to do something then it will be the end of Draegonia as we know it and I for one certainly do not wish to live in fear for the rest of my days." Both dragons finally reached the cave of Dragon Brown who they saw about to open his door. "Dragon Brown," Blue called out. "Have you a moment?" Brown seeing his allies invited both of them in and silently closed the door after them. Dragon Brown's cave like all other dragon caves was the colour of his skin. Dragon Blue's was Blue, Dragon Red's was red and here the three dragons were now standing in the middle of a large roomy cave decorated throughout in Karkheh Brown.

"So what's up?" Brown questioned. Dragon Blue was the first to respond. "Look Brown there is no one who dares to oppose Dragon Black. He is a murderer, a tyrant, and a bully, passing unreasonable laws and taxes and things are going to get worse. We have to do something!" Brown gave a weak laugh. "Do something, do something, we lost our chance of doing something when we disposed of the one and only thing that could have been used against him, namely those darts."

"I know, I know" Dragon Blue interjected, "but it's no good thinking about them, they are gone." Dragon Brown beckoned the two to crouch with him and in a calm officer tone of voice said. "OK dragons, what do you suggest we do? And before you come up with any bright ideas, let's look at the fact!" Brown, using his claws, started to count off. "Firstly, we are no match for his strength and secondly he can fly and we cannot. Thirdly, he has become leaner, meaner and faster since he was banished. Fourthly, he has a small number of guards frightened into doing his every bidding. Fifthly, he has reduced any threat to himself by arresting our strongest and fittest dragons and taken them to the north of the Island. They are in chains, forced to work in the harshest of conditions, with little food or water." Brown continued. "And if that's not enough, as you well know, he has disbanded our Police force." Blue nodded in an affirmative manner adding. "And he has imposed a curfew and I might add forbidden meetings such as ours." Dragon Gold could no longer contain himself; he had listened long enough and angrily snarled. "OK you two, so do we just give up? Is there nothing we or any other dragon can do to rid us of this evil force?"

Gold did not wait for any response but pointed to the engravings on the wall depicting a white knight on horseback stabbing a silver lance into a large reddish brown dragon. "I suppose your ancestor just gave up and did not bother to fight, beaten by an insignificant mortal eh?" Dragon Gold jeered. Dragon Blue took a closer at the engravings, each showing a different stage of a fight. Underneath each one was the inscription *'George & The Dragon'*. Dragon Brown, taken aback at Gold's accusation that his ancestor did not put up a brave fight, recalled the stories handed down over time of the Dragon Slayer who was a knight of the realm.

Legend spoke of a wicked dragon that had captured a princess and was beaten in battle by a young knight who saved her life. Brown was well aware that one of his ancestors, whose reputation was flawed, had been beaten in combat. The engravings, pictures and drawings on Brown's wall were a reminder of bygone years and wicked times. Dragon Gold and Dragon Blue looked at each other and simultaneously shouted out "George, and his friends!!" Brown laughed incredulously saying. "You really don't expect them to come back riding a white horse to slay Dragon Black, do you?"

Blue returned to his previously crouched position accompanied by Dragon Gold. Blue cocked his head to one side thoughtfully and murmured. "It's not beyond the realms of believability you know." Dragon Gold nodded in agreement. "I am sure they would help us but how would we begin to contact them and would they really be a match for Black and his Elite Guard?"

The three discussed the merits of contacting the four children who had been instrumental in Black's earlier banishment. "You realise one thing don't you?" Brown, in a more subdued voice questioned. "None of us has worked out how Black got his flame back, or how he removed his explosive collar and how come his flame is far stronger, hotter and more powerful than before?" Dragons Blue and Gold shook their heads, clearly unable to answer.

Dragon Blue was emphatic. "Dragon Black has to be dealt with, irrespective of his regained or improved powers; he must not be allowed to ruin our island or to murder any more of us." He continued. "If there is one person who can help it will be Dragon Pink. Apart from Dragon Black, she is the only other dragon with the ability to fly. I am sure Pink would be willing to get help and even if she could not find our friends, she might find help elsewhere."

Dragon Brown looked at his 'Dragon Watch', "It's getting late; we can't do anything right now I suggest we meet tomorrow at your place Dragon Blue and discuss the suggestions with Pink." Dragon Brown got up and led the other two towards the cave door and wished them a safe journey. It was getting towards dusk and the last thing either of them needed was to be caught outside after curfew.

The following day early in the morning Dragon Pink arrived as usual to attend her clerical duties. To her amazement inside waiting for her with dragon coffee in their claws were the three senior members of the disbanded Council of Dragons. "Good morning," she said. "Shall I leave you in private?" Dragon Blue waved her to crouch down. "Dragon Pink, please we want to discuss matters most urgent with you." Blue continued, explaining that the three senior dragons in front of her wanted to make contact with George and his cousins and that as she was the only dragon who had not had her wings clipped; she might be able to fly and bring back help. Dragon Pink listened, a tear slowly filling one eye. "I can't help." Pink explained that whilst she would be willing to undertake the risky task she did not have the skill for its success. "You see," she continued. "My wings are still too small in relationship to my body and the furthest I have managed to fly is just once around the island, and that was with much difficulty. It would be impossible for me to fly any distance and if the weather should change I would certainly perish." "Well that's it!" Brown grumbled. "If we can't get help we are doomed and totally at the mercy of Dragon Black."

Dragon Gold raised a claw into the air stopping the conversations short. "Dragon Pink, you sent the children the 'Magical Wish Card' could that not be used to over throw Dragon Black? Could we not wish for his untimely end, or to wish to make him go away or?" Dragon Pink interrupted. "Firstly," she said. "The 'Wish Card' only has one wish and that can only be made by the person whose name is on it. Secondly no wish can be made to harm anyone or anything, no matter how bad or horrid they might be, and," she paused then taking a big breath cried out. "And, there is really no way we can get in touch with George anyway." The three senior dragons bowed their heads and went into deep conversation trying to come up with plans that would or could work to dispose of their problem. Dragon Pink listened intently as the three explored every idea and every strategy they could think of, but after some time agreed it was fruitless. So intent were they with their discussion they had not noticed that Dragon Pink had slipped away and was trotting back to her own pink cave.

Pink had an idea. It was a long shot as her plan needed to find an important magical aid. Pink scrambled inside her pink cave, slamming the cave door behind her. Her cave at first appeared small but had many other cave rooms running off a corridor that went deep into the side of the mountain. She was looking for a message bottle. But this was no ordinary bottle. Dragon Pink was a true Dragon Princess, her mother and father had been deposed by Dragon Black many years ago very soon after her birth. Her father was from a line of kings and magical dragons that stood in the way of Dragon Black. Many believed Black was responsible for the strange and abrupt disappearance of her parents, but none could prove it. But shortly after Dragon Black became the unelected leader of Draegonia. Her father had left Dragon Pink with an inheritance of some special artefacts, gifts that had been passed down through the centuries.

The 'Wish Card' had been one such gift but she was frantically searching for another, the magical bottle. Similar to the 'Wish Card', it was a one off and could only be used once. Until now Dragon Pink had not placed any significance on the old stained glass bottle that had a metal stopper in its narrow mouth. She started to panic as clearly she could not remember where she had stored it. Pink opened closets, cupboards, boxes, chests and searched other rooms. She opened hidden safes and even dug up an area of floor where other strange objects had been hidden by her ancestors down the years.

Then in the corner of the smallest room at the end of the corridor, in amongst a chest full of washed up glass and plastic bottles given to her by Dragon White, she spotted the glow of the 'Message Bottle'. Dragon Pink breathed a huge sigh of relief and clutched the bottle to her; she was not going to misplace it again. Dragon Pink returned to her main living room and recalled what her mother had told her about the bottle. She said it had the power of delivering a message anywhere in the world. The bottles magical properties were however linked to water, its one and only method of travel. Oceans, seas, rivers and lakes could transport the bottle close to its final destination, but it could not travel on its own accord across land or through the air.

Pink was concerned that any message she put inside the bottle just might not actually get to the children. She had made her mind up that George should be the recipient but knew he lived somewhere in the land of Britannia and not too close to the sea. Still she thought, this may be the one and only chance to get a message out asking for help. Using a small twin spring metal clasp she gently pulled from the bottle its content of a greenish parchment. Spreading it out on her table she used her claw to inscribe a message and as she wrote she mumbled an incantation taught to her by her mother when she was just a baby dragon. The paper glowed eerily and when she had finished her note she rolled the parchment into a very thin tube and pressed it back into the bottle. Refitting the metal stopper, she crouched back and stared at it. Would this reach its destination, would George not only find it but open the bottle, how long would it take to find him? These and numerous other questions flooded Pink's brain. She yawned. Exhausted and tired she moved towards another cave room that she used as her bedroom. Pink had to make a decision. Was she to tell Dragon Blue about the magical Message Bottle or send it on its way in secret? Dragon Pink had never told any of the dragons what her parents had left her. She was worried that some of the gifts could perhaps fall into the wrong dragon hands. Now she was even more concerned for if it was known that she had many magical items and Dragon Black got wind of it, well she knew her life would definitely be in serious danger. No she would keep the bottle as her secret and tomorrow send it on its way, keeping her dragon claws crossed that it would reach George and his friends.

Early the following day Dragon Pink trotted out of the City down towards the Southern part of the island. She passed through thick vegetation and tropical forest eventually breaking out onto the soft white and golden sands of South Beach. This was her favourite spot and brought back memories of the first landing of the ship wrecked children so long ago.

The sea was calm with little ripples of waves lapping to the waters edge. Was she to throw the bottle as far as she could into the sea or would it break? Could she gently place the bottle in the water but surely it would only wash into the shore. Dragon Pink thought for a while and then had a brainwave. Running back up the slight slope of the beach to the tropical forest's edge she collected several palm tree leaves and vines. Making a small raft and using one of the thicker leaves made a sail. The bottle was placed in the centre of the makeshift raft and to stop it rolling or falling off she tied it with thin vines. Dragon Pink cared little for paddling or wading into the sea (dragons are not happy about water) but knowing the urgency of the situation pushed the makeshift raft whilst wading up to her small chest. Then with a final push and a huge puff she blew the raft out into the prevailing winds and currents that circulated the island. "Good luck and good speed" she whispered under her breath watching the bottle sail out of sight. Pink turned and waded back towards the beach when all of a sudden there was the sound of dragon wings and the heat of Dragon Black's flames as he landed on the beach ahead of her. "So what are you doing here?" He said looking all around. Dragon Pink moved quickly. She needed to distract Black' eagle eyes as the magic bottle slowly drifted out of sight. "Oh nothing really Dragon Black, I thought I might try to do some fishing but I am too slow and my claws are not sharp enough." Black looked all around trying to work out if the answer given was plausible.

Dragon Black had a feeling Dragon Pink was up to something. "So Pink, where were you going to put the fish when you caught them." Dragon Pink smiled and from her pouch pulled a plastic bag. "I was going to use this but really I shouldn't have bothered as I have been wasting my time." Dragon Black had no reason to disbelieve her but still had the nagging feeling there was more to her early morning visit than she was letting on. "You have grown since I last saw you Dragon Pink. You must be approaching the age of 'Dragon Wing.'" Pink gulped, and stammered. "I, I, I, I've not reached the age at least not for a little while, yet." Black looked hard at her wings she was so desperately trying hard to conceal. Black sneeringly snarled. "You're approaching the age of 'Clipping' Pink, you don't want those wings of yours to get too big and cumbersome do you?" Before Pink had time to reply there was a call from behind. Black spun round, surprised to see one of his Elite Guard's frantically racing towards them.

"We have a problem your highness; someone has painted 'DOWN WITH DRAGON BLACK' across the top of the entrance of the Hall of Dragons." Dragon Black's anger was immense and reaction swift. He roared, snarled and growled firing off red and white flames in all directions causing Pink to duck her head and with one huge flap of his powerful wings, Black soared high into the air. Ordering his Elite Guard to return immediately to the city, Black gave one almighty flap of his wings shooting off at great speed.

"Wow "Pink whispered, to herself, "I wouldn't want to be that dragon when he finds out who did it." Pink watched as the Elite Guard charged off in the direction of Black and was within dragon seconds almost out of sight. He for one was not going to keep Dragon Black waiting for fear of what reprisals would be taken against him. Pink keeping her eyes on the small flying dot disappearing into the distance whispered to herself. "Well at least that's put off Dragon Black's thought process about clipping my wings, well at least for now." Turning for the last time she strained her eyes to where she last saw the raft and bottle but nothing, it had disappeared, hopefully she thought on its way to George.

By the time Pink had returned to the city it was early afternoon and there was a high degree of commotion. Dragon Black had returned earlier to confirm that indeed several places had been painted with signs calling for this downfall.

Black had called Dragon Gold to attend the Great Hall and informed him that he should prepare the Draegonian Court. Dragon Gold had been arguing that as he had been removed as Mayor and that the Council of Dragons had been disbanded he no longer had any authority to sit as a Judge. Black's response was predictable. "I'll tell you," he shouted at Dragon Gold. "What you will and can do and when and where you will do it. If you argue, it will be the last time you ever raise your voice to me, You are to be Draegonia's judge; the dragons trust you and will believe that justice is being fairly administered.

Dragon Gold tried to express his concerns but could see that Black was becoming more and more furious with him. "Ok Dragon Black, I will do my duty as a Judge but my decisions must be binding and I must set the sentence if any are to be made."

Dragon Black was furious at being challenged and grabbed Dragon Gold by the throat. He looked into Gold's eyes and snarled, breathing wisps of hot flames all over Gold's frightened brow. "I'll ask you again, will you continue your duties as Judge and do as I say, or do I remove you to somewhere slightly warmer?" Gold knew this referred to him being disposed of at Volcano Peak and knowing that he was close to being sentenced himself took a deep breath. "Of course Dragon Black, I will do as you want, but please put me down." Black pushed Dragon Gold towards the door ordering him to get out and wait for further instructions and that Dragon Gold would be required to try those responsible for the anti Dragon Black posters.

Dragon Black's Guards were moving from cave to cave looking for yellow paint that had been used to make the letters on all the posters and signs. Of course it would have been to obvious to suspect the paint belonged to Dragon Yellow especially as he was afraid of his own shadow. He was a dragon with no courage whatsoever. His cave door was pushed open and in marched two of Black's guards. Yellow's cave was of course painted yellow matching the colour of his skin. Yellow came out of the back cave room and smiled nervously. "What can I do for you sirs?" Yellow's knees were knocking and his eyes rolling as fear was running down his yellow spine back. Yellow should not have had anything to fear as he had been in his cave all day, frightened to go out. He had used his time to repair some of the marks and scratches to his walls and of course there on the table was a bucket of yellow paint and a brush. "One guard picked up the bucket and paint brush, the other grabbed Yellow's arm. "You're under arrest for Treason." Yellow just gulped too frightened to say a word of protest too confused to understand how he could be considered involved with any form of Treason. The Guards, taking the evidence with them, marched Dragon Yellow through the streets and headed for the Police Station where Dragon Blue, although officially relieved of his duties by Dragon Black, still resided.

On the high seas drifting at very slow speed was a small wooden raft under sail containing a bottle tied to it with vines. The vines were dry when the bottle was first tied to the raft but being constantly washed with sea spray and the occasional lapping wave they were becoming soaked and pliable. The vines were no longer securing the bottle and as the raft collided with another small wave the bottle slowly slid from beneath the twines slipping casually into the cool water, its silver metal top glinting with the rays of the sun. The small raft drifted further away from its once held cargo. Then for no apparent reason the bottle started to spin, creating a tiny whirlpool that widened every second of its sonic speed rotations. The bottle stopped spinning just as a greenish glow emanated from its centre and then slowly it moved from a vertical to horizontal position. The whirlpool was still active growing wider and wider with the bottle in its dead centre revolving in its opposite direction. Then just as a compass needle locks onto North the bottle stopped its rotation, the silver top pointing to a heading of North by North East. Finally with a flash of luminous green light the bottle sank below the water and with a final blinding flash disappeared. It was on its way. The bottle could only travel in water and being strapped to the raft, it would never have reached its destination.

CHAPTER 9

Arrests are Made

Dragon Yellow was well and truly locked up, miserable and cold in a dark damp cell, unable to comprehend why he had been charged with the crime of treason. Dragon Blue appeared outside the stone prison door and slid open a small hatch to hand Dragon Yellow a brown plastic bucket containing a warm drink. "Yellow you old fool, what on earth were you thinking about daubing messages all over the place to upset Dragon Black." Dragon Blue did not believe Yellow had anything to do with the posters and banners but wanted to hear it from him. Yellow reached for the welcome drink and started to sip. "You know Dragon Blue, I couldn't have made those signs. Firstly I would have been too frightened to. And secondly, I have been in my cave all day repainting it." Blue nodded "Just as I thought," he said reassuringly. "We need to prove your innocence Yellow, and prove it fast; I will see Dragon Gold and ask his advice as to what we should or can do." Blue was just about to offer more reassurance to the trembling yellow dragon when he heard a kafuffle coming from the top of the passage way leading to the cells. Dragon Black's Elite Guards were bringing in more suspects believed to be part of some underground movement to overthrow Dragon Black.

"Open the cells Dragon Blue we have some more customers for you," the leading Guard joked, pushing the dragons before him. There was Dragon Byzantine a light purple dragon who was considered one of the wealthiest of Draegonia's Dragons. Stumbling alongside were Dragons Cerise, Sea-Green and

Dragon Ecru, a sporty dragon with a tint of grey running throughout his light brown skin. Two other Guards entered the crowded space each with another suspected terrorist. Dragon Chameleon who was usually seen sporting a reddish orange skin but had the ability to change colour at will and Dragon Iceberg, an off white dragon, much like his temper. "Don't push me" Dragon Iceberg moaned at his Guard. "I remember you when you were in dragon nappies so don't think you are too big to be dealt a dragon blow by me." The Guard took no notice of the protestations, opened one of the cells and pushed Dragon Iceberg straight in slamming the door shut, locked it and removed the large iron key. Blue witnessed all the dragons being shoved into the cells as one by one, the four guards removed the keys. "I'll take those if you don't mind, health and safety and all that." Dragon Blue suppressed a grin, after all the circumstances really did not warrant any mirth. The guards looked at each other and handed to Dragon Blue six keys, one for each of their now imprisoned dragons. "You had better make sure they stay in their cells Dragon Blue," the senior Guard growled. "If any escape your head will be on the block." "More like in the oven," another Guard yelled. Laughing at what they thought was highly amusing the two Guards left the police station to report back to Dragon Black.

Dragon Blue returned to his old office. He may have been removed from duties but there were prisoners to look after and he was not going to shirk his responsibilities, irrespective of Dragon Black. Blue placed the 6 cell keys close to others on their hooks noticing that one key was missing. He recalled that the one and only uninhabited cell remaining was the highly secure smelly and damp one that had the three special locks. There on the hooks were the keys that he and Dragon Gold had used to secure two of the locks but the third key was still held by Dragon Brown. Blue murmured under his breath to himself, "I need to remind Brown to return the key before anyone notices it's missing."

The guards had returned to the Great Hall and were now lined up listening to their senior officer making his report to Dragon Black. Black as usual was perched high on his ceremonial plinth surveying all beneath him. He enjoyed everyone having to look up to him. The officer saluted Black and reported in regimental fashion, "Sire, we apprehended several dragons today and have them all under lock and key. Dragon Yellow was caught with the type of paint used to daub the messages across the city and we have arrested six other dragons believed to be part of an underground dragon movement to depose of you Sire."

Dragon Black sneered. "I suppose they all declared their innocence, but it does not matter we shall have an enjoyable day feeding them to the Volcano." Black grinned, displaying his razor sharp brilliant white teeth protruding from mauve and fiery red gums. Black's tongue curled from his mouth and as he licked his lips, saliva dribbled from his bottom jaw. "The volcano has had little fresh meat since I left, but that's all going to change." Black's eyes glinted as he acknowledged the report and waved the guards to leave. But before they reached the Grand Archway Black growled again. "Wait; there is one important job you must deal with." Black recalled meeting Dragon Pink on the beach and noticing that her wings were starting to develop decided that she may well have reached the age of flight. The last thing he needed was a dragon with wings able to leave the island to get help. "I want you to apprehend Dragon Pink and take her into custody. She is to be placed under lock and key and await the ceremony of 'Clipping of the Wings'."

The senior officer saluted Black and somewhat hesitatingly asked. "Where are we to keep her Sire? There is no secure place other than the cells in the Police Station and they are almost full." Black angrily waved his arm, his sharp pointed claws clenched. "Then fill the place up, throw her into any of the cells, just make sure she is ready for the New Moon when the ceremony shall take place." The officer was pleased to be able to leave the wrath of Black and with great urgency saluted and scurried off with two Guards to locate Dragon Pink.

Pink had returned to her cave quite late and was surprised to see several posters, banners and daubings, all calling for the downfall of Dragon Black. She thought it best to stay out of sight for a while as Black had become aware that her wings had not been clipped, a ceremony that she wanted to avoid at all costs. Suddenly she heard a banging on the door. Pink had no time to call out when it was violently thumped again and a voice shouted out. "Open up immediately we know you're in there." Confused and unaware of what the commotion was all about, Pink tentatively opened her cave door to reveal three of Dragon Black's Elite Guards.

"We are to take you into custody Dragon Pink; you are hereby summoned under the specific directives of Dragon Black to prepare yourself for the 'Ceremony of Wing Clipping'." Dragon Pink blinked in dismay her worst fears were being realised. "Why must I be taken into custody surely you can let me stay here under guard?" The Officer, showing no emotion, growled once more. "Dragon Pink, you are ordered to come with us where you will be taken to the cells where you will await for the full moon. At that time you will partake in the 'Ceremony of the Wing Clipping'." Dragon Pink's arms were grabbed by the two Elite Guards and with the officer in the lead, was unceremoniously marched, protesting all the way, to the Police Station.

Dragon Blue could hear Pink's troubled voice over the sound of heavy marching footsteps. He opened the station door just in time to see a forlorn Dragon Pink being dragon-handled by two very officious guards. The same guards who earlier had brought in the suspects now incarcerated in all but one of the cells. "Why is Dragon Pink being handled in this appalling way?" Blue demanded. The officer confirmed what Black had commanded and that until the New Moon, Dragon Pink was to be held in one of the cells. Blue glancing at the list of prisoners and keys displayed on the wall above his desk, growled." I am afraid we have no more cells free and Dragon Pink is a young female dragon who should not be locked up with any male, it would not be right or proper!" The officer brushed past Blue and grabbed at the two keys under the sign displaying 'Out of Commission' and yelled. "We'll use this one then?" He snarled, beckoning to the guards holding Dragon Pink. "Bring her through."

The officer led them along the dimly lit tunnel towards the smelliest and bleakest cell of all. The same cell, that earlier had been used to secure the package containing the 'Dragon Flame Out' darts. The officer, using his keys for the two locks opened the gate "In you go." He said, pointing into the black void. Dragon Pink gulped and taking several steps entered the cell as the heavy rusty iron bar gate slammed firmly shut behind her.

She could hear the two locks once more being turned and over heard the officer as he handed the keys to Dragon Blue. "These are now in **your** care; I advise you not to let them or her out of your sight and above all do not open the cell door for any reason, on pain of your death." Blue did not appreciate the threat but felt it better to appear as though he was in accord with the events. "Of course I will take every care of her, don't worry, she will be secure here." Blue had chosen his words carefully, for the one thing he would guarantee was the safety of his little friend and more recently his employee, Dragon Pink.

The guards were well on their way back to the Hall of Dragons as Dragon Blue extinguished the outside lights, deciding that as curfew was now in force, there was little more he could do until morning.

Early next morning, Dragon Gold was summoned to the Hall of Dragons where Dragon Black was waiting for him within the ceremonial Great Hall. Gold stood upright in front of the evil dragon, showing little emotion, listening to his threats and orders. Although Gold was not in agreement with any of Black's dictates or assertions, he knew he had to appear to be supportive or suffer the consequences. Black had informed him that six dragons suspected of being traitors and planning to overthrow him were now securely locked up, together with Dragon Yellow, awaiting their trial set for the day of the full moon.

Black snarling and grunting, made it clear that the trial was not to last too long and that the verdict of 'Guilty' would be followed by all seven dragons being sentenced to 'Volcanic Death'. Gold tried in vain to appeal for mercy, for Black to allow for a fair trial and not to prejudge the verdict. Black roared in anger, he did not take too kindly to Dragon Gold's remarks and with flashing eyes, threatened him with severe consequences should he disobey him. Black emphasised, in no uncertain terms, that he could and would appoint some other dragon to the position of Judge, should he consider Gold was not up to the task. Gold could do nothing but acquiesce but was further taken aback when Black told him that Dragon Pink was also in custody. Black drooled as he explained that subsequent to the executions there was to be the ceremony of clipping Pink's wings. And, that he would perform it.

Gold knew that once Pink had her wings clipped it would be the last chance of any dragon getting off the island to seek help. Gold tried in vain to persuade Black to reconsider, but Black was not interested. Dismissing all of Gold's protestations, Dragon Black in final customary fashion, cracked his mighty tail three times, ordered Dragon Gold to go. Revenge was sweet.

A very worried Dragon Gold headed out into the early morning sunshine for Draegonia's Police Station and the cells. He needed to get support and his friend Dragon Blue had to be informed of all of Dragon Black's evil plans.

Blue had got up early that morning and was preparing eight bowls of dragon porridge and some hot dragon tea when in bounded a concerned looking Dragon Gold. Before Blue had chance to say good morning, Dragon Gold rattled of a barrage of grunt's, growls and sighs as he told Blue of the earlier encounter between him and Dragon Black. As soon as Dragon Gold had stopped his verbal diarrhoea, Blue responded in a subdued tone. "I know what Black was planning Gold and have been thinking hard of ways to stop his inevitable executions and the clipping of poor Dragon Pink's wings but there really isn't anything we can do other than try to get enough supporters together to immobilise the Elite Guard and capture Dragon Black." Blue hesitated then in a more worried tone gruffed. "However, as you know that idea is out of the question. Black is picking off all our strongest dragons one by one and either putting them to work in hard labour camps or locking them up pending a sham trial! We just don't have sufficient dragon power to overthrow him."

Dragon Blue seeing that Gold' was looking forlorn and depressed tried to offer some hope. "You know," he said. "There is one dragon that has not been seen for a while and coincidentally disappeared when the anti Dragon Black posters appeared." Gold straightened his shoulders and looking at Blue shouted out. "Dragon Brown, of course he was in charge of the military and I bet he is behind those posters and banners, no doubt about it." "Shush," cried Blue. "Not so loud if that information, whether it be true or not, got back to Dragon Black then Brown's life would not be worth a claw." "OK, so what do we do?" Gold whispered. Blue closed the main office door and beckoned Dragon Gold to crouch with him. "Look, we need to keep our positions or at least be close enough to Dragon Black to know exactly what he is planning. We need to find Dragon Brown and we need to do everything to save the prisoners, including Dragon Pink."

Gold nodded furiously. "Yes, Yes, what do you suggest Blue?" Blue gazed up towards the 'Dragon Clock' and 'Dragon Calendar' hanging on the cave's blue wall and replied. "Whatever we do, we only have less than one dragon week to do it. Firstly, you must do everything possible to get a message to Dragon Brown." Blue continued making suggestions as Dragon Gold listened intently to his every word. "When you find Brown, arrange for us all to meet, I suggest somewhere well away from the city. In the meantime I will look after the prisoners and Dragon Pink." Gold interrupted. "Isn't she a prisoner too?" Dragon Blue nodded. "Yes, but she is only here in custody, not for any alleged crime, but under Black's orders, just for safe keeping." "Oh!" Gold exclaimed, "then she is a prisoner, what a mess!"

Dragon Blue urging Gold to leave, re-opened the station door and bid him good luck and watched him scurry away. Once more, shutting the door, Blue returned to feeding breakfast to his 8 disheartened guests held in the darkness of their cold, damp and very smelly cells.

CHAPTER 10

A Conditional Wish

Several days had passed since George's birthday and he still had not worked out what he would wish for. Joel and Zach had each come up with lots of ideas, mainly things that they personally wanted. Grace also had made out her own wish list and was somewhat surprised that George was not using the 'Wish Card' quick enough.

The four had met with their bikes at the local youth club. Music could be heard coming from inside and the car park was bustling with coming and goings as mother's and fathers were either dropping off or picking up their children. "So, have you decided yet?" Grace wanted to know. "Yes are you going to wish for new bikes?" Joel demanded. "I want an electric scooter and model cars" added Zach. George said nothing but looking at the list of wishes prepared by his three cousins, smiled.

Electric Scooter	Super Lego
Model Cars	Mountain Bikes
Season Ticket for Tottenham	Tent
Play Station 3	Computer
A New Wii	Games
A new Dress	Flute

"You know." George spoke softly. "We are just wishing for things we want and are not really looking at the gift we have in the right way" "What is he talking about" Zach cried out! "I've been suggesting loads of things and none appear to be right, so what's the point of having a 'Wish Card' if you can't use it."

George suppressed a laugh and putting his arm round Zach's shoulders showed him the list. "Look, everything listed here is OK for us but all the items will lose their value, their appeal and also their novelty factor over time. We should be using such an amazing gift for the lasting benefit of others, not just ourselves." "Ridiculous," cried out Grace removing the list from George's hands. "These here are things you could give us and we would be very appreciative. I need, for example, a new flute, we all need new bikes and you need a new computer, so why can't you wish for them all?" "Perhaps that's being too greedy?" piped up Joel.

George moved to one of the benches overlooking the playground where apart from one girl on a swing was now deserted. Pulling from his inside jacket pocket the Wish Card, George turned it over and read the reverse, out aloud.

This wish card is given to you

But one wish and never two

Gifts not pure and thoughts untrue

This wish Card will not work for you.

"Well that explains why you have been reluctant to use it George!" Grace exclaimed. "I suppose if we made a selfish wish that was just for us then the wish may not be granted and if I understand that inscription correctly, there would be no second chance."

George nodded in agreement. "Yes that's exactly what it means, so we really do need to think carefully about how we use any wish we make." The two boys looked at George, understanding that perhaps they had been only thinking of themselves. Joel shrugged his shoulders just as Zach kicked an empty cola can neatly into an open waste bin.

"Good shot, perhaps you should be in the club's football team, they need a good goal scorer," laughed Grace. "OK Guys, I've got to get home," George yelled as he pushed his bike along the path towards the road. "I'll see you all tomorrow as we are all going with your Dad to look at a replacement for 'Princess'." Grace, Zach and Joel had been informed by their father that he had seen a sailing boat for sale at the local marina and offered to take them all, together with George, to see it. "Don't forget," Grace shouted to George as he was peddling away. "You're being collected at 8 o'clock and Dad won't be too happy if you're not ready." George, racing out of earshot, smiled to himself, knowing that if any of the four overslept, it definitely would not be him.

CHAPTER 11

A Message in a Bottle

"Come on you three" shouted Andrew, their father. Andrew was a tall muscular individual that liked everything to be done on time and with three children all deciding on what they would or would not take with them to the Marina, his patience was running thin. "For goodness sake, at this rate it will be lunchtime before we leave," he exaggerated, but the message was clear. "Get a move on."

The three youngsters bundled themselves into the car and sat behind the two front seats, one of which was occupied by their father who was at the steering wheel. Zach, the last to get in, slammed the door behind him. "You no need to slam the door Zach," his dad complained as he started the car. "Seat belts on, doors locked?" There was a pause as he waited for all three to yell out "YEP," "OK." "Mine's done." Andrew slowly drove out of the drive and turned into the quiet main road. "OK," he said. "Next stop George's."

George had been up very early and had got his own breakfast. He was watching the football news and results on TV when he heard the familiar toot of his uncle's car horn. Hurriedly, he put his jacket on, grabbed his rucksack, and ran to open the front door. "Won't be a minute," he yelled at the four in the sleek Peugeot 308 Hybrid 4 that had used the drive to turn round in. George, shouted out his good bye's to his mum who yelled back in similar fashion, closed the door and ran down his drive to the front of the car and jumped in next to his Uncle. "Belt up,

George." George laughed. "That's nice I am only in the car for a few seconds and already you're telling me to belt up!"

Andrew said nothing but set the GPS for Harleyford Marina and headed off with the excitable chatty four. The marina was only half hour away situated on the Thames between Maidenhead and Henley. The surrounding countryside featured rolling hills and various shaped fields the colours of which looked like a patchwork quilt of winter greens, yellows and browns.

The Peugeot, turning off the main road, continued down a private narrow lane towards the river. As they neared the Thames the four children could see row upon row of holiday chalets all closed up and looking quite forlorn. "**Brrrr**, it looks quite cold out there." Grace sighed, "I think I will stay in the car whilst you four look at boats." Andrew pulled into the Yacht Marina car park and was just about to answer Grace, when out from the club house appeared Alan the smartly dressed young Marina's Sales Director. "Hi Guys," he cheerily said. "I've been expecting you come in, have a sit down and I'll get you something hot to drink." The five, with Alan in the lead, entered the Club House.

The club's meeting room was palatial with several large red leather chairs, two three seater sofas and rich red flock papered walls sporting paintings and prints of sailing and yachting scenes. In the corner was an enormous TV screen showing the early morning news. The newscaster was reporting on the rescue of 16 crewmen of a stricken oil tanker, that having lost its steering had ran aground, exploded on rocks and subsequently sank in the South Atlantic. The report mentioned that the crew had survived for over a week with just enough rations to last a couple more days when a civilian light aircraft out of Barbados spotted them and alerted the authorities. The US had launched a rescue and the film clips showed the men being winched up in helicopters and taken to a USA Coast Guard vessel where they were being interviewed.

The four children sat in their sumptuous red leather chairs watching the unfolding story whilst sipping hot chocolate that Alan had brought in for them. Joel moved closer to the TV and turned up the volume. The captain of the stricken vessel was being interviewed, surrounded by his crew. "How did the sinking of the 'Shell Oil A2C', occur?" The interviewer asked. The Captain was visibly embarrassed as he replied in a well scripted manner.

"We had been battered for many hours by severe storms when our Port engine failed. Following a further three hours in horrendous seas our Starboard engine started to overheat and we had little steerage capability and were in an area of known rocks unable to manoeuvre. Our vessel was pounded by seas whipped up by storm force winds making visibility difficult. Our navigation aids indicated we were close to a known danger area but our manoeuvring ability was zero. Despite dropping anchor we were unable to avoid the disaster." The Captain coughed, cleared his throat and continued. "Once the situation became totally unmanageable and lives were at risk, I gave the order to abandon ship."

The Interviewer nodded and then poignantly asked. "But captain why the explosion, what caused the tanker to explode and to sink beyond any possibility of salvage and why was there so little oil spillage, is it true you were attacked?" The captain swiftly glanced at his First Officer and with some hesitation answered. "We are not certain of all the facts surrounding the explosion or what caused it, obviously we will wait for the investigation report following the enquiry into this incident." The Captain hurriedly continued. "We still have to attend a full debriefing and until such time as all the facts have been established, I do not wish to say any more."

The interviewer thanked the Captain and turning to camera summed up. "An unconfirmed rumour has it that the tanker was attacked and sank as a direct result of a missile or bomb hitting and blowing a hole through the main deck igniting the oil and causing catastrophic explosions. Further unconfirmed reports are alluding that some form of aircraft the shape resembling of all things a dragon was used in the attack. The military are naturally playing down any possibility of deliberate sabotage or sinking of the vessel and as you can see behind me the 16 survivors are now under the jurisdiction of US Naval Intelligence. I am Keith Powers for 10 Live, back to the studio."

The four children had not really been taking much notice until the word dragon was heard. "Do you think?" Joel started to ask, just as Andrew and Alan returned. "OK you lot, we are all going to take a trip down the Thames in a medium size cruiser, no sail this time but reliable engines eh?" Andrew was recalling the incident two years earlier, when the four had lost their small sailing craft in a storm and felt now that reliable engines of a power craft would be far safer. "Can I drive?" Zach called out as he ran to the exit. "No me first," yelled Joel. "Oh here we go again, I can see arguments occurring before we even get on the boat," murmured Grace.

Andrew quickly calmed things down. "Sorry kids none of you will be at the wheel this time. Alan will take command as this boat is very expensive and only covered by the Marina's insurance. It does not allow any person under 21 to take the helm."

The six walked out to where a large boat was moored called MIANN, a 42' Grand Banks built in the 1980's. The condition and layout on board was luxurious despite its age. The main cabin had a large teak table to sit four that could be extended for six situated in the corner of the cabin where an L shaped corner seat afforded a great deal of comfort. "Hey look at this," Grace cried out. "It has an ice maker!" George and Zach were more interested in the electronics situated in panels just in front of the teak spoke wheel. George identified the electronics with awe and enthusiasm. "Look at these, radar, GPS, depth sounder and a Moving Map Display." "Yes I know, it's also got autopilot and stabilisers," added an impressed Zach, "this boat has everything."

Up above on the flying bridge Andrew was listening to Alan who had started the twin Lehman engines and was instructing his berth staff to cast off. As the last of the warps were placed on board Andrew made a move "I'll go down below and ensure the children have their life vests on." Alan nodded in agreement and putting the craft in reverse slowly backed out of the berth.

A few days earlier a small greenish tint bottle had turned itself into an undersea projectile. It knew where it had to go and had been travelling at great speed avoiding dolphins, whales and sharks who all thought it was some new form of delicacy. The messenger bottle was fast approaching the UK streaking underwater along the English Channel having successfully navigated the rough seas of Biscay.

The magical bottle, hidden from view above, maintained a purposeful course to its programmed destination only a few feet beneath the surface of the deep seas. As it approached ships, rocks, or any obstacle in its path, it would deviate, taking a safer and less damaging route. The bottle, travelling inbound from the west, soon approached the Needles off the Isle of Wight and passing along the channel cleverly avoided the infamous sand banks and Isle of Wight ferries that traversed between Lymington and Yarmouth.

The bottle continued its relentless journey, seemingly gaining its speed from the way it revolved at tremendous velocity. Soon it passed the main harbour of the Isle of Wight, Cowes. Here the bottle momentarily paused as though trying to take stock of where it was and where it needed to go. The bottle, still spinning but at a slightly slower speed, glowed and glowed an eerie green, then with a flash shot off heading out past the town of Cowes towards the open channel and south east coast of England.

Still submerged, the magical messenger passed Brighton, Hastings, and Dover, swinging round the east coast of Kent passing Ramsgate, quickly heading for the mouth of the capital's major river. Its long journey was nearly at an end but the bottle carrying its all important message now faced the final leg of its mammoth 5000 mile journey, the more difficult and challenging sectors of the River Thames.

The River Thames is some 215 miles long from its source to the sea and tidal up to Teddington Lock (Richmond being both tidal and non tidal). Situated along the Thames are 45 locks which allow medium and small sized craft to be lifted from sea level up some 240 feet to its highest point of St John's at Lechlade, about 184 river miles from London.

The bottle with its all important message firmly locked within, patiently waited at the first lock for travelling craft moving upstream, to enter. The enormous heavy lock gates slowly opened to allow an assortment of small craft to enter. They were closely followed by the bottle hugging close to the lock's side but well out of the way of any crushing craft. The lock quickly filled with ear shattering, swirling water, raising its contents up to the higher level. After a few minutes the lock's exit gates opened exposing the route ahead. One by one the small fleet of craft, followed by the spinning submerged bottle, continued their journey upstream towards the next of thirteen more locks the bottle had to transit, before reaching its final destination, of Marlow.

The cruiser Miann, with its crew of four children and two adults was heading for Marlow Bridge. Alan, eager to sell the boat had made prior arrangements to moor at the Complete Angler, a prestigious hotel and restaurant, situated above Marlow Weir. Here the river ran very fast, dropping some several feet with river passage assured through the Marlow Lock. Boats of all sizes were either raised or lowered depending which way they were heading. The noise of cascading water thundering over the weir was deafening as early winter rain had made the river run very fast. Not wishing for their motor vessel to drift away from the Complete Anglers VIP area, the four children assisted with the ropes. They securely tied the warps (ropes) holding the bow, stern and amidships to stainless steel rings protruding from the purpose built mooring. Having double checked their knots Alan, still extolling the virtues of the Grand Banks 42', led the five for an early lunch.

Meanwhile, the bottle was continuing up river climbing higher as it passed through each lock towards Marlow and was soon within minutes of its destination as two adults and four children, having had a good meal, returned to the Grand Banks.

Joel and Zach untied the mid ship warps and with them climbed back on board. Alan had looped the bow rope through a metal ring on the concrete mooring and was by the starboard side cabin door holding it firm for Andrew to cast of the stern. The engine was ticking idly over ready and waiting to go.

The spinning bottle was still in the middle of Marlow lock and some minutes away from exiting as the cruiser Miann turned away from the weir and headed back upstream, towards Medmenham and the marina. Alan, at the helm, was in deep conversation with Andrew discussing in depth the running and mooring charges associated with the craft. Behind them, to the rear of the flying bridge, holding onto the steadying sail mast, were Grace and Joel. Below in the warmth of the cabin and sitting in front of the consul were Zach and George. The two were looking in awe, mesmerised by the displays of flashing lights, moving maps and digital sound's emanating from the array of electronics.

Marlow Lock, now several hundred meters behind them was reopening with two small craft exiting. The wide river was in flood and running extremely fast towards the lock, yet there in the middle, was a wake of water created by an unusual object. A metallic tip had surfaced and was now powering up stream against the flowing current. The magical bottle's silver cap was catching the afternoon's winter sun, reflecting rays of needle sharp dazzling light in different directions as it revolved.

The bottle was following Miann and every now and again propelled itself out of the water dolphin style, only to fall back to continue its travels unnoticed. The four up top and two within the boat's cabin had no idea that something was trying to gain their attention. Miann entered the marina basin and moored against the polished wooden pontoon displaying the 'For Sale' notice.

"Well what do you think?" Alan enquired. Andrew did not immediately reply. He was studying the cruisers sales leaflet and took one more look at the boat. "Yes I think it's really good and meets all our needs if not more but the price is way beyond my budget." Alan tied the last warp and looked up. "This is a really good craft and has quite a history but been well looked after. You know it's more of an investment and unlike a new boat will not devalue as quickly, especially if it is well maintained." Andrew was not entirely convinced but at Alan's suggestion followed him into the office to discuss things further. "Don't go too far." Andrew bellowed out to the children. "Keep out of trouble and above all don't fall in and whilst you're near the water keep those life vests on." The four children each made a gesture of understanding and agreeing with the more than reasonable request, walked across to where a small bridge afforded an advantage point to all craft entering into the marina.

The bridge overlooked a small number of boats that were entering and exiting. "It's not very busy is it?" Grace said. "Well it is still winter you know and not many people go out in boats at this time of year," George responded. "Then why are we here, I'm freezing?" said a shivering Zach. Joel made no comment; he was gazing at a dazzling light that seemed to be coming from beneath the bridge, dead centre in the water below. "Look," he cried. "What's that?" The three followed Joel's finger that was pointing at a bobbing metallic top of a discoloured bottle. "Oh it's nothing, just an empty old bottle, leave it," shouted out Zach. Grace was not of the same opinion and rushed back down the steps closely followed by George. "If it is a bottle then it should not be left in the river," she shouted. "It may break and the broken glass could cause someone an injury, we have to get it out it out."

The two boys on top of the bridge did not move but just watched as Grace and George found some long sticks and tried to reach the bottle. They did not have to exert any effort. The bottle reacted like a magnet to a metal pole and headed immediately for the tip of the stick being held by George. "That's weird," he said. "I have never seen a bottle do that before." Grace nodded in some amazement and bending over, stretched out and grabbed the bottle. "Wow" she said. "It's quite warm and there seems to be something inside it."

The two boys watching events unfold ran from the top of the bridge, their interest aroused and on reaching Grace, Zach suggested, that Grace opened the bottle. "What do you think I am trying to do? It won't budge," she frustratingly cried. Joel gently took the bottle from his sister had a go. He twisted and pulled at the stopper with all his might but he too could not budge it. Zach was more businesslike. He grabbed the bottle from Joel and went over to a large metal container with a sign saying 'Industrial waste'. With an almighty sweep of his hand he brought the bottle down hard on the containers steel edge.

But instead of breaking into thousands of pieces and releasing its content, the bottle just bounced back into the air. Zach tried again but with the same result. "Enough" shouted George just throw it into the container and leave it there, we need to get back." Zach did as he was ordered and started to walk towards the three, but as he did so the container shook and a green glow emanated from within. As Zach moved further away from the container the greenish haze seemed to fade and melt away. A bewildered George walked past Zach to the container and peered in. As he did so the glow from the centre of the bottle increased and as he continued to stare the green glow faded to a pin point light, and then disappeared completely. "Weird," George mumbled under his breath. He turned and walked towards the three who were discussing what might have caused the glow just as the waste container started to violently vibrate yet again and the same glow, but much brighter this time, enveloped the area in which it stood.

George turned back, leaned over the container top, reached in and grabbed the bottle. It felt strange sending through him a warm, good feeling. Taking the bottle over to where the others were standing he peered into the bottle making out something buried inside. "You won't' get that out, we have all tried without success," Grace cried. George placed a finger and thumb on either side of the metal stopper and twisted. The stopper not only turned but continued to turn on its own accord as George held the bottle in his quivering hand. Unbelievably the metal stopper was now, on its own accord, slowly rising out of the bottle and as it rose a few more centimetres above the bottles mouth, disappeared completely in a red glow that took a few seconds to fade. **"Wow"** Zach blurted out. "How did it do that?" Joel shouted. Grace moved closer to George and whispered, "Is it safe?"

George said nothing but carefully turned the bottle on its side and watched as the parchment from within slowly appeared and floated in mid air in front of him. Then, there was a blinding flash. No noise, but a brilliant flash of vibrant colour the centre of which oscillated between green, yellow and red. Once the four had re-accustomed their eyes from the array of spectacular blinding lights they saw that the bottle had vanished and that the contents had now expanded to twice their original size and was being read by George. "What's it say," Grace enquired. "Yes speak up, I can't hear" Zach cried out. George was concentrating hard as he read out loud the written message.

URGENT

We are in danger and fear for our lives. We have been imprisoned, face unjust laws and cruelty. Many dragons have been killed. The evil Dragon Black has returned. He has greater strength and has regained the ability to spit flame more powerful than before. We are desperate and in need of assistance, otherwise it will be the end of Draegonia.

Dragon Pink

There was silence as the four digested what George had just read out. "Oh!! Grace exclaimed. "What on earth can we do? We have no idea where the island is, we have no means of getting there and even if we did, we certainly are no match for a flame throwing evil dragon like Dragon Black."

"We agree" said Zach deciding to speak on behalf of his brother as well. "We remember the cell Black locked us up in and the narrow escape from being thrown into the island's volcano, no point in taking unnecessary risks."

George shook his head, was he dreaming, did a bottle really appear to follow him, did it disappear leaving behind a message for help? He pinched himself to make sure he was not dreaming. "Ouch." "What did you say George?" Grace asked on hearing his tiny yelp. "Nothing, look it is getting late and we need to get back or your dad is going to do his crust." Grace and her brothers needed no further encouragement and with George following sped off to where Andrew was finalising his discussions with Alan and was now walking towards the Peugeot. "Good timing, jump in," Andrew beckoned as he shook Alan's hand saying he would be in touch. Shutting the rear door behind Joel, who was last to get in, Andrew slid into the driver's seat and started the engine.

The drive back to George's house was a little subdued making Andrew somewhat concerned. "You lot OK?" He said. "What's up, you're ever so quiet?" Grace was first to speak. "We're just tired that's all, probably all the fresh air eh!" George grinned and added. "Yeah we have had a great day, did you buy the boat?" Andrew coughed and at the same time chuckled. "Hey George, if you happen to have a cool £100K on you we could go back and do the deal, if not it's back to looking for something perhaps smaller, and cheaper." Zach yelled out. "Well I've got £50.00 in my savings." Everyone laughed, except Zach, for he really did mean it and as far as he was concerned £50.00 would be more than enough for a deposit.

The traffic was light and as the car sped through the winding country lanes George turned and looked at his three cousins sitting behind him. "After football tomorrow I'll be down the club, can you make it as we have some very important things to discuss?" Andrew made it easy for them to all agree by offering to drive them saying. "What time are you planning on being there George?" George looked again at the other three and winked. "Oh, let's make it half past two, after lunch and if it's alright with you they can stay over, Mum won't mind."

The car turned off the main road into a cul-de-sac and stopped outside George's house. George opened the door, exited and as he ran up the drive, turned, waved and shouted. "See you all tomorrow; you know we have something very important to do." George patted his inside pocket once more, knowing that he had received a rather special message, in a bottle.

CHAPTER 12

Finding Dragon Brown

Dragon Gold, as promised to Dragon Blue, had been investigating the appearance of the posters, banners and graffiti's that were cropping up all over Draegonia, each one calling for the downfall of Dragon Black. Black had quickly responded by putting out a reward of 1,000 Draegonias for information and conviction of the perpetrators. He had also ordered the Draegonian Guards, loyal to him, to interrogate every dragon who lived close to the provocative slogans. These actions led to two more dragons being arrested, put in chains and led north to join others imprisoned without trial.

Dragon Gold made himself ready for the dangerous journey ahead. Earlier he had met with Dragons Red and Grey, hoping to obtain a lead or at least some information, but neither Dragons Red nor Grey knew anything about the insurgence, yet they were both intrigued to know who the leader of the audacious underground movement might be.

Gold had spent most of that morning asking questions, digging for clues and without success searching for the one dragon that seemed to be conveniently missing. "I wonder," Gold muttered to himself. "Dragon Brown is nowhere to be found and yet a resistance movement has appeared out of nowhere, is it coincidence?" Still mumbling to himself, Gold headed north, towards the bleakest part of the island. Gold wanted to see for himself how the recently arrested and much stronger dragons were fairing. Black had considered them as a major threat and without trial sentenced them to hard labour. Gold guessed that they would be held under appalling conditions and now was extremely worried for their safety and wellbeing.

The trek to North Island Beach is hard at the best of times, but to-day as the late afternoon sun blazed down, the heat reflecting off the barren rugged hard ground was unbearable, even for a fit and healthy dragon.

"Poor Devils!" Dragon Gold murmured as he rounded the last obstacle in his path to reveal eight of Draegonia's toughest dragons all in chains, moving rocks almost as large as themselves. The three very untidily dressed Draegonian Guards were growling at their captives to move quicker. The guards flicked and cracked their tails, using them as whips, against the tired bodies of their captives. A reddish brown coloured dragon by the name of Russet saw Dragon Gold approach. "What are you doing here? This is a restricted area by orders of Dragon Black." Gold pulled himself up to his full height and glared at the Guard. "Who are you growling at, stand to attention when addressing the appointed legal representative of Dragon Black." Gold bluffed, he knew that Dragon Black had forbidden anyone to visit North Island Beach. "I am here to observe and report and to ensure you are all doing your duty. I must also check that all prisoners are accounted for, let me see the role call register?" The guard was taken by surprise. He knew Dragon Gold used to be the Mayor before being relieved of his duties by Dragon Black, but had not realised that Black had re-appointed him again as, what did Dragon Gold say?

"Legal representative?" The Guard queried. "Yes that's right" Gold emphatically responded, "I am Dragon Black's appointed Judge and representative. I will be arranging for all trials and soon will be sentencing all guilty dragons for crimes against Draegonia." Gold held a hard and angry expression, staring at the Guard full in his face. "And, I will also be reporting back on anyone who is insubordinate or unhelpful in my duty." The Guard stood to attention, saluted and asked permission to speak. Gold nodded. "Sorry sir but we were not informed of your visit. There is no role call register, but I can confirm all prisoners are present and correct pending Dragon Black's orders."

Gold nodded again and walked towards two of the chained dragons who had just positioned a huge rock on a newly constructed key forming a sea break and asked. "How are you both are you being fed and where are you put in the evenings to sleep?"

Before the imprisoned dragons had chance to respond, the Guard jumped forward and growled at them, "No talking, get back to work." He then glared at Dragon Gold with some alarm and taking on a more authoritative stance said. "Dragon Gold, I am sorry sir but you must be aware that Dragon Black ordered that these dragons were not to speak, for any reason, at any time, or with anyone and I am sure, that means you as well."

Gold shrugged and in a contemptuous manner walked off and turning his head back over his shoulder curtly informed the Guard. "That order was before he reappointed me Judge and as Judge I am required to investigate many matters prior to a trial. I need the names of those to be tried and of course the list of crimes that they are alleged to have committed. I am also instructed to report back on security, your effectiveness and how you are handling the prisoners. However, if you are going to be difficult, then I might as well return and inform Dragon Black accordingly."

Gold, moving his head back, took a deep breath and with a sly grin trotted off shouting out. "I am sure when I inform Dragon Black how co-operative and helpful you have been, I am sure he will reward you accordingly." "STOP," yelled the Guard, "if it's only names and crime details and just general information you now joined by their commander who appeared from the darkness of the rear extremities of the cave.

"So how do you like our barracks?" Dragon Brown asked as he moved towards Dragon Gold with outstretched paw. Gold shook Brown's paw enthusiastically. "We have all been wondering where you were Brown and guessed that the anti Black posters were most probably of your making, but I for one had no idea you had actually raised an army."

Brown laughed and pouring two large jugs of clear water offered one to Gold. "Look Gold, Black has only been here a short while but has wreaked havoc. We have dragons murdered, burnt to a crisp, dragons in jail and my best dragons, who could be considered a threat to Black, all chained up doing hard labour. They are being worked so hard that it is unlikely any will survive more than one or two dragon months, so I decided something had to be done!"

Gold nodded in absolute agreement. "So what can we do Dragon Brown?" Brown took another swallow of the cool water, licked his lips and ushered Gold over to a larger rock table situated in the centre of the room, where a colourful diagram of the island was displayed. To the side of the diagram was a parchment containing a list of dragon names?

Draegonian Forces

Dragon Brown   *Commanding Dragon in Chief*

Dragon soldiers available for action

Tuscan Red	Sergeant
Umber	Corporal
Wenge	Private
Wine	Private
Zinnwaldite	Private

Prisoners (8) Hard Labour North Island

Wild Watermelon	Tool Box	Mango	Tango
Magenta-Dean	Krugerrand	Candy	Apple red

Dragon Soldiers (13 Deceased)
Carbonised by Dragon Black

Electric Yellow	Egyptian Blue	Golden Poppy	Lapis Lazuli
Golden Yellow	Hansa Yellow	Indian Red	Indian Yellow
Drab	Pale Aqua	Vivid Auburn	Twilight Lavender
Meat Brown			

Dragon Brown pointed to the list. "You can see Gold, we have a problem. Dragons of Draegonia are in the main peaceful and have neither the experience, will or desire to fight. Our Draegonian army originally was made up of a compliment of 27 including myself. The list shows we have already lost 13 killed by Black when he first arrived. There are six of us here and eight below doing hard labour under tight guard and in chains." Gold nodded in agreement, paused for a moment, then in a low tone, growled. "But can't you still overthrow Dragon Black with half of your original team?" Brown turned his head from studying the list and with a very worried frown stared at Gold. "Gold, if we had not been so stupid in getting rid of the 'Flame Out' weapon, then we might have stood a reasonable chance of success, however as you can see there are only six of us here who could put up a reasonable fight we would be unlikely to succeed against Black's Fire Power backed by his formidable Elite Guards. And, there are no other dragons willing to risk their lives or indeed any who are trained to fight." Brown continued in a more urgent tone. "We might stand a better chance if we can rescue those in chains below, but as you probably saw they are guarded at all times." Gold interjected, "Yes I know, but are you aware there are only three guards and they would not expect any attack and I am sure that the six of you could surprise and over power them." Gold continued with some excitement, "If you could release the remainder of your forces, then at least you would have a 14 strong army."

Brown, a grim expression on his face, shook his head. "I am afraid not Gold, the prisoners have been worked so hard and fed so little that they now have serious injuries requiring time to heal. More importantly, because of malnutrition, their flames are so weak they would initially be of little use and before they could gain sufficient strength, Black and his guards would hunt us all down."

Brown looked very thoughtful, his brain working overtime, continued, "For the time being we are no more than just an annoyance and fortunately for us Black is unaware of who has set up the Anti-Dragon Black movement." Gold growled in contempt. "So, you're going to leave your troops to die eh? What's the benefit of doing nothing, it makes no sense to me?" Brown glared in annoyance at Gold and growled back. "It's not a question of doing nothing; it's a question of not losing any more dragon lives, and if you think you can handle the situation better, then be my guest!"

Realising that the discussion was becoming somewhat heated Gold removed from a concealed pocket the file he had earlier obtained from the senior dragon guard.

"Look," he said. "I know which assignment and which Guard has been allocated to each prisoner. This tells us the times of their breaks and importantly the times when the guards will be relieved." Brown took the file from Gold and eyes squinting, peered at it. "Umm the information is of course useful as we had no knowledge of their assignments or timings. This does tell us when they are planned to be relieved. But, and I am not trying to put a dampener on things Gold, but, even if we took out the Guards, we still would have to release our comrades and quickly get them up a very difficult track in order to hide them here." Brown frowned once more adding. "Then, even if we got them here we would not really have sufficient room or food, or indeed facilities for fourteen of Draegonia's largest dragons of which some will undoubtedly require medical attention." Gold furiously nodded in frustrated agreement. "Yes, Yes I agree, but what if we get Dragon Grey up here to deal with the medical issues and I get assistance from Dragons Red and Blue to move up all the supplies you need...." Brown shook his head once more and in a much more subdued voice sighed. "Your enthusiasm and desire to assist is of course appreciated, but let's look at the facts. Firstly, the only way up to this cave is by following the track you managed to locate hidden below the cliff face. Secondly, the entrance into the rear of this cave cannot be reached easily and dragons trekking up to this area are going to be seen as very conspicuous. Thirdly, and this is important, if we do manage to overpower the guards and we do release the prisoners and we do manage to get them up here without any loss and we are able to get all of us into this space, **what** do you think Dragon Black's retaliation would be?"

Gold was just about to answer as Brown furiously clapped both his paws together and at the same time swiped the floor with his tail. A startled Dragon Gold reacted nervously as resonating, thunderous sounds, echoed throughout the cave. Dragon Brown laughed at Gold being so obviously frightened and knowingly said. "If that made you jump, imagine what Dragon Black would do to us all and it certainly wouldn't be a clapping of hands and a thrashing of his tail. Unlike us, he can fly; he has tremendous flame throwing powers and is far stronger than any of us. His Elite Guards are totally loyal, doing his every bidding and if we get it wrong, he will make examples of us all." Gold slumped back on his haunches and as Gold entered. He was covered in dust, his eyes were watering and he was panting furiously. "Whatever is the matter Gold?" Blue asked.

Dragon Gold shut the door behind him and leaning with his back against it asked for some 'Dragon Water'. Blue quickly poured some cool, crystal clear liquid, into a large blue plastic tub and handed it to Gold who gulped it down in one large mouthful. Wiping his jaws with his right paw Gold explained what he had been doing, how he had entered the hard labour camp, his conversation with the senior guard, the obtaining of strategic information and how he had located Dragon Brown.

Blue listened in some amazement, nodding and raising an eyebrow every so often at Gold's exploits. Was this really the cautious, usually pompous Mayor Dragon Gold who rarely took risks? Blue waited patiently for Gold to pause for breath. The moment came and as Gold took an enormous intake of air, Dragon Blue spoke in a cold precise tone. "You have been either very brave, or very stupid." Gold looked at Blue wide eyed with an expression of exasperation. "What do you mean? I have not only located Dragon Brown but agreed with him a plan of action to get rid of Black and his murdering followers, what's stupid about that?" Blue moved closer to Gold and patted him on his shoulder. "Look," he said," I am not suggesting you have not done brilliantly in finding Dragon Brown or organising with him a counter movement against Black's tyranny. But, by making the senior guard believe you were given permission to take that file and pretending to be acting on Dragon Black's orders, what's Black going to do when he finds out you have been lying?" Gold had not given any thought to the consequences of his actions and just shrugged his large round shoulders. "Hopefully, Dragon Brown's attack on the guards will prevent the senior guard returning." Blue reacted immediately. "You told me Gold, that Dragon Brown is going to wait for the current guards to be replaced. They will return to the city leaving behind the new guard. So, the officer you hoodwinked..........."Gold realising the significance of what Blue was suggesting blurted out "Oh, what on earth can we, I mean, I do?"

Blue slowly shook his head from side to side. "Gold, I think you had better come up with a plan to counteract the guard's inevitable report or join Dragon Brown and go into hiding." Gold looked thoughtfully at Blue, turned and opened the door ready to leave.

"The guards will be changed tomorrow and I am too tired to do anything tonight. I will go home and sleep on it. I suggest Blue that we meet up tomorrow, immediately after Dragon Black's regular morning meeting, by then I may have thought of something. In the meantime, can I rely on you to accompany me to discuss with Dragon Grey our plans and the need for his medical skills to be available for Brown's team?" Blue bowed his head in agreement, his face showing signs of major concern.

Gold cautiously looked out of the Police Cave door, watching for any movement of the curfew guards. Then, with a wave of his paw and the ringing tones of Blue's last words of "Good Luck, see you tomorrow," slid silently into the empty quiet street. With quickening strides, dodging the harsh shadows created by the brightness of the moonlit night, made it back to the comfort, protection and safety of his cave.

Dragon Gold closed the cave door behind him, lit a 'Draegonian Lamp' and breathed a sigh of relief. Deep down he knew that his actions and meeting with Dragon Brown had now placed him in very grave danger.

CHAPTER 13

A Good Plan & Perfect Strategies

The sun as usual started another long day's trek as it slowly emerged out of the east, where the dark pinks and blues of the early morning sky seamlessly joined the mirror-reflective rich dark blue of the flat sea. The senior Draegonian Guard looked at his 'Draegonian Watch' and blowing a large whistle signified that the eight dragons, their chains biting deep into their skin, could stop for their morning 10 'Draegonian Minute' break.

The two remaining guards herded the imprisoned dragons into an enclosure specifically made as a holding compound, with large, heavy posts, sunk deep into the rocky water's edge. One by one the dragons were shackled by their chains to thick iron rings embedded deep into the hard wooden posts preventing any chance of escaping. Two open topped barrels of water and a trough full of what looked like thick lumpy cold porridge was placed within the reach of their mouths. "Hurry up and eat, you have ten 'Draegonian Minutes' only, then back to work," yelled one of the guards. The senior guard, Dragon Russet, whipped his tail across the heads of two of the closest tightly secured dragons. The prisoners ducked and began sucking at the tasteless muck made from stale bread and water. They were starving and as there was insufficient for so many dragons the trough was soon bare.

Russet teasingly laughed out loud and pulled from an old wooden locker, positioned beside one of the huge posts, an enormous fish he had caught earlier and swallowed it in one go.

"Umm, that was delicious," he sneered, licking his lips for all to see. "I bet all of you would have liked that?" The eight tired and worn out dragons made no comment. They knew that if they did respond it would mean just another whipping, no more rest and probably, no more food or water for the remainder of the day.

"LOOK" shouted one of the guards pointing along the beach. "It's our replacements and about time I have had enough of this place." The approaching Guards were all related, their skins of a similar creamy fawn colour differentiated only by shades of dark, light and neutral.

Dragon Almond was the senior of the approaching three. He was followed by Dragons Moccasin and Wheat. They were all dressed in bright red and blue tabards, a new uniform that Dragon Black had decided all his troops should wear. The three dragons that had been on duty for a week looked down at their own threadbare tunics of dirty white and red material faded through age by the sun and covered in stains. "I am looking forward to getting my new uniform when I return and shall pick up yours at the same time," Dragon Russet grunted at his subordinates. The replacement guards were now in hailing distance and all fired out a tremendous burst of flame signifying they were about to take charge and relieve the old guard.

Earlier the three old guards had packed their kit bags and were now standing by them, eager to depart, as their relief team finally drew closer. "Guards, attention" Dragon Russet barked. "Guards salute." As he shouted out the last command Russet stepped forward and presented his counterpart with keys to the chains, office and a pack of comprehensive prisoner notes and schedules. Russet's replacement took the items, growled and turned to his two eager subordinates. "Guards, attention, take your positions and assume duty." With the last command ringing in the ears of all those around, the two brightly regaled new guards went over to the prisoners enclosure and immediately started whipping their tails across their prisoners backs, causing each of them to wince in pain. The new senior guard, with flames emanating from his crooked mouth sneered. "Dragon Black believes you may have been too lenient with the prisoners Russet and has instructed us to make them work a 22 hour shift with one break in 11. They are to be worked until they drop." Russet just nodded, saluted once more and with the command of **"Quick march,"** trotted off with his tired two dragon soldiers. They moved quickly along the beach heading for the long trek back to the city and their well earned rest.

Dragon Brown watched as the old guard disappeared into the distance and then focused his attention back to the three new ones who were now pushing their chained captives back to work. One dragon tripped over his chains pulling a second with him into the sea. The nearest guard thrashed his tail into the water and then violently flicked it across each prisoner's back making them yell with pain. "Get a move on," the Guard growled.

A concerned Dragon Brown could see the pain being inflicted but felt helpless; he was unable to immediately do anything to relieve them of their suffering.

Brown, in deep thought, returned to the cave that now was officially the control and command post for what would be the implementation of his audacious plan. He issued instructions to his assembly of five dragons. "We shall today take the first step in removing Dragon Black from power. Let us review our plans and strategies. At sunset, Dragons Tuscan-Red, Umber and Wenge, you will overpower and replace the guards." Tuscan-Red, raising a paw, interjected. "Sir, may I speak? I am concerned that our skins are somewhat darker than the three guards we are to replace. We most certainly will stand out and surely not fool Dragon Black during his daily patrol."

Brown nodded in agreement. Bending down he picked up large clawed handfuls of the whitish grey dust from the cave floor and hurled it at his sergeant. The dust spread over a part of the sergeant's wing and as he tried to brush it off he saw that his reddish brown skin was fading into a much lighter fawn colour. Dragon Brown still pointing to the floor barked out his orders. "All three of you will cover yourselves in this dust. Just stay away from the water as Black passes by. After the three guards have been overpowered you will put on their new tabards and from a distance anyone should be fooled into believing you're the regular guards." Dragon Brown, steely eyed gazed at the two other dragons. "Once we have neutralised the guards, Dragon Zinnwaldite and Dragon Wine, you will return with them and secure them in one of the inner caves. Then, Zinnwaldite you will assume position as lookout from the top of the cliff and Dragon Wine your role will be to patrol the North Beach and immediately report back anyone seen approaching, any questions?"

There was a hesitant silence broken by the odd grunt as five dragons nodded their heads signifying their total support. "Right," said Brown. "You all need to get some rest and in the right mood for a jolly good fight, it is time we teach Dragon Black and his supporters that we will not put up with their murdering and bullying anymore. We have a plan and perfect strategies that will put an end to our misery." Outside the cave, in the oppressive heat of the day, silence was broken only by the rumbling chuckle of dragon laughter as Dragon Brown concluded his motivational message to his troops.

CHAPTER 14

A Wild Dragon Chase

George had been waiting patiently outside the club house. It was now 3 o'clock in the afternoon as three, very out of breath cousins, raced towards him. "Sorry we're late George" Grace puffed. "Yeah we had a bit of a problem convincing Mum and Dad we could stay over with you tonight," piped up Joel. Zach, swinging his rucksack in circles above his head laughed and shouted. "But we convinced them and Dad has spoken with Auntie Paula who said it would be OK." George grinned at their enthusiasm but he knew that there would be no-stop over that evening, well at least not at his Mum's house.

"OK, guys let's see what you have brought with you," George said, keenly eyeing their bags. Zack was first to open his rucksack to reveal, a silver wind up torch, some chocolate bars, a change of clothing, a notebook and a plastic bottle filled with milk. Grace had a hold-all containing, a change of clothes, paper, pen, compass, a small laser pen light, some candles and a box of matches. George moved closer and peered into Joel's rucksack. Inside he saw clothes, a second pair of flip flops, a large black plastic torch, a small pair of binoculars, an assortment of sweets, a pen knife and a woolly bright red blanket. George pulled out the corner fold of the blanket revealing it to the others. "Why a blanket Joel?" Joel dropped his head in some embarrassment snatched his bag back and closing the flap took a deep breath, explaining. "You all know the island can pop up in any ocean or sea anywhere in the world and it may be cold, so I have brought a blanket and some plastic sheeting as well as my hoodie." "Oh, I am sure the island will be somewhere warm, dragons don't like the cold," Zach added in amusement. George gave Joel a friendly smile and a wink. He knew that the Island of Draegonia had its own eco-climate. Only the North Beach and seas surrounding Draegonia were affected by its location, be it in the South Pacific, or freezing seas of the Antarctic. But not wanting to hurt Joel's feelings, he nodded in some agreement taking from his pocket the 'Wish Card' he had carried close to his chest since its arrival.

Facing his three cousins he signalled them to listen. "*Shhhoosh*, let's get this wish sorted out." Then, from another pocket, George removed and held the message that had been retrieved from what all four agreed, had been a fantastic magical bottle. "We know that Dragon Black has returned and that Draegonia is in trouble. We also know that we have been asked to help, so do we use the 'Wish Card' to get us there or not?" "That's a stupid question," retorted an indignant Grace. "Of course we should help our friends and especially if Dragon Black has returned, but why don't we just wish for him to disappear, never to be seen again?" Before George could say anything Joel piped up. "Look, why don't we just wish for Dragon Black to lose his flame and become weak again?" "We could of course wish he would just die or be executed," Zach contributed with an air of defiance. George removed the 'Wish Card' from its envelope for all to see and turning it over reminded them of the inscription. "We cannot use our wish to do harm, even if our wish was against evil. We only have one wish and I think we are all in agreement it must be used for us to get back to Draegonia, where I am sure we can at least help, in the fight against the black dragon." The three, simultaneously, shouted in support. "Then let's go," yelled Zach. "I'm with you George," Grace chanted. "Let's get him," said Zach between gritted teeth as all four entered the now deserted club house.

George drew a circle in the dust on the club room's parquet floor. "All stand in the middle of the circle." The three clutched their belongings as George, now with the 'Wish Card' firmly held in his somewhat sweaty hands closed his eyes to make his wish. "Do we have to close our eyes as well?" Grace whispered. George was oblivious to her question and in a slightly nervous voice made his wish. "I wish that all within the circle I stand be transported safely to Draegonia." **"Wait,"** cried out Joel. But it was too late.

A column of bluish white light encompassed the four. The club house room could still be seen, although not clearly, as the room appeared to be spinning. Faster and faster the room spun and brighter and brighter their encompassing beam of light became, until all about them no longer resembled the club house hall but was now replaced, by a misty green haze dashed with shadows of differing colours, shapes and sizes.

What seemed like minutes was in fact just seconds as the four were whisked away, moving at the speed of light, high into the sky inside their mini tornado of pulsating colours.

Then silence. From inside their protected sphere, the four saw, through a misty haze, images of spinning trees, rock formations and sandy beaches. The circular beam of towering light that had encapsulated them started to shrink and as it did so the images around them became sharper. They had indeed arrived on the Island of Draegonia, somewhere on the steeper eastern slopes, close to some tall granite looking rocks and to their left the uninterrupted views of the sea.

"Wow," said Zach. "That was awesome." Grace said nothing but brushing her hair from her eyes turned to Joel then asked. "Why did you shout out for us to wait?" Joel, hands in his pockets, kicked away a small stone and just shrugged. "It's too late now." "What do you mean?" George enquired. Joel, picking up his rucksack searched for the bag of sweets he knew was inside and just shrugged again. An exasperated Grace, arms folded, glared at Joel waiting for him to explain. Joel did not reply but took a sweet out of the paper bag, removed the foil wrapper and was about to put the chocolate fudge in his mouth, as George demanded yet again to know what he had meant.

"Well it's like this; you were making a wish for us to be transported to Draegonia, right. But your wish did not include anything about returning us home. I shouted wait, because I was going to make a suggestion, but it was too late." He's right," Zach cried. "How are we going to get back home?" George and Grace, turning their heads towards each other, for the first time looked worried. They both realised that Joel had raised a very important question and one that they had stupidly overlooked in their haste to return to Draegonia.

"OK Joel," George said, patting him on his back. "You are right I should have thought of it before making the wish but we are here now and our first priority is to seek out some of our dragon friends who will hide us. In the meantime, I suggest we make camp by those rocks over there and get some rest." The four ambled towards the rocks and as they did so peered up towards the peak of the Volcano that was unusually dormant, with only thin wispy plumes of light grey smoke, drifting high into the windless sky. "You know," Joel mumbled between sucking on his second mouth-watering sweet. "It appears to me that perhaps we are on a 'wild goose chase'." "Nope we're not," Grace with a glint in her eye laughed. "We are actually on a wild dragon chase."

CHAPTER 15

Grey Has An Idea

Earlier that day, Dragon Black had presided over his daily gathering of dragons held in the main square. He had informed them of the new laws and regulations he was to impose on Draegonia and its inhabitants. Clearly, the new regulations were designed to tighten his bullying grip and restrict the free movement of dragons. He announced that no dragon would be allowed to leave the city limits without special permission and that the evening curfew would commence earlier and now be 1 hour before dusk as of immediate effect. Black had also threatened that unless he received information of the whereabouts of Dragon Brown and others believed to be in his company, he would take reprisals on the families of all missing dragons, making examples for all to see. The congregation of dragons shivered and crouched in fear, knowing that if any were brave enough to object, then their own lives would be at risk.

Dragon Gold had not slept well that night and tiredness was making it difficult for him to concentrate. He listened in abject horror, knowing that the freedom of all dragons had been severely compromised and that Dragon Black had, by imposing such unreasonable laws, now made their city into an open prison.

Black's final proclamation of the day, before terminating his enforced meeting, informed everyone that he was also introducing conscription. With immediate effect all able and fit young male dragons would be recruited into his newly formed army. Those who refused would be dealt with as traitors.

Two young dragons, (Vegas-Gold and Dandelion) crouched out of immediate sight towards the rear of the crowd, looked at each other and nodded in silent agreement. They were the right age to be conscripted but they were also dragons who had strong opinions about fighting, irrespective of the reasons or justification. They were known as 'Conscientious Objectors', dragons who refused to fight on moral grounds. Black's decree was the 'final straw'. Both had made their minds up to depart the city as quickly as possible, to hide in the dense forest in the southern part of the island, out of the clutches of Dragon Black and his guards.

Dragon Vegas-Gold slipped away first, followed by his closest friend Dandelion, who casually sauntered after him, as though in no real hurry to catch up, so as not to draw attention from Dragon Black's Elite Guards.

The two young dragons eventually caught up with each other on reaching the deserted Draegonia Hospital. "Vegas," Dandelion whispered, peering all around to ensure they were not seen or heard. "Don't you think we should go back for supplies, I mean to say, living in the forest won't be easy for us without some of the comforts of home?" Vegas, a slim, rich golden yellow dragon grinned. "If you value your life Dandelion you will forget returning back to your cave for a few luxuries. Our first priority is to get as far away from the city as possible before the guards seal off the only two ways in or out." "But," Dandelion started to protest. "Enough." Vegas responded, raising his voice in annoyance. "We need to move quickly, carrying anything will just slow us down. Also carrying any baggage would make us look a little obvious, don't you think?" Dandelion said nothing, but just listened to Vegas who although younger, was very bright and a born survivor.

"Dandelion, you head for the eastern pass and I will aim to get through the much heavier guarded southern exit. By our splitting up, one of us is surely to escape." Vegas started to make a move, patted Dandelion on his shoulder as a motivational gesture. "You'll get through this, so don't worry, just make sure you keep out of sight, move quickly and we'll meet up within the southern perimeter of the forest late this evening." Dandelion, still displaying a concerned look on his yellowish face, that was becoming a paler yellow by the second, moaned. "I do hope your right and we do make it, but I have a horrible feeling that something terrible is going to happen to me." Vegas knew that speed and urgency was of paramount importance, turned away from Dandelion and with final words of encouragement quietly said. "Be positive, take care and you will be fine." Then silently, he disappeared out of sight, heading south.

Dragon Black ended his routine morning meeting with the square once again returning back to some normality. Dragon Gold was wiping his brow with a rich velvety red cloth displaying the gold embossed Draegonia Insignia, given to him when he was Mayor. Gold breathed a sigh of relief, he had heard that the officer of the recently replaced guard had requested some sick leave and would possibly be out of action for a few days. Gold wiped his brow, one problem solved for the short term at least, he thought. Gold was a truly hot and bothered dragon, facing real dilemmas. The situation with the guard maybe temporarily resolved but he had other worries to consider. How was he to get information to Dragon Brown and more importantly, in view of all the new restrictions, how could the essential supplies of food and water possibly reach Brown and his team? Gold knew he needed help and that his priority was to find a way to elicit the support and assistance of Dragon Black's personal physician, Dragon Grey. Stern faced and with several deep lines of worry across his brow Gold hastily galloped towards the Police Station where Blue had been ordered to guard the prisoners and of course Dragon Pink.

Gold arrived at the police station still conveying the look of a dragon carrying the woes of all. His brow furrowed his eyes wide with fear, tongue hanging out and gasping for breath, he rushed through the open door.

"Dragon Blue we need to talk, we have to devise some sort of plan, firstly to prevent Dragon Russet when he recovers from his illness, from reporting to Dragon Black my encounter with him. Secondly, we need to find a way to prevent Dragon Pink's wings being clipped and thirdly we must secure a way to assist Dragon Brown's efforts to overthrow Black."

"**Shush,** for goodness sake Gold, keep your voice down and shut that door, do you want us to spend our last seconds being roasted by Dragon Black?" "I'm so sorry Dragon Blue." Gold cried. "But if we do not do something and soon, life will be totally unbearable and there will be many more horrendous laws imposed, increased taxes, restrictions on our movements, and....." Dragon Gold paused for breath, then exclaimed. "And, there will be many more dragon deaths." Blue nodded in agreement and expanded his wings revealing that, at an early age, his too had been clipped. "Gold, look at these, we have all had our wings clipped, none of us are able to fly, our flames are no match for the strength of Dragon Black's and," Dragon Blue gave a sigh, raised his paws in a gesture of acceptance and continued. "Now, he has a number of dragons forming his Elite Guard protecting him from any attack. So," Blue emphasised. "**What** do you propose we should do?" Gold winced in the pain of knowing that hope was dwindling and that little appeared to be able to be done. "Dragon Blue," Gold quietly but firmly stated. "I have no idea what we can do, but I do know we must do something and perhaps we should look to the immediate threat to poor little Pink's wings." Blue with a nod of agreement responded. "OK, so how do we stop Black from carrying out his decree of the 'Clipping of the Wings' ceremony planned for the New Moon and also, I might add, the execution he has planned for the prisoners?" Gold thought for a moment, scratched his head, paced up and down and then with a glint in his eye, cried out. "I have an idea, why don't we approach Dragon Black with a good reason as to why HE should not demean himself by actually undertaking the clipping?" Blue looked on, somewhat quizzically, but before he had chance to speak Dragon Gold added. "Dragon Black loves to have everyone believe he is our leader and that he is above us in intellect, knowledge, strength and position, AND, that we all respect him. That is his weakness, a weakness we could focus upon and use to our advantage."

Blue crouched down in his usual relaxed position but with a somewhat bewildered look upon his face and quietly asked. "Gold, what are you getting at, what have you in mind?" Dragon Gold smiled. "Look," he said. "Why don't we meet with Dragon Black on the basis we wish to agree the format of the trial and events that inevitably will lead to the execution of the prisoners. We will let him believe we are entirely in agreement with the planned executions but believe he would be more popular and respected, if he was to show some compassion and not hold the 'Clipping of the Wings' ceremony on the same day as the executions." Blue was about to question the logic as Gold continued in a more excited tone. "Look, I don't suggest he does not clip Pink's wings but just has the ceremony or operation undertaken on a different day, perhaps at a different location and importantly, he does not administer the surgical procedure himself."

Dragon Blue, eyes widening and frown disappearing waved his paw in a circular motion indicating he wanted to hear more. Gold obliged. "My plan is that we should convince Dragon Black that the clipping of any dragon's wing is far too demeaning and should be left to one of his lowly subordinates. We should emphasise that he should be seen as the one who delegates and orders whilst being totally responsible for the *execution* of fair and true justice." Blue nodded in some enthusiasm. "I see, your aim is to get Dragon Black to believe that clipping dragon wings is beneath his position and that he should be seen as a true and just leader that earns him our"..... Blue paused, and then sneered, *"Our respect!"*

"Exactly Blue and we should suggest or better still recommend that Black would earn even greater respect if he was to show a little compassion and have Pink's wings clipped by his Chief Physician, Dragon Grey." Blue stroked his hairy spiky chin and once more nodded in approval. "The plan is good but it still results in Dragon Pink's wings being clipped, even if it is professionally administered." Gold shook his head and moving closer to Dragon Blue, whispered. "But Pink's wings will not be cut we will persuade Dragon Grey to make it look as though the ceremony has been completed but we will have agreed in advance with Grey not cut and remove the tendons of her wings that we all know would render them useless forever."

Blue growled and then laughed nervously. "If Dragon Grey goes along with your plan then we stand a chance of saving Dragon Pink, but if any of this should leak back to Dragon Black, then we are in serious and I mean serious, deadly trouble." Gold moved towards the station's door and beckoned Blue to follow. "Look Blue, we have really nothing to lose in at least discussing the strategy with Dragon Grey. If he agrees to carry out our plan then our next step is to convince Dragon Black that the 'Clipping of the Wing' ceremony should be seen by him as a minor event and be left to the Draegonia Hospital surgical teams overseen by his Chief Physician. If Grey refuses to cooperate with us," Gold paused, then with significant exasperation exclaimed. "I just do not know what we will do." Blue, pushing Dragon Gold ahead of him, slid into the late morning sunlit deserted street, closed and locked the heavy cave door behind them and with a flurry of his empty clawed paw pointed in the direction of the hospital. "OK Gold, let's meet with Dragon Grey and see what he has to say about it." Dragons Blue and Gold walked off together at a quickening pace and once out of sight of the Dragon Police Station, ran the rest of the way, towards Draegonia's Hospital.

Rounding the last corner a tall stone archway with its towering, open rusty iron gates of the hospital, came into full view.

"Gosh," said Dragon Gold. "It's so quiet, where is everybody?" "I know," Blue retorted. "Ever since Black's return the hospital has had fewer patients but significantly more dragon bodies and everyone is frightened to even visit the small number of patients that are still remaining. The two, moving swiftly through the hospital's brightly lit cave corridors finally came to a large green wooden locked door carrying a phosphorescent glowing sign. In large green letters it displayed the words;

RESEARCH & DEVELOPMENT

Dragon Blue, with a clenched dragon fist, knocked aggressively on the door, the sound of his banging resounding throughout the corridors. There was no answer. "Let me," Dragon Gold offered. Using his tail Gold cracked it sharply against the door and simultaneously shouted out as loudly as he could. "Dragon Grey, I order you to open this door immediately." Before either dragon growled one more word, the door was swiftly pulled opened by a stern faced Dragon Grey. Dressed in his white laboratory coat, displaying a variety of 'Dragon Pens' in his top pocket, he stood before them. "What's all the noise and commotion? Oh it's you Gold and Dragon Blue, what on earth is the matter?" Dragons Blue and Gold pushed past Grey instructing him to close the door after them. The laboratory was off limits to everyone other than the two assistants that usually worked with Dragon Grey, but today, they were nowhere to be seen. The oblong room contained two full length tables running down its centre. Each table displayed weird looking bottles of different shapes and sizes containing a variety of differing coloured solutions and liquids. Several glass containers were perched on metal tripods, their bubbling contents being heated by flames appearing from pipes and tubes that disappeared through holes in the table top, down into the very smooth highly polished stone floor beneath. Hanging on the walls were numerous graphic pictures of dragon body parts and at the very end of the room a full size dragon skeleton appeared to watch their every move. Before Grey had time to question his new arrivals, Dragon Gold let out a blast from his fiery mouth, quickly explaining why they were there. Blue looked on in support, whilst Dragon Grey listened, not saying a word. He heard how Gold had found Dragon Brown and the need for his involvement. He raised his eyes at the suggestion that he should put his life on the line by looking after the injured prisoners and pondered thoughtfully on hearing of the plan to assist Dragon Pink. "So what do you think Grey? If we persuade Dragon Black to defer the date, time and venue and agree that he will abdicate the responsibility of clipping Pink's wings over to you." Dragon Gold paused and rather hesitatingly continued. "Would you be prepared to undertake the responsibility and importantly find a way not to permanently cripple Dragon Pink's wings?"

Grey had been listening with interest making the odd growl as he nodded in some agreement with the strategies being presented. He slowly removed his white laboratory coat and hung it carefully on a rack near the door. "Ummmn," he started to say. "You know I have no love for Dragon Black but he is definitely not one to cross. Whatever we agree to do, we need to also fully appreciate the risks." Both Gold and Blue looked at each other in concerned agreement. Blue, straightening himself up and with a look of authority, stepped forward. "I am sure we can persuade Black to command you to carry out the procedure Dragon Grey and our plan will be for the operation to be undertaken here, in the hospital." Blue again hesitated for a second then questioned. "But do you think you can make it look convincing enough to fool Dragon Black if he were to either be there to watch or inspect your handiwork?"

Grey moved awkwardly across to one of the smooth flat walls and halted next to a diagram of a dragon's wing depicting in great detail all the muscles, ligaments tendons and veins. Grey had an idea and pointing a claw to the diagram, he thoughtfully confessed. "There is a way of appearing to cut these key ligaments and tendons but actually only cutting into muscle tissue. To the untrained eye it would be hard to differentiate." Grey turning to face both dragons lowered his head and in a much sterner tone growled. "We do have one small problem though." Before Gold had time to open his mouth Blue quickly interrupted. "What problem, surely it's just a question of you fooling Dragon Black into thinking you have clipped Pink's wings?" Dragon Grey smiled knowingly. "It's not Black I am concerned with, its Dragon Pink." Grey continued. "You see, if we let Pink know that she is not really going to have her wings clipped for real, then she will not display the fear, horror and anxieties that all other dragons have done in the past and Black will soon see through our subterfuge." Dragon Grey rubbed his chin and with an air as though of talking to himself, continued. "The false procedure will however cause great pain to Dragon Pink and if she is not aware of our plan she could well believe that the correct procedure has been undertaken and hopefully, display convincing emotions." Grey was now in deep thought mumbling. "And because the muscles will have been cut Pink's wings will feel heavy, she will not want to move them, thus giving the exact impression they have been clipped."

The two dragons, fully appreciating the importance of Grey's opinions were in awe. It was Blue who first broke their silence. "OK, we appear to have a plan to safeguard Pink but what do we do in support of Dragon Brown and his dragons?" Grey immediately retorted. "Dragon Black has made it clear anyone leaving the city will be dealt with and his guards have been ordered not to take prisoners. I regret Brown and his makeshift army will have to fend for themselves."

Gold and Blue nodded their heads in reluctant agreement. "Right," Blue loudly growled. "Gold, we need to speak with Dragon Black and put into place the first steps of our agreed plan. Dragon Grey I suggest you get ready to accept Black's orders and prepare to receive Dragon Pink."

CHAPTER 16

Black Makes A Killing

The four children had decided that they needed to make plans before attempting to take on the task that lay ahead. Their first priority was to set up a camp well out of sight but in a position that provided good views of the ground around. The tall rocks afforded excellent cover, especially as Joel had cut branches from the tall leafy shrubs and placed them across the openings to provide the four with sufficient camouflage. Grace laid out sleeping bags on plastic sheeting, Zach searched for wood to make a fire. George smiled; he was delighted that his cousins were working as a team but apprehensive of what might lay ahead.

George called the three together. "I am sorry Zach but we cannot afford to light a fire but the wood you have collected won't be wasted. Importantly I think we need to have a lookout at all times, no good us just arriving only to be caught unawares." George pulled some paper and a pencil from his pockets and started to write. "I'll take the first watch and will take cover behind those rocks over there." George pointed towards a group of boulders some 10 meters from where they were standing. "Zach," George continued. "You relieve me in a couple of hours. Grace I would like you take over from Zach and Joel I suggest you get some sleep now, as you will take the first of the night shifts." Joel blinked and looked at his wrist watch. "Sleep, it's the middle of the afternoon and you want me to sleep, I can't sleep, I'm not at all tired." Grace tapped Joel on the shoulder. "Look Joel, we have enough to do to keep ourselves safe let alone worry about whether or not we can adapt to a sleeping pattern." George grabbed his bag and moving some of the branches placed earlier by Joel, exited the encampment, as his did so, turning, he faced his three friends. "Look guys we're in an extraordinary situation and we will have to do some extraordinary things if we are to help our dragon friends and now is not the time for any moans or groans." George did not wait for any response but quickly headed for the cover of the small boulders and rocks that would be his look outpost for the next two hours.

A few hours earlier Dragon Dandelion had left both Dragon Vegas-Gold and the Draegonia Hospital, cautiously making his way out of the city towards the safety of the southern forests and planned rendezvous with his closest friend. Nervously, he kept looking over his shoulder, expecting to see one of Dragon Black's elite guards ready to arrest him. The eastern exit of the city was narrow and very rugged. The track ran round the island's volcano, its narrow path overlooking steep drops to barren and inhospitable ground below. The eastern route was not often used and Dandelion was experiencing first hand all the reasons why.

As he moved his large frame along the narrow and winding route his feet occasionally breaking the edges sending cascading rubble on their echoing journey beneath, he wondered if he would ever reach the safety of the lush forest that seemed so far away. Dandelion took a deep breath, mumbling to pull himself together. He closed his eyes and with his back to the rugged mountain cliff face continued his journey. Finally, exhausted but relieved, Dandelion reached the base of the volcano and stood on ground that gradually sloped between undulating ground towards greener and more visibly attractive surroundings. The vista ahead was interspersed with large boulders and tall shrubs either side of a winding track. Dandelion took one last frightened look all round him and set off for what he believed would be a meeting with his friend Vegas-Gold, in the safety of the lush forest.

Meanwhile, Dragon Black was sitting on his throne in the Great Hall as Dragons Blue and Gold appeared. Black stared at them; his piercing red eyes did not flicker as they approached. **"So what do you want?"** Black snarled, as he shifted his long tail to curl beneath him. Gold spoke first. "Your Highness, Dragon Blue and I have been finalising plans for the trial and execution of the prisoners. We have also been reviewing the 'Clipping of the Wings' ceremony and would now like to report to you our recommendations for your approval." Blue, moving to Gold's side, stood to attention and saluted. Blue really did not respect Dragon Black but knew that if he played to Black's ego they just might get him to cooperate with their plan. Blue dropped his saluting paw sharply to his side. "Sire," he said. "We have looked at the timings of the trial and have a recommendation that we feel will be of great benefit for you." Before Black had chance to respond Dragon Gold interjected. "Yes your Dragonship." Gold recalled that Dragon Green used to refer to Black as 'Your Dragonship', a title that Black apparently quite liked. Gold continued. "We have looked at the timings for the trial of the prisoners and know that you wish for all of Draegonia to see you as being fair and just. We estimate trial time for each prisoner to be at least 30 minutes if we were to let them offer any defense." Black began to raise himself up in a gesture of intense anger just as Blue quickly responded. "Sire, it is clear that you want to ensure that all Dragons of Draegonia see you as a just leader and one that they can trust will show true justice who they can respect. I feel that if they did not believe this, then we may well have some who will oppose you and possibly form a movement of opposition that will take up unnecessary time to put down." Black contained himself no longer. He roared with flames firing off in all directions creating an army of formidable shadows that appeared to march across the walls, in and out of the numerous tunnel entrances. **"What,"** Black bellowed. "Do you think I care? Do you think I am scared or worried by a few stupid dragons that may choose to disobey me?"

Gold smiled and again tried to flatter Black in an attempt to calm him down. "Your Dragonship, we know that there are none on Draegonia who are a match for your strength, intellect or courage. Indeed we are all in awe of you, but why create irritations when there is another way of meeting all your needs and desires?" Black cocking his head to one side lowered himself back to his throne. He bent his body forward, his head now close to Gold's. Dragon Gold felt the heat of Black's breath and saw the glint in his evil eyes as he wanted to hear more. "You see Sir," Gold quietly but with great conviction pontificated. "The prisoners will no doubt be found guilty but why should you take the blame or full responsibility for their sentence when we can pass this onto a jury." Before Black had chance to respond Blue quickly interjected. "The outcome will be the execution and of course Sire you will no doubt assume the role of executioner but it will be the Jury who will have passed the sentence and not you, so no one can reasonably blame you for their deaths."

Dragon Black grinned and raising his head coughed with little plumes of smoke wafting from his nostrils. "I see, as judge I shall uphold the sentence but it will be the dragon jury who will find the prisoners guilty, I like that." Gold saw his chance and hurriedly spoke again. "We of course have one minor problem but we also have a solution." Gold paused. There was a brief silence, broken by an irritated Dragon Black. "Well spit it out what's the problem?" Blue was the first to react and quickly intervened. "Dragon Black, I think Gold is referring to the fact that Dragon Pink is to have her wings clipped on the same day and that the ceremony will be a major distraction from what should be seen as a day where you stamp your authority on Draegonia." Black whipped his tail back and forth in exasperation. "Dragon Pink's wings are to be clipped and that's final," he bellowed.

Dragons Gold and Blue had rehearsed exactly how they were going to handle Dragon Black and now as they had planned, Dragon Gold offered the solution. "Your Dragonship, we do not expect Dragon Pink to miss out on such an important ceremony as wing clipping, but do you really want all eyes on her and the obvious sympathy *she* will gain from those gathered around her. Surely *you don't want her* to be considered *as a martyr?*" Black cocked his enormous head to one side his brow wrinkling as he thought through what Gold was saying. Black was just about to let out another of his angry outbursts as Gold thumped the floor with his tail, immediately gaining Black's undivided attention. Gold grinned and held a proclamation sheet between slightly shaking paws. "Your Dagonship, I have prepared a proclamation that only requires your signature. It will result in the immediate instruction to Dragon Grey to carry out the operation on Pink's wings within the operating theatre of the Draegonia Hospital. It also states that the procedure will be observed by you." Blue wanting to support Gold quickly added. " Sire we have checked with Dragon Grey and he has informed us that he can undertake the procedure tomorrow and that he would be honoured for you to attend."

Gold handed the proclamation to Dragon Black and with it a 'Dragon Pen'. "Obviously" Gold calmly stated. "By signing and ordering Dragon Grey to undertake the wing clipping you will be seen to be totally in command but also demonstrating a little compassion." Black was somewhat taken aback. Here were two of the most respected dragons of Draegonia actually supporting him, offering what appeared to be helpful and good advice, why? Black frowned for a few seconds but could not think of any disadvantage to their proposals. Snatching at the proclamation Black clawed on his mark. Handing it back to

Gold he commanded. "Inform Dragon Grey that I will attend tomorrow after my daily meeting to witness the operation and that I expect Pink's wings to be irrevocably cut and no mistakes. Now go and affix the proclamation to our notice board for all to see." Gold and Blue nodded in pretence of respect and without looking back scurried out of Black's sight, relieved that their strategy had worked.

Dragon Black saw them disappear out of the Great Hall and for the first time since his arrival felt that something was wrong and that possibly he was not fully in control. The two dragons appeared to respect him, they had presented reasoned arguments and there was nothing to suppose that his wishes were not being carried out, but still, as he prepared to go out on patrol, flying round the Island of Draegonia, his concerns were growing.

Dragon Dandelion was now well on his way and feeling a little more confident as he placed more 'Dragon Miles' between the city and himself. The safety of the lush green forest was still a long way off but the ground was a little easier to cover as the mid afternoon sun began its decent towards the west. In his haste he occasionally slipped on the loose gravel beneath his feet. Then he heard it, a sound of a roar followed by a noise of powerful wings. Dandelion stopped in his tracks. Turning slowly, he saw an enormous black shadow and as he did so his heart missed a beat. His worst nightmare was happening. In the distance, swooping left and right was Dragon Black, his body casting upon the ground beneath him a huge black image of himself. Dandelion froze for a split second before realising that he was easily visible from the air and that he had to find a place to hide and do it quickly.

George had been on lookout for just over half an hour hidden behind several large rocks that were interspersed with thick bushes that easily concealed his small frame. He too heard the beat of powerful dragon wings as he peered towards the volcano. Then he saw him, a much larger, fitter and more frightening dragon swooping from side to side. Dragon Black was obviously searching for something. His powerful wings propelled him across immense areas within seconds. Black's daily patrols rarely revealed anything of interest as he knew that all dragons feared him so much that they would not dare to break any of his laws. Yet, what was that! Dragon Black swooped lower and as he did so he spied the back of Dragon Dandelion running at full pelt towards some cover of tall prickly shrubs close to a number of boulders and rocks of differing shapes and sizes.

A furious Dragon Black dived headlong towards the very frightened dragon that was running in fear for his life. Black's first pass was clinical and precise. As he descended Black took in great gulps of air, his cheeks bulging under the pressure being built up within his clenched mouth. The two dragons were now only a few meters apart as Black opened his enormous mouth, teeth glistening with the reflection of the sun's rays and spat the full force of his flames. Dandelion first felt the heat of the flames then the powerful blast of hot air that lifted him high into the sky.

George could see the attack clearly. Dandelion's body was immediately singed to a reddish brown, his body tumbling over and over with the blast from Black's fearsome fire power. Dandelion came to an abrupt halt only forty meters from where George was and less than 25 meters from where his cousins were in hiding. What could he do? Should he rush to Dandelions aid? Should he move as quickly as possible to join his friends? Before he had time to fully think through his options, Dragon Black could be seen circling to come in from the rear of Dragon Dandelion for what appeared to be a second attack.

Black felt good. He thought to himself what fantastic exercise he was having, what fun, and a chance to show off his fighting skills. As he turned for the final kill, he saw a motionless charred dragon. **"Ummm"** he spoke out loudly. "This is too easy and no fun, I would have expected any dragon to put up at least some fight." Black spread his enormous powerful wings and continued to dive towards the smoldering dragon.

George was dumbstruck. He had expected Dragon Black to be a force to be reckoned with but had not dreamt that he would have returned stronger and more powerful than before. He followed Black's descending glide and could not believe what happened next. Black, with no flames being expelled, drifted silently over the still body of Dandelion, coming to rest on top of some very large boulders surrounded by bushes and shrubs. Underneath where Black had just landed were three very concerned children.

Grace had been peering out towards where George was on lookout not understanding why he looked so worried. Turning her head to her left she just caught sight of an injured dragon that had smoke drifting from its now charred skin. Then, all of a sudden without any warning, the sky was obscured as Dragon Black, wings fully extended in a wind break position, landed on top of their camp site with a thud. Grace rushed across to her two brothers and with a finger across her mouth indicated absolute silence. The three huddled together not daring to make a sound and waited for events to unfold.

George seeing Dragon Black now on top of the boulders that afforded cover to his three friends sank back so as not to be seen. Black was surveying the area preening himself and with the occasional lick of his long brilliant red tongue, wiped the dust from his amour plated black skin. He felt good. One deserter expediently dealt with and no one would know. As he looked from side to side, his gaze passing over where George was in hiding, he saw movement. Standing up to full height

Dragon Black inhaled, expanding his lungs to their maximum size and smiled, he was about to make a final killing.

Fortunately for George the movement Black had seen was from the raised head of an injured dragon. Dandelion had not been killed but severely injured and had passed out. Now dazed he raised his head only to be consumed by a jet of ferocious white hot flames fired at some distance by Dragon Black.

Dandelion stood no chance. It was quick and painless. All that was left of one of the nicest of all dragons was a charcoal image. Black had made a killing.

CHAPTER 17

Back to the City of Draegonia

George watched as Dragon Black finally rose into the air to continue his patrol of the island. Once out of sight, George ran and threw to one side the bushes concealing the camp's entrance and rushed inside. Grace, tears of sadness in her eyes cried out. "Oh why did he have to kill that poor dragon, Dragon Black is evil." Zach and Joel did not speak they were still in shock having realised that they too had been so close to death. George sat down and drew a diagram on the dusty ground. "Look we cannot stay here, I am sure that Black will return to remove the evidence of his deeds. We were all very lucky that he had not seen us but if we stay I am sure our luck will not hold." George, pointing the stick to areas of the map he had scribed into the ground continued. "We are here and rather exposed not only to being seen but also to the elements. The only food we have is what we have brought with us and we will run out of fresh water in a day or so." Zach looked at the roughly drawn map and pointed towards the southern edge of it saying. "I think the safest part of the island is there where we left the life raft on our last visit to the island. If the raft is still hidden we could use it as our camp, it's large enough for the four of us and importantly provides water proof shelter." Joel interrupted. "We could also drag it further into the forest and cover it with palm tree leaves to make it less conspicuous." "That's a good idea," George praised. "And at least we know there is a spring where we can obtain fresh water," Grace added. The four hurriedly repacked their bags in silence. The urgency of moving to take cover within the thick forest before dusk was now a priority.

Dragon Vegas-Gold had managed to avoid Black's Elite Guards who were oblivious to him transiting the route to the south of the city. Vegas Gold darted from cover to cover and in the open spaces maintained an even more vigilant lookout. Finally he was in sight of the back edge of the forest. Shrubs were getting thicker and taller more and more trees were coming into view. Vegas-Gold with even greater urgency continued his journey travelling further and deeper into the humid dense forest. As he progressed It became darker and darker as the fullness of the canopy above him blotted out most of the late afternoon sunlight. Vegas-Gold was feeling somewhat safer. His rich gold coloured skin was blending well with the rich greens and browns of the dense vegitation. All of a sudden he froze, not moving his body he raised his eyes upwards and through the thick leaves above he could just make out the glistening body of Dragon Black. Vegas-Gold considered how lucky he had been for thirty minutes earlier he would have been fully exposed and possibly caught by Dragon Black.

Black had left the charcoal remains of his evilness behind him and this was the final route of his patrol before returning back to the city. Beneath him were miles of thick dense forest leading down the softer more gradual slopes towards the sandy coral shores of the southern beaches. Black did not realise that beneath him was Dragon Vegas-Gold and that some distance behind him four children were also about to enter the security and safety of the forest. Little did he know that their meeting would start a chain reaction that would threaten his existence. For now, Black was in good spirits and decided to head eastwards and then north, returning back to the City of Draegonia.

The four were exhausted. It had been a busy and frightening day and here they were rushing towards the cover and safety of the forest. "We do need to get to the raft before dark George." Grace chanted, "I do not want to have to sleep in the forest without some form of protection from the insects around me." The boys laughed but it was Joel who offered an agreement.

"Yes sis, I'm with you. No point in sleeping out in the open if the raft is in good condition and dry." George and Zach were ahead of the other two moving thick brush, leaves and branches out of their way in a bid to make a path. "How much further George?" Zach somewhat breathlessly asked. "I really don't know Zach but I expect we have at least another hour or so before we reach the beach." Zach looked at his watch. "If we are not quick enough it will be dark before we reach the beach and travelling at night through the undergrowth could be dangerous." Grace hearing the conversation pointedly shouted out. "If you two expect me to travel through this undergrowth in the dark then you have another think coming." All of a sudden Joel stopped and whispered to the others. "Shush, be quite, listen." The others froze, what was Joel indicating with his quivering arm. The three struggled to see what Joel was pointing at when all of a sudden the trees and bushes parted and there standing in front of them was Dragon Vegas-Gold. He looked at the four in utter amazement not quite believing what he was seeing. "Is that really you George and Grace you have grown and surely that's not Zach and Joel?" The four children more in relief than amusement laughed out loudly. "You really frightened us," said George. Grace nodded in agreement and just smiled as both Zach and Joel ran up to Vegas-Gold wrapping their arms around him in an enthusiastic greeting. "Oh are we pleased to see you," Zach expressed with delight. "Joel said nothing he just gripped Vegas-Gold tightly knowing they had found a really good ally and friend.

The pleasantries of renewed introductions were soon over as George briefly informed what they had seen earlier. Vegas-Gold said little not indicating that Dandelion had been his best friend. He listened, anger brewing, as the four explained the events leading to the demise of Dandelion. It was Grace who realising it was getting late called for them to stop talking and get a move on. "What's the hurry?" Vegas-Gold enquired. Grace explained that they were finding the going hard and that they needed to get to where they had hidden the life raft, before night fall. Vegas-Gold just smiled, turned and gruffed. "Follow me." He parted the thick shrubs as though they were thin stems of wheat making a wide and accessible path for the children to follow. An hour later the five broke through the edge of the forest to see the golden sands being washed by the deep blue blackness of the sea. "I know where we are." Joel shouted. "We left the raft under cover over there." Zach was already on the move racing towards some thick clumps of brightly coloured bushes surrounded by palm trees. "Here it is," he yelled picking up the rope tied to a steel eye on the dinghy's front. "It's in good condition," announced Zach pushing with all his might to release it from some vines that had grown over it. "Hold on a moment you two," called out George. "If we each grab one of the web handles at the side of the raft we should be able to lift and move it together."

Vegas-Gold looked on in bemusement. He found the four children refreshing. They worked together, looked out for each other and still had time for others, especially the Dragons of Draegonia. Vegas-Gold ambled towards the struggling children who had made the raft somewhat heavier by loading into it their bags and belongings. "Let me," Vegas-Gold offered gently picking up the raft in between his lips avoiding his sharp pointed teeth. The four followed their dragon friend deep into the forest where Vegas-Gold placed the raft on the ground and with his tail thrashed out a circular clearing. "There," he said. "This will make a good place for you to set up your camp. The trees are thick enough to provide cover and the thing you call a raft makes an interesting cave." "You mean house don't you," giggled Grace. The dragon ignored her digging his claws deep into the ground. As he did so he revealed several smooth almost round rocks that he placed to one side. The four looked on in bewilderment. What was he doing? Vegas-Gold cleared and smoothed an area with his long tail ensuring that anything flammable close by was removed. He placed the rocks in a neat pile in the middle and fired with pin point accuracy a thin beam of very hot reddish blue flame until all the rocks were a glowing orange giving off a great deal of heat.

"This will keep you warm as the sun goes down and will help you boil some water without you having to light a fire." "Good idea," agreed Grace. "We certainly don't want to give our position away with smoke signals do we?"

Vegas-Gold crouched down to observe the four preparing the raft as their new makeshift home. Inside the raft was the pump necessary to inflate its sides to its maximum pressure making it comfortable to lean tired backs against. The bright orange canopy and yellow side panels were covered with palm leaves and leafy shrubs providing a natural camouflage. The sun had now gone down and within the canopy of the trees only the glow of the hot stones afforded any semblance of light. The four children all entered through the unzipped canopy into the comfort of the raft. Vegas-Gold placed his head close to the entrance his wide warm eyes giving them confidence and support. The four children quickly rustled up some food and water and settled down to make their plans. George took control, well he was the eldest, it was his magic card that got them there and he felt he had a duty of care for his friends. "Tell us Vegas-Gold; are there plans to get rid of Dragon Black? Why were you and Dandelion the only ones outside the city and what are dragons Brown and Blue doing to combat Black's tyranny?"

Vegas-Gold took a long deep breath and in greater detail than when they first met informed the children of how Black had systematically reduced any threat by imposing curfews, restrictions, laws and stiff regulations. He told them about the strongest dragons being forced to work in the north under hard labour conditions. The four listened in amazement especially as Vegas-Gold explained about the day Black returned and the number of dragons who were injured or turned into charcoal statues. Grace and George became more alarmed to hear that

Dragon Pink was to be the centre of attraction at the 'Wing Clipping Ceremony' and that several dragons were on the very same day apparently going to appear before a sham trial, only to be found guilty of trumped up charges, before being executed. Vegas-Gold paused for breath allowing Joel to speak first. "Horrific and Black deserves everything that is coming to him but you still have not explained why you and Dandelion were alone and heading this way?"

Vegas-Gold looked a little embarrassed explaining that Black was conscripting all the younger and fitter dragons into his army where he could keep them under tight control. Vegas-Gold paused, then in a quieter tone of voice explained that he and his friend were conscientious objectors and that they did not condone any form of fighting. Zach looked hard at the dragon and in a questioning manner asked. "Are you a coward, do you not think that if every dragon had your views Black would rule for ever and what about your best friend are you going to let Black get away with it?" Grace piped up in a somewhat supportive manner. "Look Zach I am sure that Vegas-Gold is not a coward. Some people have strict views on fighting and not everyone is the same, I am sure …….."

Grace was stopped in mid flow by the dragon shaking his head. "No the little one is right. We should not allow murder or oppression to be tolerated and for me and Dandelion to run and hide is cowardice. I might not have to fight, I might not have to be involved in causing anyone any injury, but I can stand up and be counted." The dragon looked thoughtful for a moment then smiled. "You know the four of you are demonstrating to me what I should be doing. You have come to help us yet here I am running away to hide, I should be ashamed of myself, but what can I do?" George had been thinking hard. Clearly all the dragons had been frightened by Black and his grip on Draegonia was so tight that no one dared to stand up to him. Dragons had obviously lost confidence and needed hope. "Look Vegas-Gold," George stated. "You must get back to the city and appear as though nothing has happened. The curfew means you are likely to be in great danger if caught but you must get back tonight otherwise your non appearance at Black's daily meetings will be conspicuous and he will order a search for you"

The golden dragon nodded in agreement as George continued. "We need you to gather intelligence. We also need to develop some sort of plan to protect Dragon Pink. I assume that Dragons Blue, Gold, Red and Brown are still alive?" Vegas-Gold thought for a moment, then displaying some concern replied. "Well yes, I believe so, but in all honesty I have not seen Dragon Brown for some time, oh I hope he's OK, in fact some say he has gone into hiding." Grace could contain herself no longer and yelled. "Dragon Vegas-Gold get yourself back to Draegonia now and find dragons Blue or Gold and let them know we are here. Try to find out where Dragon Brown is and how many dragons we can count on to form any resistance movement." Joel and Zach punching the air shouted. "You can count on us, can we count on you?"

A motivated Vegas -Gold stood up and enthusiastically spat a few flames, singing the surrounding bushes, briefly illuminating the circular camp. "That's all we need is to start a forest fire," shouted Zach. The dragon just grinned he had it well under control. With a thrash of his long tail he whipped and thrashed the scorched bushes until the last flickering spark faded into the blackness of the night. Joel was the first to move and grabbing a torch passed its sharp beam of light across where Vegas-Gold had been crouching, but he was nowhere to be seen, he was gone.

Vegas-Gold had never really lacked courage and he certainly was not what some had believed to be a coward. His teeth gritted, his eyes focused, he fought his way through the thick forest, breaking out onto higher ground and the stony rough track leading past his charcoaled friend, back to the City of Draegonia. His new found friends had given him new strength and the death of his best friend, a new purpose.

CHAPTER 18

The Campaign Begins

Dragon Brown refused to display the concerns building in his mind, but as time passed and dusk was turning into the blackness of night, the worry started to show on his steely eyed face. His sergeant, Dragon Tuscan-Red, had been on lookout and now reported that no sightings of Dragons Gold or Grey had been made as planned. Brown had known the risks were grave and pondered on the thought that Gold may well have been apprehended by Black's Elite Guard and that probably Grey was oblivious of plans made earlier. However his primary objective was for the release of those eight dragons held captive below.

Dragons Wenge and Wine, under the command of Dragon Corporal Umber, had already set off and were now positioned well out of sight and earshot of Black's guards and their prisoners. The heavily chained dragons looked bedraggled, exhausted and could be seen sporting major injuries. Still being beaten, they were now being herded towards the hard woodenround posts, where they were to be secured for their ten minute break.

Corporal Umber, briefly turning his head back from observing the prisoners, addressed his two dragon privates in a hushed growl. "We need to take those three," he said, pointing to the three guards who were now feeding themselves on vast amounts of fresh fruit and fish. "We need to wait until they settle down for the night leaving just the one sentry on duty. I will overpower him, but you two need to make sure the other guards are well taken care of at exactly the same time. And don't forget it is important we have their tunics, so wait until they have removed them before you attack." Dragons Wenge and Wine nodded, their faces and bodies covered in black commando stripes making them look a frightening fighting duo.

Umber pointed to a cut out in the giant rock face to the right of where the guards were all crouching together, oblivious of the fact their every move was being carefully observed. "You two," continued Umber. "Move to that position and keep out of sight. As soon as the prisoners are taken back to work I will creep up behind the guard and overpower him. Once you see the guard has been neutralised, quickly move in and capture the other two." Wenge and Wine both saluted and moved silently to their new positions.

Several minutes passed before the officer in charge marched to where his prisoners were huddled together. Whipping his tail across their backs he unlocked them from their holding posts and linking their chains together, proceeded to return them back to their hard labour tasks. **Crack, crack** and another **crack** could be heard as the officer's tail, drawing blood, whipped mercilessly across tired wet bodies. "Move it," the officer was heard to yell.

Dragon Umber gritted his teeth in controlled anger, waited for the moonlit skies to be obscured by a flurry of thickening cloud and crawled silently towards the guard. The guard was enjoying inflicting pain. Just as he strode through the deepening waters, a sickly grin on his face, his feet were violently pulled from under him. Umber had waited for the tail whipping guard to be caught totally unawares and grabbing his hind legs had forced his head under the cold black sea. The closest of the chained dragons, Dragon Candy, responded instantaneously and with one movement, placed his tail across the back of the guard's neck preventing it from being raised. A second chained dragon, Dragon Mango, pounced and held the guards tail. There was a sound of thrashing with huge plumes of spray seen shooting into the night's sky, as finally the guard was overpowered.

Meanwhile, hidden within striking distance to the other two unsuspecting guards were dragons Wenge and Wine. As soon as they saw their corporal move into action, they immediately rushed towards their prey, spitting out huge spreads of lethal white hot flames. The battle was over within seconds, the two dragon guards, taken completely by surprise, did not know what had hit them and so fierce was the attack, only charcoal replicas of their former selves remained.

Dragon Umber urged his imprisoned friends to wade back to shore where he released their chains. Wenge and Wine grabbed the guards' food supplies and ran to where the relieved dragons were stretching their tired and injured limbs, they were free. Whilst they all tucked in to the first decent meal they had since their incarceration.

Corporal Umber made his way to the centre of the feeding dragons and in true army fashion briefed them. "The success of your release is, I am afraid, based on your willingness to stay here and assist us." "What do you mean?" Dragon Tool –Box cried out. "Are we not free to at least fight for the safety of our families?" The earlier silence of the night was well and truly broken by the gathering of the injured, questioning, angry, mainly frustrated dragons, many of whom were now glaring in bewilderment at Corporal Umber. Umber raised and lowered his paws to indicate he wanted silence and some order. He appreciated that those crouched before him were suffering from malnutrition, injuries and exhaustion and really could not be blamed for their outbursts. "Dragons let me explain our plan and how you must play your part if we are to overthrow Dragon Black." Umber coughed, cleared his dry throat and continued. "You can see that Dragons Wenge and Wine have in their claws the tabards worn by your guards. We will be covering Wenge and Wine's bodies with a substance to make their skins appear similar to the guards and they will tomorrow wear the tabards and assume the position of your captors." Umber did not wait for any comment. "Of course it is no good us pretending to be your guards if we have no dragons to guard and that is why we need you to still appear captive and in chains, working as Dragon Black passes overhead on his daily patrols. Sergeant Tuscan-Red and Private Zinnwaldite will be taking turns as look out and will alert us should they spot Black or any of his Elite Guards approaching."

There was stunned silence eventually broken by Dragon Goldenrod who stopped licking his wounds and stood up. "I for one would be pleased to assist. If we carefully think things through, we will all see that there really is nowhere to hide and if Black thought we had escaped, he most certainly would hunt us all down." Goldenrod paused, letting his words of wisdom sink in. Then, having gained a silence of agreement from all the other dragons, asked. "What do you and Dragon Brown want us to do?

Corporal Umber explained that they needed the dragons to regain their strength and this required rest, good food and time. Umber explained they only needed to put on their chains and pretend to be working if any of Black's entourage approached. He explained that they had to be strong and be fit enough to overpower the next relief guard and be ready to join forces with Brown, to defeat Dragon Black. Dragon Mango, a younger and more severely injured dragon moved forward. "What about our injuries can we at least have a 'Dragon Nurse' or doctor to attend to our wounds?" Umber shook his head. "I'm sorry, but we were hoping for Dragon Grey to be here with Dragon Gold. Gold was to organise medical supplies and food." Umber paused for a second. "But something must have gone wrong as we have not heard from either of them." Umber coughed and began to turn to report back to Dragon Brown the evening's success as Goldenrod stood up. "You do have our co-operation corporal and inform Dragon Brown, he can totally rely on us.

Umber made his way back along the stony beach, the sound of waves rippling furiously over jagged rocks projecting from the sea. Shadows slid back and fore gliding over the tall cliff face, appearing, disappearing and reappearing as the moon cast its illuminating beams between a series of complex cloud formations. After some minutes Umber came to the partly hidden track that climbed steeply, up along the cliff face and finally winding its way to Brown's command center.

Brown in deep conversation with Sergeant Tuscan-Red was discussing the need to obtain intelligence and news from the City as Umber marched in. Umber reported the removal of two guards and the apprehending of the officer confirming that all the prisoners had been fully briefed. He also reported that one dragon was very badly injured.

"Well done Umber, I knew I could depend on you and your team. I think we need to concentrate on getting the injured dragons fit and well as quickly as is possible. Whatever happens we must be ready in time for the changing of the next guard. In addition, I will place you in charge of looking after the dragons below and of course your team needs to assume the identity of the guards you have removed." Brown continued barking out his orders. "The one and only guard remaining should be chained and be seen as one of the prisoners. This will make it possible for the dragon with the worst injuries to be brought here to convalesce."

Brown waved his paw to Umber in a gesture to go and bade him farewell. As Umber exited the cave Dragon Brown stroked his chin and with a searching look focused his eyes on his sergeant. "We need to work fast Sergeant. I'm going to the city to find out what's going on. You're to assume total command and maintain a 24 hour watch for Black or any of his Elite Guards. Is Dragon Zinnwaldite on lookout duty?" The sergeant puffed out his chest in pride and saluted. "Yes sir, I will relieve him in the next hour or so and you can count on me. And sir, I trust you will take care, we cannot afford for you to be captured." Brown smiled in gratitude for his subordinate's concern and using the rear corridor that climbed skywards exited on top of the cliff and headed into the stillness of the night, towards the City of Draegonia.

and released the prisoners and now need supplies and the services of Dragon Grey, also..." Brown had now turned to face the door he had entered through and saw Gold standing with his back to the wall. "So this is where you have been hiding Gold?" Brown barked. "I have not been hiding Dragon Brown; in fact I have been working with Dragons Blue and Grey in a bid to save the lives of the prisoners held in the cells and the wings of Dragon Pink." Gold went on to explain about the new curfew times and the fact that no dragon was allowed to leave the city for any reason on pain of death, when all of a sudden Brown spotted Vegas -Gold.

"What's he doing here; shouldn't he be at home with his mum?" Brown had no time for conscientious objectors. An embarrassed Vegas-Gold stepped forward with a hurt look on his face and snapped. "Whatever you may have thought of me in the past Dragon Brown now is not the time to refuse any form of help. I have seen the remains of a very good friend put to a painful death by Dragon Black. I have more reason than ever to rethink my views and for the time being, I am at your service." Vegas-Gold paused, took an intake of breath and in a loud growl, reinforced by flickering flames shouted, "I am ready to fight."An amazed Dragon Brown smiled warmly and patting Vegas-Gold on his back congratulated him saying. "Well done, we need all the assistance we can muster."

Brown continued to ask many questions in order to bring him up to date with the new laws that had been passed, the plan by Black to use conscription to bolster his army and the fact that a strategy was in place to save Pink's wings that relied on subterfuge and the assistance of Dragon Grey.

After some time Dragon Blue took a long look at his pocket watch and called out. "We all need some sleep and there is little point in any of you attempting to leave here tonight so I suggest the following. Let's wake up Dragon Pink and let her sleep in my room. Vegas-Gold and you Dragon Brown use the cell where Pink has been held, it might not be ideal but at least it has enough space for you both. Gold you and I will sleep here in the office." There was a scurry of activity as all four very exhausted dragons settled down for what was left of the night.

Vegas-Gold looked on with some distaste at the rough bed now vacated by Dragon Pink. The cell had been cleaned during Pink's incarceration but it still smelt musty and damp. Brown lit another torch lantern and affixed it to a clamp held in the rugged damp rock wall. "I am glad we only have to stay here one night." Vegas-Gold mouthed under his breath. Brown's sharp ears made out the comment. "I am with you on that Vegas-Gold, but just spare a thought for the prisoners in the other cells who have been held here for some time." Vegas-Gold blinked finding it difficult to focus in such a dimly lit place and slumped onto the hard makeshift bed, his long tail dangling over its side. Brown crouched down with his back to a wall in the far corner and rested his head against one of the numerous protruding rocks. "I suggest you curl your tail up Vegas-Gold and place it under the bed just in case during the early hours of the morning I inadvertently step on it." Vegas-Gold rapidly coiled his tail and slithered it under the bed. He dreaded the thought of one of the heaviest of dragons stepping on it. Slowly, they drifted off to sleep, their lodgings may have not been the most comfortable, but they were quiet.

Unlike the peace and quiet of the cells, the tropical forest was filled with chattering and screeches, sounds that were always magnified at night. Nocturnal animals appeared to make the most noise and this night held no exception. "I can't sleep with this cacophony," Grace cried. "Ca-coff-onee, what's that?" yelled back Zach in complete ignorance. "Why don't you speak using words we all understand?" Joel laughed and held tightly onto his somewhat frustrated younger brother. "Oh she's just showing off Zach, all that cacophony means is much noise or mixture of sounds." "I am not showing off" Grace replied indignantly.

George, intervening what obviously was starting to be a heated discussion, immediately took the passion out of the situation. "I agree," he said. "We can't really sleep with all this noise and it's useless just camping here when all the action is going on in the city. I think the best thing is for us to travel through the night, under the cover of darkness and try to get to Dragon Blue before dawn." "You see Grace," Zach with a cute grin on his face chanted. "George explains things so well without the need for....." Zach paused, turning his grin into a broad smile and chanted... "Without the need for convoluted, extraneous or superfluous words." Grace took Zach's clever, very pointed response, with good humour but still wanted to have the last say. "Very good Zach, I'm impressed, but don't use words you cannot spell." "Enough you two," interjected George. "Grab the bags, stay close together and let's go, we have a long journey ahead. It's time we helped to set up a resistance movement.

CHAPTER 20

Meeting Up

Dawn was fast approaching, the early rising sun illuminating the eastern sky a blood orange, interspersed with dark grey clouds indicating some pending rain.

The four children had struggled valiantly through the night, often becoming entangled within the thick foliage and hanging vines of the tropical forest. It had been difficult in the almost total blackness to see where they were going. Joel led the way with his sister, his black plastic torch providing sufficient light to avoid major obstacles within their path. Grace fortunately had packed her compass before arriving on Draegonia and its illuminated needle ensured a correct heading north towards more open ground. Following behind was George, who was more than happy for Grace to take the lead. The three were kept in sight by Zach, who pointing his silver wind-up torch, illuminated their every footstep.

Some hours had past and without stopping for any rest the four finally reached the rocky dusty track that led to the eastern pass and access into the City of Draegonia. The four momentarily halted. Ahead were two of Dragon Black's Elite Guards sprawled across their path? The snoring dragons were fast asleep, unwittingly secure in the knowledge that they would not be disturbed.

"Quick take cover," George whispered. The four slid behind a large triangular jagged boulder that had in the distant past been spewed out of the volcano that now overshadowed them.

"So how are we going to get past those two?" Zach whispered. George did not immediately answer but ushered the three to get closer to him. "Look," he said. "I am not sure how we're going to get past them, any ideas?" His three cousins made no comment, they were in deep thought. "This is going to be tricky," George sighed. "I know," said Zach. "But why don't we creep up to them and tie their legs together so if they wake up they can't chase us?" Grace smiled at Zach. "And where do we get the rope or chains from then and even if they were tied up don't you think they would think it strange when they awoke?" Joel smiled in support of his younger brother and spoke in his defense. "At least he is trying Grace, have you any better suggestions?" Grace felt a little humiliated at being admonished and was just about to respond as George held up a finger to his mouth. "Shush, we have to work together and any idea or suggestion is welcome, no matter how weird or improbable it might sound. Zach your suggestion is welcomed but I have an alternative suggestion. We know that dragons sleep at night awakening only at early light. What we need to do is keep as quiet as is possible and one by one silently creep by them, whilst they are asleep." George lowering his voice continued. "We have about 15 minutes before the sun's rays illuminate the area where the two dragons are asleep. As soon as it does, then I am sure they will wake up. So, Zach you go first, don't run and try not to scuff the ground or make any noise."

George handed to Zach a small pair of binoculars he had removed from Joel's rucksack. "You can see there is a small gap between them and that is our way through." Grace shook her head. "No George, I should go first. If I get past them without waking them, then Zach and Joel should have no problem." Grace winked at her brothers, picked up her bag and silently slipped away, tiptoeing towards the two ugly sleeping dragons.

As she got close, the sound of the snoring and wheezing got louder. Her hands were sweating; her mouth was dry, she started to feel very, very nervous. "So far so good," she murmured under her breath. Then her heart missed a beat. The dragon guard to her left moved. His previously curled-up tail unwound and he swept it lazily to his side, grunting and puffing as he did so. Grace froze, her right foot not quite touching the ground as she focused upon every dragon movement. Were they waking up? Was all lost?

Three pairs of worried eyes looked on, none daring to make a sound or movement. The dragon's tail came to rest and as it did so the sound of his snoring could once more be clearly heard. The abrupt motion had frightened the life out of Grace but there was a benefit. By moving his tail he had widened the gap between himself and the other sleeping dragon. Grace seized the opportunity and cautiously moved towards the gap, not daring to breath. She was now between them both, just as again, the dragon's tail moved once more. The dragons would soon wake up, she had to move quicker. Grace did not panic and taking a few more steps was seen by the other three to disappear round the curved narrowing track.

George hugged the two relieved brothers. "OK, you're next Zach and as time is running out Joel, you go with him, no talking and be as quiet and as quick as you can. Once you get past them, do not look back but join your sister and wait for me."

The two young lads grabbed their bags and moved quickly towards the direction of Grace. George averting his eyes from his two pals was following the fading and disappearing shadows, as the rays of the sun fought to penetrate the cover of the sleeping dragons. There was no more time to lose he had to immediately follow the boys. George moved much more quickly than the two ahead of him and within a few strides was at their sides. He again placed his finger to his mouth and indicated he wanted absolute silence. Holding onto Joel he gestured to Zach to continue.

George and Joel watched with bated breath as Zach silently slid by the dragons that were beginning to regain consciousness from their night's sleep. George glancing at Joel once again whispered. "Quickly Joel, go." Joel did not require any more prompting and with clenched fists and a look of absolute determination followed his younger brother. George held his breath, waited for Joel to pass through the gap between the two dragons and made his move.

Creeping forward, he reached the midpoint between the slumbering two, just as the dragon to his left lifted his head, opened its eyes and blinked. George froze and remained motionless. The dragon opened his mouth and yawned and as it did so started to move its rear legs in a clumsy effort to stand. The dragon to George's right was woken by the movement, made a terrific growl and also started to rise up.

George wasted no time and under the cover of the noise and movement of the two wakening dragons ran for all his worth to join his concerned onlooking cousins. "That was close," Grace said as she hugged him in relief. Zach and Joel grabbed George's hands and pulled him out of any chance of being seen by the now upright dragon guards. They had secured the pathway. No one would be allowed to pass either in or out.

Dragon Blue was explaining to Dragon Pink that Dragon Gold and he had been ordered by Black to escort her to the hospital for the ceremony of 'Wing Clipping'. Pink's eyes showed signs of her forcing back tears as it was explained to her that the procedure was going ahead but would be carried out by Dragon Grey and not by Dragon Black. "Oh well, I suppose that's something." Pink, in a somewhat small, nervous voice, sighed. "I would have liked to have flown properly before my wings were clipped but........" Pink was interrupted by Dragon Gold who had entered the cave. "Be brave Dragon Pink, we have ensured that the operation will be as painless as is possible and you will be well cared for. I am afraid we have to go through with it or Black will........." It was Pink's turn to interrupt. "I know, your lives would be at risk if you did not carry out his wishes, I understand." Dragon Blue and Gold looked at each other, both knowing the secret they had to keep from her.

Gold took a deep intake of air and growled. "There is quite a great deal of ill feeling because Black is insisting you have to go through with it. In order to ensure we have no demonstrations we are going to get you to the hospital before the sun is fully up." Blue nodded in agreement. "Yes we need to move quickly so grab anything you wish to take with you and we'll leave straight away."

Blue was in a hurry and gruffed loudly as he scurried down the corridor towards the cells. "Dragon Brown, Dragon Vegas-Gold, we are leaving now, please feed the prisoners for me and we will see you a little later." As the three dragons exited into the main street on their way to Draegonia's Hospital, it was Dragon Brown who waved them a farewell. "Not a problem, see you later," he cried out.

Vegas-Gold, awakened by the loud shouts of orders of Dragon Blue, stretched out in the dimly lit cell room. He was about to get up from his uncomfortable night's sleep, when he felt something touch him. His long tail had been tucked out of harm's way curled under the heavy wooden log bed. "What on dragon earth is that?" Vegas-Gold murmured, slowly moving the tip of his tail back and fore. Vegas-Gold felt nothing and was just about to remove his tail when something seemed to roll into it. Vegas-Gold carefully ran his tail back towards the rear corner of the bed and felt the moist cold wall that lay immediately behind it. Very slowly he ran his tail along the wall, curving it as he reached the other end. Then with great care he gradually withdrew the entire length of his tail in a semi-circular motion. As he did so, he could hear something rolling on the hard granite-like floor. Squinting his eyes in the very poor light to a spot between his hind legs he thought he could see something. Crouching down, his nose almost touching the floor he then thought he could both see and feel something. What was it? What had he found? Should he just ignore it and join Dragon Brown who could be heard giving the prisoners their breakfast?

Brown had returned from feeding the last of the prisoners a hearty breakfast of various fruits and fish. "Humph," he snorted, "they have better food than my troops and yet still complain." He was referring to Dragon Iceberg whose growls and groans could be heard reverberating throughout the station.

These however were overshadowed by an enormous yell cried out by Dragon Vegas-Gold.

CHAPTER 21

Joining Forces

George and his pals were moving with some stealth and speed, heading for the safety of Draegonia's Police Headquarters, the early morning sun now visible on the horizon. Grace whispered. "Keep close to the walls and out of sight, we're nearly there." George placing a restraining hand on her shoulder replied. "Hold on, stay low, don't move." He had seen three dragons just disappear out of sight heading in the direction of the hospital. "I think that was Dragon Gold but I couldn't make out the other two," he said. The four carefully surveyed the area not wanting to take any chances of being seen. The street once more was empty and with the sign of the Police Station only a hundred meters ahead George gave the signal and in an authoritative but hushed tone mouthed the word, "Run."

The two younger boys immediately sped off at an alarming rate closely followed by their sister. All three ran as though being pursued by Dragon Black himself. George smiled, thinking that such a simple command should yield such energy and followed, but at a somewhat less frenetic pace.

It was Grace, having overtaken her breathless brothers, who arrived first outside the locked blue stone cave door. She tapped on its solid wooden frame not wishing to make much noise as her brothers appeared to her side. "Let me," shouted Zach as he punched the door with his fist. "Open up," demanded Joel. "Oh for goodness sake keep quiet," an annoyed Grace murmured pulling her brothers to one side. Despite the banging and thumping, the door remained resolutely shut.

"Listen you three." It was an exasperated George. "I am not sure what you're playing at but this is not the way to avoid attention and if you make any more noise you'll give us away, so be quiet and let me get through." George was concerned that their shouts and bangs would have been overheard by the resident dragons that lived nearby and as he could not know which were trustworthy, the last thing he needed was any of them to peer out of their cave windows. George knocked firmly trying hard not to make too much noise. He waited a few seconds and then heard the turn of a heavy iron key. The door opened a few inches to reveal the bright eyes of Dragon Brown peering at them.

Brown could not believe what or indeed who was before him. He fully opened the door and with one sweep grabbed all four children pulling them into the cavernous room. Slamming the door shut, he locked it behind them. "Well," he laughed. "What have we here, the cavalry has arrived." The four hugged him, they knew that this was one dragon they could trust and one who knew them well.

George gasped for breath as Brown released his hugging grip on the four. "I thought," George said. "You would be in hiding with your dragon soldiers, what are you doing here and where is Dragon Blue?

Brown beckoned them to make themselves more comfortable and offered refreshment of squeezed fruit juice, something he recalled they enjoyed. He told them about the plan to save Pink's wings. He covered in great detail his strategies to reduce the number of Black's Elite Guard and explained that he had to rescue the seven dragons in the cells before they were to be sentenced to Volcanic Execution. The children listened in silence not realising that Dragon Black had become so powerful, stronger and more deadly. They now realised the enormity of their task.

The four were explaining how they had arrived, the attack on Dandelion and their transit through the pass avoiding the sleeping dragons, when out of the passageway leading to the cells, Vegas-Gold appeared. The children greeted him enthusiastically as he too gave each of them a hug, but at the same time, clutching something tightly between his claws.

"What's that?" Brown demanded in his typical officer manner. Vegas-Gold opened up his hand revealing a chemical dart. Brown could not believe his eyes, grabbed it and stared. "Where did you get this?" He demanded. Vegas-Gold had not realized what the pointed slender tube was when he withdrew it a little earlier from under his bed.

The four children were informed of how the Council of Dragons had ordered the destruction of the chemical weapons and that one must have been missed when several had spilled out of the packing during their storage. Vegas-Gold rolled his eyes as he learnt of the dart's potential power. Had he known the true implication of it pricking his tender palms, he would not have held it so tightly.

"Great," said George. "You now have a weapon that will remove Black's ability to shoot flame and......" George was interrupted as a key was heard turning in the lock and as the door opened, there in the sunlight stood dragons Blue and Gold.

Recognising the four children, Gold rushed forward and gave a wet lick kiss on Grace's right cheek. Grace taken a little aback smiled embarrassedly, wiped her face and thanked Gold. Blue just crouched down surveying the now very crowded station room and gave out a tremendous roar. "Well! Look what we have here," he said with a tinge of astonishment. "It's the Dragon Slayers." Blue gave a wink as he had recognised the significance of their surnames shortly after their departure from Draegonia some years earlier. Blue closed the door and turned to explain. "Here we have George Slayer and his cousins, Mistress and Masters Garond." He paused, and then with a roar of laughter wrote on a piece of parchment, lifting it up for all to see and read out loudly.

"G.A.R.O.N.D is an anagram for DRAGON

The surname of George is........ SLAYER,

They as a team make............Dragon Slayer."

The three other dragons nodded, calling it a coincidence. Blue retorted that he did not believe in coincidences but fate and that the problems they were facing needed something special to happen and as far as he was concerned the four children were very special. He was sure they would be the catalyst for change.

Brown chuckled seeing the link that Blue was expounding and thrashed his tail on the dusty hard floor to gain attention and held up the chemical dart. "OK, good to have some fun but we need to agree a plan of action and thanks to Vegas-Gold we may have the means to destroy Black's power." Gold not believing what he was seeing, wanted confirmation. "Is that really one of the darts, is it full, can it be used?" Blue looked on thoughtfully, his gaze centering on the dart's tiny metal needle like tip. "That does not look to me as though it is strong enough or even long enough to penetrate the armour plated skin of Dragon Black."

Dragon Brown, turning the dart in between his claws responded with a snort. "Yes, I share your concern Blue, it's a real pity we had not completed the development programme and you're right, these were never tested to penetrate amour plated skin similar to that of Dragon Black's." Vegas-Gold, not wishing to interrupt could contain himself no longer. "Even if we were confident about the strength of the darts tip, what would you use to propel it, or how could it be injected it into Dragon Black?" Vegas-Gold paused, took a deep intake of breath and with a final exasperated tone cried. "And how close would anyone have to be to administer the chemical inside?" There was silence, no one had any answers.

Gold looked at the station wall clock and noted that they had only a few minutes to get to the square for Black's daily gathering. "I think we had better go now, especially you Vegas-Gold if you don't want to create any concern or alarm in Black's mind. The fact that your best friend Dandelion was slaughtered by Black will no doubt ensure that he will be specifically looking to see if you're there." A subdued Vegas-Gold nodded in agreement. Blue patted together all his sprawled documents making them into slightly neater piles on his cluttered desk, raised his head and gruffed. "I'm going to go with you as well and if Black asks me about the prisoners, I will just confirm that as he ordered, they are secure in the cells. We need to continue to make Black think he has everything and everyone under **his** control.

Grace was not really listening, her thoughts were on other matters more important to her and she spoke decisively. "Whilst you three are away we should use the opportunity to visit Dragon Pink. She will only have Dragon Grey with her if all dragons have been summoned to Black's meeting and I am sure she will feel a little better if she knows we are here for her." Brown was just about to object on grounds of their safety as George, in a loud voice of agreement, backed his cousin. "Yes I totally agree Grace and it will give us an opportunity to discuss with Grey how we might administer the dart that Dragon Brown is holding." Brown's reservations were immediately vanquished as he thought it an excellent idea to elicit the aid of Grey. "Fine," Brown said, carefully placing the chemical dart on the table top. "All of you go, I shall look after the dragons in the cells as well as work on some strategies for all of us to discuss and agree on your return.

Brown held the station door wide open as dragons, Vegas-Gold, Blue and Mayor Gold quickly headed for the square, the four children running in the opposite direction, headed towards Draegonia's hospital.

Closing the door behind them, Brown marched across and lifted off 7 large iron keys that were hanging on wooden pegs embedded into the painted blue wall. His next move was fraught with some anxiety as he was about to release 7 imprisoned dragons in order to convince them they should join his small troop of dragon soldiers to overthrow the dreaded Dragon Black.

Brown unlocked the cells, releasing each dragon in turn and ordered them to wait within the main station room. The final dragon to be released was Dragon Iceberg, who still moaning, ambled along the corridor to join the others.

The seven bewildered dragons, in stony silence, crouched in a semicircle round Dragon Brown. Brown stood upright, his steely eyes penetrating the gazes of his onlookers. "Dragons of Draegonia, I am going to make this brief and to the point. If you decide not to join me you will be returned to your cell and face the trumped up charges levied against you that will, I am afraid, result in your inevitable execution." Brown paused to let his statement of fact sink in. "We have no choice then, have we?" It was Byzantine who responded first. "So what do you want us to do?" added Dragon Chameleon. Before Brown could reply, Dragon Sea-Green stood and growled. "Whatever you have in mind it seems to me we are going to die either way and I for one would wish to keep my options open. I know

Black is a tyrant but he also has a tendency to be lenient if he is not made angry." The six dragons crouching round Sea-Green glared in anger. Dragon Iceberg lost his patience and grabbing Sea-Green's paw dragged him unceremoniously back to the floor. Iceberg snarled. "Sea-Green, we had a bad experience with one of your relatives and no doubt you will recall his rather warm ending (referring to the volcanic demise of Dragon Green). I advise you not to be so silly to think you can or could possibly win the favors of Dragon Black. Brown is an officer and indeed has my absolute trust." Iceberg took a deep breath and continued pointedly. "Trust is something that your family has not only to gain but also to show." The crouched dragons applauded as Sea-Green dropped his head shamefully and in a dragon whisper was overheard to say. "I'm sorry but if we join Brown, there is no going back." Dragon Yellow listened on, trying not to be noticed, his head bowed low. Was he to show his fear, was he to support Sea-Green. Now was not the time to be seen as a coward, a reputation he had tried so hard to live down. Brown seeing Yellow's worried scowls and clearly hearing the comments made by Sea-Green, decided to ignore them both and continued with his briefing.

"Right I gather you're ALL with me. This is my plan to save you and Draegonia. Black has ordered that you are all to be taken to Volcano Peak to be tried and sentenced. We will make our move at that time when our numbers have increased." Brown explained how he intended to reduce Black's Elite Guard and how he was planning to release the imprisoned dragons in the north, who would, once they regained their strength, take their positions within his expanding army. "You can see," Brown continued. "We will have a combined strength of some 20 fighting dragons and importantly, we will outnumber the Elite Guards, any questions?"

Dragon Cerise growled aloud. "Yes" she said, "If we are to join you and **I am** ready to fight, we need to have specific responsibilities so as not to overlap or duplicate effort." Brown was impressed; Cerise was the only female dragon he knew who had the skills of intellect, strength and ability to be part of a true fighting force. So confident was he that he took all the dragons slightly by surprise. "Dragon Cerise, you are quite right and as every good unit needs a good leader I appoint you as officer in charge of the team." Apart from Sea-Green who was displaying a little of his families trait of envy, the remaining dragons congratulated Cerise on her appointment.

Brown gazed down on his new recruits. Would they be a force to be reckoned with? Could they work as a team? Time would tell. "Right," he bellowed. "I need you all to return to your cells. It must appear, should Dragon Black make an unscheduled inspection, that everything is in order. What I will do is make sure you have plenty of food and water but obviously we cannot make the cells any more comfortable. Cerise, you stay behind and I will provide you with additional information you may later pass on to your team." As six dragons returned to their damp and cold quarters, Brown and Cerise became heavily engrossed in discussions of tactics and the plan to ultimately join forces with those in the north for what was hoped to be the final battle.

CHAPTER 22

A Heartfelt Kiss

The iron gates of Draegonia Hospital were still wide open as the children entered the deserted courtyard. Blue had told them where the laboratory could be found and the four were heading as quickly as they could towards it.

"Why didn't we get Dragon Blue to call ahead so that Dragon Grey would expect us?" Zach enquired. It was a question that Joel was quick to answer. "It's always great to have ideas after the event Zach, but we should have thought of it before we left." Grace was the first to reach the tightly locked door of the laboratory and in the empty corridor her three heavy thumps on the hard wooden door echoed throughout the maze of tunnels. Grace did not wait for any immediate response but again tapped on the door, a little less noisily and listened. "Who is it?" A stern voice from behind the door was heard to growl. "It's Joel, Zach, George and I," Grace announced. "Can we come in?"

Dragon Grey, a slender fit, studious looking dragon, opened the door. He displayed little emotion and appeared not to be too surprised at seeing them. "I thought it wouldn't be too long before we saw the four of you. Dragon Pink has told me she sent a message requesting your assistance."

The four swiftly entered the lab, the door closing firmly behind them. All four surveyed the clinical room bathed in a phosphorescence light searching for their pink friend. Zach pulled at Grey's tail and asked "Where is Dragon Pink then, she is supposed to be here?" Grey placed a clear bottle containing a yellow liquid on a long narrow bench that ran completely around the cave wall. Peering down at the four he grinned. "She is safe, in one of the pre-operating rooms waiting for my team and Dragon Black to attend the procedure to clip her wings." George, turning towards Dragon Grey confirmed that they were fully briefed about the planned subterfuge. "We won't let on that she will still have the use of her wings after the wound has healed but we do wish to see her before you carry out the procedure." Grey could see the concern and resolve on the four little one's faces. "Yes, I know, she means a great deal to you and I am sure she would be pleased to see you, but you don't have a great deal of time before Black is due." George knew that Grey was right. "OK," agreed George. "We need to move fast. Grace, you and Joel go and see Pink and wish her well. Don't let on what is actually going to happen but tell her that we do have a plan to overthrow Black." "Have we?" Zach, in some amazement queried. "What plan is that then George?" Ignoring Zach's question, George informed Dragon Grey that he and Zach would stay behind to discuss with him a number of ideas and to elicit his advice. Grace needed no further encouragement and with a wave of her hand motioned Joel to open the door requesting Dragon Grey to give directions to the pre-operating room. Grey trotted across to one of the long tables and from the wall above it removed a sketch showing the floor plan of the hospital caves, corridors and rooms. "Here take this," he said. "I'll mark the place where she is resting, it's not far." Clutching the marked sketch provided by Grey, Grace led Joel out of the laboratory to search for their friend.

George closed the laboratory door behind them and with some urgency spun round to face Grey. "Dragon Grey as we have little time I need to have some quick answers in order that Zach and I can formulate a working plan of action." Firstly, we have found one dart that we understand holds a viral based chemical that if injected into any dragon would immediately create the condition of 'Flame Out'. Is it possible therefore to replicate the chemical?" Grey was just about to answer when Zach interjected. "Yes, and more importantly are there any more darts available?" Grey frowned. "I am surprised that even one dart survived as they were all condemned to be destroyed and I saw, what I thought was their full disposal." Grey turned to face Zach and looked into his eager face and smiled. "Zach, I am afraid that there are no more darts and...." Grey paused, turned towards George. "And, there is no way we can replicate the chemical as the formulae was also ordered to be destroyed." Grey slowly shook his head and with a worried look crossing his face bent down, moved his head from side to side, and peered at the two before him. "Even the fact you have one dart, I am afraid, holds little comfort. You see, they were still in their experimental stage and we had not designed any method of delivering the dart. Also, we had experienced major problems with the dart tips, as they required to be hollow to inject the chemical, but we found were not strong enough to penetrate the toughest of dragon skin, let alone the amour plated skin of Dragon Black."

George and Zach thought long and hard. It was Zach who broke the silence and in a very clear, deliberate tone of voice questioned. "Everyone has an 'Achilles Heel', what's Dragon Black's?" Grey smiled, he knew of the legend that in bygone years there was a handsome warrior called Achilles, one of the heroes assembled to fight against the city of Troy. *(Achilles was known to be invulnerable in all of his body except for his heel. As he died because of a small wound on his heel, the term 'Achilles Heel' had come to mean a person's principal weakness).*

George had moved towards the rear of the laboratory and was now looking hard at a detailed picture of a dragon's head depicting its anatomical structure. George pointed towards the diagram. "Dragon Grey, it looks to me as though most dragons have a weakness just under their chins close to their throats." Grey sidled over to where George was standing, peered at the diagram, also pointed his claw and nodded. "Yes, dragons have a soft patch of skin just here. It is necessary for us to be able to move our heads in almost a 270 degree sweep and this area of the upper throat has several folds of softer skin." Zach now moved closer to George as Dragon Grey faced them with a frown. "I have to tell you however that if you were thinking of using the dart to penetrate Black's throat, then think again." "Why?" Zach cried out. "Well, just think. Firstly, Dragon Black is very well protected by his Elite Guard, it would be impossible for anyone to get close enough to inject him. Secondly even if you were able to find a way to propel the dart you would have to be at the right angle to fire it and before you even had time to take aim," Grey paused to give proper emphasis. *"Black would turn his attacker into a charcoal statue,* no I just don't think the chemical dart is an option."

George shook his head in disgust. "We are not going to give up that easily." Grey shrugged his powerful shoulders in a gesture of annoyance and growled back. "I admire your willingness and courage George, but let me make it very clear the Dragon Black who has returned is nothing like the weakened dragon we banished some years ago." Zach, moving closer, patted Grey on his hind leg. "We understand your frustration Dragon Grey but we have learnt that you don't give up at the first hurdle and when the going gets tough, that's when we must all pull together." George still pondering on everything Grey had been saying suddenly shouted out. "There is someone who could get close enough to inject him isn't there Grey?" Grey knew what George was alluding to but with a deepening frown, just growled. "If you think I could walk up to Dragon Black, ask him to lift his head for me to administer an injection into the top fold of his throat, all without him being suspicious or questioning my reasons, then you really do underestimate him.

Black trusts no one and that includes me." Grey's eyes focussed upon the 'Dragon Clock' hanging on the wall. "It's getting late; Black will be finishing his meeting soon and then immediately after he will be coming here to witness Pink's operation being carried out. You had better make yourself scarce, go now find Grace and Joel and for all your safety, keep well out of sight." The two boys, fully realising time was short, thanked Dragon Grey and hurried off towards the operating theatres to join the others.

Grace and Joel had finally found Dragon Pink slightly subdued lying on a very large flat piece of thick marble that had a number of smooth perfectly round small tree trunks acting as rollers underneath. This was the pre-operation table that also performed the function of being a dragon patient's bed. When an operation was ready to be started the flat marble base together with its patient would be rolled into the adjoining cave room, divided by a curtain of heavy sail canvas. Both of the oval shaped rooms were extremely clean considering they were hewn out of the inside of a mountain. The walls had been covered in a brilliant white paste filling most of the crevices and undulations, creating a shiny, hard, almost perfectly flat surface. Pink's body stood out well against the clinical background as the two children entered.

A wide grin spread across Pink's face as she spied the two. "Oh am I pleased to see you both but where are George and Zach, are they OK?" Joel ran across to Pink almost tripping up in his enthusiasm and yelled. "They're with Dragon Grey working on a plan to dispose of Dragon Black and......." Grace quickly interjected knowing that Joel was going to add something such as, 'and save your wings'. "And Dragon Pink," Grace continued. "We are going to find a way to protect you." Pink smiled, her flushed face still showing signs of anxiety. "You are all amazing and I knew when I sent to George the distress note that you would find a way to come to our aid, but I think it is too late. I will lose any ability to fly once my wings are clipped later today and the chances of destroying Dragon Black are indeed pretty small." Grace shook her head and placing a hand on Pink's tiny right wing, knowingly said. "Pink, we will look after you, just trust us, we do have a plan in place and George knows exactly how we should deal with Dragon Black." Joel could see how worried Pink was but did not quite know what to say next. His sister had made a timely interruption stopping him from giving away their entrusted secret about the planned subterfuge. Joel turned his thoughts into being more constructive. "Dragon Pink," Joel pointedly asked. "We need some weapons to protect ourselves and recall you had lots of bits and pieces in your cave that we might find useful......" Pink raising her head turned towards Joel. "I think you have more chance of obtaining what might be more useful to you from Dragons Cream and White and to be honest, most of the items they collect are now logged and stored in Dragon Blue's offices."

Pink explained that her new role as administrator necessitated her to record and enter into storage all washed ashore items. She listed a few of those most recently found as Joel listened with increasing interest. Pulling from his pocket a piece of paper and a pen Joel jotted down everything recalled by Pink. Pink smiled at the obvious enthusiasm and dedication being displayed. For the first time in days she felt secure, more so than ever before, as Grace and Joel spent their time encouraging and re-building her confidence.

Their chatter and laughter was abruptly interrupted as George and Zach hurtled into the room. "Hi Dragon Pink, it's only us," yelled Zach. George a little quieter but nonetheless enthusiastically ran across to where Pink was crouching and gave her an enormous hug. "Gosh," George cried out. "You really have grown since we last saw you." Pink's face went a slightly darker shade as she blushed, her eyes showing small droplets of tears. "I am very pleased to see you George and Happy Birthday. You all have made me feel much better. I am now prepared to face the 'Clipping of the Wing' ceremony." George not wishing to be drawn into this conversation changed the subject. "Look guys, we need to leave Dragon Pink to rest and get out of here before Black and his entourage arrive. If they happen to find us here I don't think it will just be **our** wings he will clip." Pink raising a half hearted smile, knowing the consequences of Black's impending arrival, waved her paws in the direction of the door and bade the four a swift farewell. Grace was the last to leave and as she exited through the open door, turned to face Dragon Pink. Raising her hand to her mouth she blew a kiss. Pink caught the invisible gift between her paws and with a huge smile, clutched them to her heart.

CHAPTER 23

George has a plan

Dragon Brown looked at the clock on the station cave wall thinking to himself that he had better make tracks back to North Island and his team when the door opened. In rushed an out-of-breath George and three other children. Acknowledging them with a faint smile on his face, he growled. "I'd given you four up for lost and was just about to leave, do you have any news?" Grace ignored the abruptness of Brown's question and raised her own. "We have been busy finding a way to capture Dragon Black as well as visiting our friend thank you, but more to the point, why are you still here?" Brown's smile broadened into a grin as he looked down at the little ones who showed little fear. "You're courage is commendable Grace but do not underestimate Black, he is far more dangerous since his exile and yes you are right, I should have already left for North Island, but I have been briefing...." Brown paused, pointed a razor sharp claw in the direction of the cells and exclaimed. "...My new recruits." Brown explained how he planned to enlist the prisoners thus increasing his dragon power to match the strength of Black's fighting forces.

Zach and Joel could contain their impatience no longer. Moving towards Brown, Zach spoke out. "We have been looking at the problems and we do not believe an open attack on either Dragon Black or his guards will work." Joel interjected and pulling on Zach's sleeve moved in front of him. "What Zach means is that we appreciate that Dragon Black is more formidable than ever and that with his ability to fly any attempt to remove him from power will be thwarted by his strength and maneuverability. So what we have to do is incapacitate him and to do this we will need to have the chemical Dart."

Dragon Brown roared in frustration. "We have discussed why the dart cannot be considered as a weapon. The delivery method has just not been developed and we only have one, unless Dragon Grey has told you he can produce more." George to gain attention raised his hand. "Stop, for goodness sake it's no good just going over old ground, you get off Brown to rejoin your team in the north and concentrate on getting them up to fighting strength. Leave us to prepare a plan and we will contact you as soon as it is formulated. In the meantime you should concentrate on getting your dragons fully fit to fight."

Grace moved to the table where earlier the dart had been placed and picking it up, carefully wrapped it in one of her clean handkerchiefs. "I will look after this," she said. "We will find a way to use it as it is the only thing we know that can cause an immediate 'Flame Out' but," she continued in a much more authoritative tone. "Our second key objective is how to combat Black's ability to fly. If we do not have a strategy for that, then he could escape only to fight another day." Brown nodded in full agreement. "You are right, we have to incapacitate Black as well as remove his flame and that dart will not do both."

Brown once more glanced at the clock and picking up a pack of supplies taken from the station stores quickly marched towards the door. "Inform Dragon Blue I will replace these once we have removed Dragon Black and his cronies." Brown laughed as he could see the funny side of things being that if Dragon Black was not removed then replacing supplies would be the least of all worries. "I'll leave now before Black's meeting finishes. Take care, Dragon Cerise is in charge of the new team chair and apologised. " We are tired," he said, "it has been a long day for us and we mean no disrespect but really think we have a better chance of perhaps finding a way how the one and only means of causing 'Flame Out' might be used to your advantage. In any event it will be safer with us as Dragon Grey has advised us that the chemical has no side effect on humans."

Blue smiled, he knew that the children were there to help, they were demonstrating genuine care for the dragons' predicament and that they were indeed risking their own lives. "OK," he said in a lowering tone of dragon growl. "What are your plans for the rest of the day and where will you stay?" George and Grace looked at each other in some amazement. "Where do we plan to stay?" George spluttered, "Well here we thought." Blue shock his head. "I am sorry but that will not be possible as Dragon Black informed us that after he has attended Pink's wings being clipped he intends to visit here and inspect the security of the prisoners, he must not find you here." Zach on hearing that Dragon Black was likely to appear quickly got off his chair and grabbed Joel by his hand. "Come on let's get out of here while we can, I don't want to be roasted by Dragon Black."

George had an idea and turning to Blue pointed to the log book that listed all the items that were securely locked away. "Where are these things kept?" Blue pointed a claw towards the tunnel leading to the cells. "The storeroom is set back off another tunnel to the right of the cells but surely there is nothing there that's of any use?" George looked hard at Dragon Blue rubbed his head and started to move towards the tunnel entrance. "I expect the storeroom is locked Dragon Blue, I hope that it is the one place Black will not think of visiting." Blue could see what George was thinking and interjected. "I am afraid that there is insufficient room within the store room for you all and anyway it would not be very comfortable. The cave room is hot and the air's very thin' making it ideal to store all the items we have collected but not a comfortable place for you to stay in for any length of time." George waved a hand of acknowledgement, he had a plan. "Look we cannot afford to leave right now as we know Black is due any minute. We also know Black's Elite Guard will be on patrol, the streets will be busy and we do not want to give ourselves away. The storeroom may or may not contain items that might be of use to us, but we should at least check them out and whilst we are doing this, we will be hidden from Black's visit." Grace in support moved towards George's side. "George is right the storeroom provides temporary cover and I believe there are things in there that could be used as weapons, but we will still require a permanent safe place to stay." Vegas-Gold had been listening to the discussions taking place his head moving from side to side observing everyone as they spoke in turn. "I have an idea, why don't they stay at my place they can leave under cover of dusk and I will have a room prepared for them."

Blue peered at Vegas-Gold and with a smile congratulated him. "Good thinking Vegas-Gold, I am pleased that you're willing to lay down your life to support our guests, for if you were ever found out that you were harbouring these four, Black would insist on your slow and painful death." Vegas-Gold looked startled. He had not really thought of any consequences of his pending actions and moving towards the station's main locked exit, nervously replied. "Please unlock the door Blue and let me leave now before I change my mind." Vegas-Gold then turning back to look at the four children sported a large grin and encouragingly said. "Don't worry, I won't let you down. Just be careful and don't be seen. I will have a room prepared for you and see you later this evening." "Just one thing," shouted Joel. "Can you prepare our room not only for us to sleep in but also as a workshop? I have a feeling we are all going to be rather busy."

CHAPTER 24

Operation Subterfuge

Dragon Pink was sitting upright on the large brilliant white marble slab used as an operating table. Dragon Grey and his two assistants were ready and waiting for the procedure of wing clipping to commence. Grey peered over his face mask at the operating room clock and sighed. "Where on earth has he got to?" Grey was of course referring to Dragon Black who not unusually was keeping everyone waiting. Pink, sank back on the cold slab. She had been given some special pills that had made her feel drowsy so much so that right now all she wanted to do was close her eyes and sleep. Suddenly the peace of the operating room was broken by the roar of Dragon Black. **"Out of my way, be quick about it, what room are they in?"** he was heard to demand. Grey's assistant opened the Theatre Door and politely asked Dragon Black to wipe his feet before entering and to stay back from the operating table so as to minimise the risk of infection.

Black roared again, thin wisps of smoke and violent red flame curling from his snarling mouth. **"I'll do what I want thank you, just get out of my way."** Pushing aside the assistant, Black moved towards where Pink was lying now fast asleep. "So get on with the procedure Grey, I have no time to waste and why is she asleep?" Black paused, and then eyes evilly glinting growled. **"She is supposed to feel the pain of the ceremony."** Dragon Grey was quick to respond. "Dragon Black, we intend to cut very deeply and remove the tendons completely, this will cause some of Pink's blood to spurt out and the last thing you need is to be covered or splattered by it."

Black immediately stopped in his tracks but as he was being followed so closely by his Elite Guard, they crashed with a thump into his rear. Black swung round and with a deft flick of his iron strong tail clipped both of them firmly across their heads. **"You stupid dragons,"** Black growled. "Get back over there and keep out of my way." The guards, rubbing their bruised heads scrambled to the corner and watched as their lord and master Dragon Black crouched down to view the procedure.

Dragon Grey took a position slightly obscuring Black's gaze but as he did so he turned his head and asked. "Dragon Black would you like me to create a wound that will be visible for all to see demonstrating that the ceremony has been accomplished." Black nodded furiously. **"Yes of course, the larger and the longer the cut the better."** He roared. Grey had thought well in advance to what he was going to do and being a skilful physician made the first incision under the edge of the wing close to where it joined her body. It was at this point that Grey knew he would be cutting into a number of veins that would bleed profusely, looking more severe than it really was. Black looked on eagerly. He was witnessing the removal of the ability to fly from the only dragon, other than himself, capable or equipped for flight. Pink would no longer be a threat. She like all the other dragons of Draegonia would be confined to the island. No longer would she pose any risk of leaving for help.

Black watched as Grey appeared to score a second more diagonal incision beneath Pink's wing and pulled what looked like thin cords and appeared to cut them. Grey's first assistant was ordered to stitch the cuts and as he did so Grey moved to the opposite side of the operating marble slab and with the second assistants help lifted Pink's other wing. Dragon Black could not see what precisely was happening. This was just as well for Dragon Grey was now into what could be considered 'slight of dragon paw'. Grey appeared, from Black's perspective, to make the same incisions and cuts under the wing that neither his assistants nor Black could fully see. What was in fact taking place was a carefully rehearsed act of subterfuge. Grey had earlier prepared a container filled with a liquid that closely resembled dragon's blood. As he passed his paw under Pink's wing he picked up the container and poured its content over the floor whilst capturing some of the sticky red liquid, rubbing it across the wing where the cuts should have taken place.

Black, from his vantage point, thought he saw a profusely bleeding wing with cuts that appeared much deeper than the first wing. Black smirked with appreciation for his Chief Physician's skill and willingness to inflict such pain on a fellow dragon. Black moved a few paces forward eager to see the damage done. Grey moved quickly and with a bloody looking thick swab speedily taped it over the simulated cuts. Black immediately noticed that no stitches were being administered but before he was allowed to say anything Dragon Grey, in a very clinical and authoritative voice spoke. "I see no point in making this too easy for Pink." Dragon Grey smirked under his face mask for his ongoing comments were tinged with hidden insult. "Making it less painful, your Dragonship, would make dragons think you have become soft. The wound will take longer to heal if not stitched, be more painful and leave more visible scaring." Black did not pick up on the contemptuous reference to 'Dragonship' but applauded Grey and once more roared so that all could hear. "Dragon Grey you are an inspiration to all other dragons. I wish more had your intelligence and willingness to serve my wishes." Black had seen enough and looked on by his bewildered guards, spun round and headed for the exit. "Come on you two, jump to it; we now need to see the prisoners being held by Dragon Blue."

Grey looked on as Black and his entourage departed and smiled. The plan had worked and now he was to add the finishing touches. It would be essential for Dragon Pink to believe that the operation had been carried out. Her right wing had been cut to simulate the 'Wing Cutting Ceremony' and of course there would be some pain but, she would still be able to fly once the muscles had healed. Her left wing had not been surgically operated upon at all so to prevent Pink realising this, Grey tightly bound the wing and strapped it to her side, similar to the right wing. Next, Grey ordered his assistants to clear up the theatre as he gently moved Pink on to a nearby intensive care bed.

Turning to his assistants he once more ordered. "Once the area is clean please return Dragon Pink back to her room and stay with her until she awakes." The assistants moved quickly, one cleaning the marble operating slab the other washing the floor, removing the evidence of the false procedure.

Dragon grey removed his face mask and smiled knowingly. Operation subterfuge had been a complete success.

CHAPTER 25

Bits and Pieces

The four children were rummaging through the mass of flotsam and jetsum that had been collected over the years; now labeled and racked in the dedicated store room of the police station.

"Gosh it's stuffy in here and why is it so hot?" Zach asked. Grace mopped her brow in agreement. Joel just wheezed he didn't react well to the lack of air. George seeing that the three were in some distress explained. "I think this part of the cave is very close to where there is a crack in the fissure of the volcano and as a consequence the air in here is heated. Just feel the walls, they're quite warm. Also there is no vent and the air is not circulating; that's why it has that musty stale smell." George pulled a small wooden bucket with tarnished brass rings towards him and inserted an old rum ladle, that may well have seen action in the 17th century, into some clear fresh water. "Here, drink some water," he said. "It will stop dehydration and make you feel better."

Grace was first to sip from the ladle but being impatient her two brothers grabbed a couple of tankards perched on one of the shelves bordering the cavernous room and plunged them into the bucket. "Oh!" exclaimed Grace, "such manners." George took no notice of the brotherly and sisterly banter, he was well used to it but concentrated his eyes on the entries of the log book.

"Look, "he said, pointing towards a packing case with partially legible labeling. "That's the locked waterproofed packing case listed in the log, what does the label say?" Grace, returning the ladle back into the bucket crossed the cave room to where George was pointing to the case and tried to read the label.

orks display unit p dry

"Well," she cried, "this is an easy one. The label obviously said;

"Fireworks display unit..Keep dry"

"I think you're right Grace!" George exclaimed. The two younger boys, realising that the packing case might hold fireworks, eagerly joined them. "Do you want me to open it?" Joel asked. "No let me, I can do it with this." Zach yelled out as he picked up one of the pirate swords from the cave floor. "No, we need to be very careful." It was George bringing the enthusiastic two to order. "If there are commercial fireworks within that case the explosives may be unstable and the last thing we need is for an explosion, no matter how small, to be set off in this confined space." Joel laughed and thought back to the time they had tested explosives causing much havoc in the Great Hall during their last visit. "I agree," he said. "We need to be careful but we cannot be seen carrying it to Dragon Vegas-Gold's dwelling and really we need to establish what's in the case and if it's safe to move it." Zach gave a wink to his sister and in support of his brother agreed. "*Yus.*" (Zach had a habit every now and again of accentuating the word yes in an upper crust manner). "I agree with Joel and we should check it out right away."

George and Grace, seeing that neither of the boys were going to wait, told them to get back and allow them to deal with it. The first thing of course was to remove the wax seal that held the padlock to the case. The stainless steel lock was going to be difficult. There was no way it could be cut, even if they had the tools. Grace had been pondering. "How are we going to remove the lock George?" George made no reply; for once he did not have the answer. It was the youngest of the four who, not bothering to stay in one position, had wandered off looking at all the bits and pieces stored in what he now considered was an 'Aladdin's cave'. Zach opened drawers of old ships cabinets, peered into buckets and barrels, each holding items ranging from screws and nails through to sponges, fabrics and ropes. Dragons White and Cream had been very busy over the decades.

Towards the rear of the cave, hidden in part by well-worn rope fishing nets, was a row of coloured jars. Zach took each one in turn, shook them and unscrewed some that had caps, carefully examining their contents. All of a sudden Zach let out a tremendous yell. "What's up? Are you OK?" A concerned Grace inquired. Zach rushed back to the three clutching a brownish glass jar. The contents were rattling and jangling as he approached them. "Look what I have found, will these help?" Zach upturned the jar and released its contents of different keys. Yale, padlock, gun case, security, there were numerous shapes and sizes. Bending down, George grabbed a handful. "How on earth were dragons able to find these? Where did they come from?" Grace was more selective picking up keys that looked as though they might fit the packing case lock. Eyeing George she whispered. "It really doesn't matter how or where they found them, what matters is will any of these keys fit the case?" One by one she tried her handful of keys in the lock. Several minutes passed as the other three looked on, each hoping that one of the keys would fit. "It's no use," cried out Zach, "I think we are going to be more than lucky if any of those fit." All of a sudden a loud **Click** gained everyone's attention. "Was that what I think it was?" Joel yelled in glee.

George casually walked towards the packing case just as Grace removed the now opened lock. "Well done Grace, obviously

luck is definitely with us. Now let's see what we have in here."
George carefully raised the hinged waterproof sealed lid to
reveal what looked like brown plasticised paper. It was in fact
a covering of waxed paper used to wrap and keep things dry.
Very carefully George peeled off the top to reveal a number of
shrink wrapped commercial *fireworks (See Glossary for
History of Fireworks). These looked nothing like the fireworks
he and his friends let off each November 5th. They were larger
and heavier than anything any of the four had ever seen before
and had names stenciled on their sides. Pack by pack the array
of explosive devices were removed and laid out on the dusty
floor as Joel and Zach studied each one in turn.

There were six packs, each one used for a different effect. The
four reviewed the names stenciled in black on their dark orange
coverings.

Aerial Firework Shells (Category 4)
Mines (10)
Roman candle (20) Battery
Tubular Fountains (24) Set
Thunder Shells (12)

The final pack removed from the bottom of the case was the
largest. It had formed the base and took some effort for Joel
with the help of Grace to extract. This pack was slightly
different as the outer wrapping was transparent plastic but
with the stencilled identification confirming they had indeed
removed,

(12) Venus Exploding Rockets

"Are these going to be of any use in our fight with Dragon
Black?" Zach asked. Joel, rubbing his eyes in bewilderment
replied. "I really have no idea. The explosive charges within

these specialised pyrotechnics are beyond me and I suggest we do not try to play around with them. Fireworks need careful handling at the best of times and these," Joel paused. "These look to me quite dangerous in the wrong hands." "Quite right," agreed Grace. The chatter of the children abruptly stopped. George whispered. "Did you hear that?" The noise grew louder and louder and finally all four recognised the ferocious growls of Dragon Black.

Black with his two Elite Guards entered unannounced into Draegonia's Police station. Blue had, just a few minutes earlier, finished feeding a midday meal to the last of the prisoners, when he heard the angry growls of Dragon Black. Returning into the main station room he saw the tail flicking, flame spitting, red eyed monster. Before Blue had time to say anything he was met with a barrage of abuse. "So where have you been you useless thing? The station door is left wide open and you're nowhere to be seen, I suppose you have been sleeping on the job again. I don't know why I keep you on Dragon Blue, you're well past your best!" Blue did not reply. He knew that anything he said would be misconstrued and only inflame the situation. "Well," an annoyed Dragon Black continued. "Where were you and what were you doing?" Blue smiled and in a cool, clear growl explained. "I have just been completing my hourly checks on the prisoners and giving them their only meal of the day of bread and water. Your commands to me, Sir, were that I had to keep my eye on the prisoners at all times...and that's exactly what I have been doing."

Black lowered his head; his fury only exaggerated by his wicked piercing red eyes and stared full in the face of Blue. "I am not sure about you," he gruffed. "I hope you're not trying to play games with me Blue, there's something that I don't trust about you." Dragon Blue swallowed hard but holding his nerve sidestepped the accusation. "Sire," he said. "You know you can count on me to provide you with everything you deserve, your command is most respected and…" "**Enough,**" Black bellowed. "I have no time to listen to you. Show me the prisoners."

The dragons held in the cells could not help but overhear Black's verbal tirade on Blue. All were busy hiding under their rough stone and wooden formed beds the food that Blue had delivered to them earlier. Dragon Cerise threw dust over her to make her look unkempt, dirty and pretended to be ill. Dragon Iceberg crouched down, paws clenched tightly over his eyes and mouth. He was not scared but wanted to stop himself from speaking angrily out of turn, something he was noted for.

Black entered the narrow tunnel leading to the cells, his enormous body leaving little space either side of him. One by one he peered though the spy holes into the cells and noted the fear, poor condition and weaknesses on display before him. "Good," he growled. "They look miserable and weak and soon I will put them out of their misery." Black was just about to back up when he saw the door leading to the store room. "What's in here?" He snarled pushing against the door. Dragon Blue gasped as Black forced open the door and looked in. Blue stretching his neck popped his head through the open door and together both dragons could be seen carefully scrutinising the interior of the room.

The four children realising that Dragon Black was in the building covered the fireworks with an old tarpaulin. Zach was the first to make a move to hide. Jumping into the now empty fireworks chest and pulled the lid down. Grace ran to the furthest and darkest corner of the room and hid behind a large spiked wheel washed up from a wrecked pirate ship of years gone by. Joel seeing his brother and sister making themselves almost invisible ran across to where the thick rope fishing net was hanging from the cave's roof. Climbing the net as though it were a rope ladder, Joel quickly reached its highest point and hid behind a suspended sail. George heard the cave entrance door being pushed. With the need for speed and survival he ran to its side just as the door opened and Dragon Black's head followed by the worried looking Dragon Blue's looked in. George held his breath daring not to move, hidden from view behind the open door.

For a few minutes Black said nothing but moved his head from side to side and up and down surveying all about him. Blue was more specific in his gaze. Where on earth were the children, did they leave without him knowing? Blue's thoughts were broken by the sound of Black's growl. "What's all this, why do you keep all this rubbish here when the space could house more prisoners. Get rid of it. Blue seized the opportunity and withdrew his head. "You're right Dragon Black, I will see to it right away. This is only junk really and could be quite easily be disposed of." Blue paused, waited for Dragon Black to remove his head and pulled the door firmly shut then marched back to his office followed closely by Dragon Black.

The four children waited a few minutes until they could no longer hear a sound and one by one reappeared. "Wow," said Zach, "that was awesome; I really thought we would be caught." Joel laughed nervously as Grace turning to George whispered. "Do you think we are safe to stay in here?" George did not reply, he was in deep thought. "Did you hear what I said George, what are you thinking about?"

George smiled, "I think we have found the way for us to have all of this," he pointed at all the bits and pieces "transported for us to Dragon Brown's hide out with the full blessing of Dragon Black."

CHAPTER 26

Goal, Objectives and Strategy

Dragon Gold bowed his head in fearful respect as Dragon Black and his Elite Guards exited the Police Station to return to The Hall of Dragons. "Come in Gold," Blue beckoned. "How is Dragon Pink?" Gold explained that the staged operation had been a complete success and that Pink was now recovering in the hospital. From the direction of the cells George and the others entered the main room clutching a list of washed up items. "Hello Dragon Gold." All four cried out in unison. Gold gave a big grin and started to close the door behind him. "We don't want you to be seen do we?" But before the door could be fully closed it was smartly pushed open again by Vegas-Gold.

"Have you heard the news?" He breathlessly panted. "A cave by cave search is being carried out looking for you four." He pointed to the children and continued his update. "It appears the Guards on duty at the Eastern Pass found a pair of binoculars and rather than disturb Dragon Black during the clipping of Pink's wings, they have set about looking for all of you." "But how do they associate us with the binoculars. They could have been washed ashore and dropped by Dragon White for all they know." Grace cried out. Vegas-Gold chuckled. "Well I suppose that is possible but on the binoculars there apparently was the name of JOEL. And, there is only one Joel that we dragons are aware of." Joel fumbled for his school bag and rummaged inside. Yes the binoculars were gone, but did he or George forget to put them back? "What's done is done." George quickly stated. "I think the best thing we can do is exactly what Dragon Black has commanded and dispose of all the items in the store room. The only difference is that half will be taken to Volcano Peak with the other more interesting and useful items taken to where Dragon Brown is in hiding." George continued. "Our Goal is the removal of Dragon Black. However, we have several objectives to consider.

1) Save the lives of the seven held in the cells.
2) Prevent Dragon Black from finding out about the subterfuge and importantly provide protection for Dragon Pink.
3) Assist Dragon Brown to overthrow Black before Saturday (the day of the full moon).
4) Prevent any more dragons from being carbonised."

George had a strategy. He had seen several items in the store room he believed would be key to their plans. "Dragon Gold we need you to call Dragon Red and get him to bring his truck round. Vegas-Gold you will be required to help load it when it arrives with as much of the storeroom's...." George paused, grinned and continued with a chuckle. "Well, in the words of Dragon Black, *the rubbish* he so kindly has ordered to be removed. Gold, you know exactly where Brown's headquarters are. You will first drop off specific items that Grace and I will identify to be loaded last. These are to be stored in Brown's command centre where we will develop the necessary weapons to use against Dragon Black. I am sure Dragon Brown will appreciate our intervention and support as he must realise that even with additional dragon power now at his disposal, he is still outnumbered. The items we do not offload must then be quickly driven to Volcano Peak by Red and Vegas-Gold. I want all the items to be evenly distributed on each of the twelve execution plinths for their disposal, just as Black has ordered."

Grace and the two boys listened in amazement. What was George planning? What were the specific items George was referring to and importantly, how *were they*, to reach the safety of Dragon Brown? George seeing their questioning eyes urged

Gold to make the call and as Gold removed the 'Dragon Communicator' from the wall, George explained further. "Don't worry about how we will travel as I plan for all of us to be hidden amongst the bric a brac on the truck."

George continued in a more excited tone and pointed a finger to some specific entries within the log book. "Look at the items listed here. We have already examined the case containing the commercial fireworks, but these look interesting! There is a set of compressed air cylinders, fire extinguishers, thick plastic tubes, optical lenses, rope, nets and numerous other things that have given me an idea how we might be able to deal with Dragon Black."

George, now with the undivided attention of all, continued. "The best way to defeat Black is when he is at his most vulnerable, at a time when he feels totally secure and non-threatened. That time will be when he is sentencing dragons to their deaths at Volcano Peak. And we know he has scheduled that for the day of the full moon, which is this coming Saturday." "Whew," Joel exclaimed. "That means we have less than a few days to prepare." George smiled and gave Joel a wink of encouragement just as Dragon Gold replaced the 'Dragon Communicator', informing them all that Dragon Red was on his way.

George pulled from his pocket a marker pen and began ringing key items listed within the log book. "Here Vegas-Gold, take this and leave the items I have marked until the very last. Separate them from those we will be leaving at Volcano Peak with one of the tarpaulins, and place a second cover over everything so that we can hide beneath." Grace however looked worried and wanted to share her concerns. "Dragon Blue, as soon as Dragon Black hears about the binoculars you can bet he will either summon you to the Hall of Dragons or appear here himself. What do you think he will do, any ideas?"

Blue rubbed his chin and was just about to shake his head, when a sudden thought crossed his mind. "I do have a suggestion but you may not like it. We need at least three of you free to carry on your important work. We also need to stop those searches currently being carried out." Joel fearing the worse looked worried and slowly spoke. "I don't think we are going to like this, are we Dragon Blue? What's your plan?"

The two dragons and four children listened in absolute stony silence as Blue unfolded his very scary and extremely dangerous plan. "I am sure that Black has not received any report that the binoculars have been found, he has only just left here and headed straight for the Hall of Dragons. No doubt he will immediately depart there to conduct his usual afternoon patrol of the island. As you all know, this usually takes a couple of hours or so, but when he returns it must be me that informs him that the owner of the binoculars has been apprehended, tortured and that it is fully established he, and he alone, was the only visitor to land on our island."

None spoke, their gazes affixed on Dragon Blue as he eyed Joel up and down. "I suggest we elicit Physician Grey's help. He will dress what will look to be wounds and bruises inflicted on our newest and youngest prisoner." Blue stopped what he was saying for a brief moment to study the confused, concerned and very worried face of Joel.

"Now you hang on a second, are you suggesting **I am** going to be seen as captured and tortured and displayed in front of Dragon Black? You all must be joking; seriously I'm not doing it." Zach seeing his brother in some distress placed himself in front of him. "I'll, I'll do it, I'm not afraid," he bravely but hesitatingly cried out. Grace shook her head. "No that's too dangerous, I will not allow it."

George, realising that Blue's suggestion had some merit turned to his three cousins. "Dragon Blue has a point you know," he said quietly. "As soon as Dragon Black hears about the binoculars he will do everything to find its owner and anyone else who is with them. You all know Black would not stop searching. We would be unable to move about at all and we know that Black will take many reprisals If we are not found." George placed his hand on Joel's shoulder and whispered to him. "You do not have to do it. It is your decision and whatever you decide we will support you." George paused and then emphasised. "BUT, you must think of the consequences if you decide to decline what is a really dangerous mission."

There was a hushed silence as three dragons together with three very concerned children all stared at Joel who just hung his head without speaking. Slowly, he raised his head and gave a very weak smile. "OK, I'll do it." A relieved Grace and George patted Joel on his back. Zach cried out. "Well done Joel you're really brave." Vegas-Gold looked on in some amazement, recognising the strength of character being displayed by such a little guy.

Before anything else could be said the roar of Dragon Red's truck was heard. George was first to make a move. "OK, Dragon Blue you speak with Dragon Grey and explain what we need him to do. It will be vitally important you also get to Black before anyone else does. Joel, get yourself ready, try not to worry, we will look after you. I suggest you place yourself in the cell that held Dragon Pink. That will please Black should he come to visit you. Vegas-Gold you go and ask Dragon Red to join Grace and me inside the store room where we will make a start to separate the important items. Zach, you stay by the door on lookout, we don't want any uninvited visitors just right now do we?"

As George and Grace hurried off in the direction of the store room, a very worried Grace was heard to say. "We know our goal is to depose Dragon Black. You obviously have outlined the objectives but do you really believe your strategy and plan will succeed? " George stopped for a brief moment but before he could reply, Grace pulled hard on his arm and in a louder voice exclaimed. "If we get it wrong, we could lose our lives!"

179

CHAPTER 27

The Most Painful of Deaths

Dragon Brown was greeted with military enthusiasm as he finally reached the command centre north of the island. Sergeant Tuscan-Red saluted and quickly updated him. "I am pleased to report that the officer in charge of Black's guards has been more than willing to cooperate and has replaced the injured Dragon Mango. As you know Sir, his wounds were the most critical and he requires complete rest. Black has not visited yet and all is going to plan."

A delighted Dragon Brown entered the large cave where Corporal Dragon Umber was standing close to the table used for planning purposes. Stamping his feet to attention and saluting, he bellowed. "What news from the city, Sir?" "At ease Umber, I will brief both of you now and you may convey the information to the others later. Incidentally who is on lookout?" Umber spoke again. "I was just about to relieve the sergeant Sir before you arrived." Brown studied his tired looking dragons. "Have you had any rest?" The sergeant responded. "Well Sir the problem is that with only five of us and three having to be seen as Black's guards, there has been little time available to sleep." Brown thought for a moment, then gave an order that quite surprised Tuscan-Red. "I want both of you to get some sleep right now. Black will be conducting his routine patrol soon and I presume that we have everything in order below. You're no good to me exhausted, so you are both relieved; get some sleep, that's an order." The two dragons, not requiring to be ordered twice, moved silently to their quarters.

Brown leaned across the expansive table top and opened a box containing chess pieces. The King, Queen, Bishop, Knights and pawns all resembled miniature dragons, the castles, well of course they were replicas of Castle Turrets. The figures were made out of calved ivory dating back to the Chinese Ming dynasty. Brown rolled the characters between his claws and thought out loud. "I thought these might be useful one day." Brown placed the black ivory pieces on a large map of the island. The Black King depicted Dragon Black. The Knights, Bishops and Castles represented Black's Elite Guard, whereas the pawns reflected the conscripted dragons that had been forced into Black's recently formed army.

Having positioned all the black chess pieces Dragon Brown removed and carefully placed the white pieces. He considered himself as a Castle, an immovable object. His sergeant he depicted as a brave knight and the remaining four of his troops together with the eight recuperating dragons, he represented by way of the pawns. Brown laid on their sides eight pawns to demonstrate their non-availability and continued to study his campaign map. He placed a knight and one bishop close to where the police station was clearly highlighted. "They represent Cerise and the other prisoners." Brown, still mumbling to himself, picked up the Queen and placed her alongside the King and smiled. "Dragon Gold, the queen, Dragon Blue, the king, I am sure they would both see the humorous side of those characters." Brown crouched down onto his haunches and once more looked hard at the black and white characters and sighed. "We are definitely outnumbered; I think we are going to need a great deal of luck if we are to really rid ourselves of Dragon Black."

Dragons Red, Gold and Vegas-Gold were clinging on for dear life as the red truck raced, bouncing and rattling as it did so, over the very rough terrain. Red was at the wheel, his thoughts focussed totally on the safety of the three children hidden in the rear.

It was approaching dusk as they finally arrived at the highest and most inhospitable tip of the North Island Cliffs, very close to the secret entrance leading down to Dragon Brown's command centre. No-one on watch, Dragon Gold placed a claw to his mouth and signalled for his two dragon friends to be silent. Grace had partially removed the edge of the cover that concealed them and signalled to the others not to say a word. Dragon Gold climbed a few metres then disappeared from view.

Brown had left his two subordinates asleep long enough and barked an order for them to wake up. Tuscan-Red and Umber responded immediately jumping to attention. "At ease," Brown barked. "I trust you are rested and ready to relieve Wenge and Wine?" Brown was just to bark out another order when from the darkness of the caves rear tunnel popped out a very dusty Dragon Gold. "Oh, here you all are, I am surprised no-one is on guard, I have Dragons Red and Vegas-Gold with me as well as George, Grace and Zach, plus a truck load of .." Dragon Gold paused, not quite knowing how to describe the truck load of bits and pieces and laughed. "Well the youngsters describe the things as potential weapons once they have built them, but for the time being they need to be stored here and we need to be quick about it." Brown had a number of questions but thought better to raise them as he could see Gold was most agitated. Brown barked out ordering Umber to go with Dragon Gold and help unload.

Meanwhile back at the truck, George, Grace and Zach had started to unload the special items and gave Vegas-Gold the task of carrying them in the direction where Gold reappeared. Gold accompanied by Dragon Umber took the load from Vegas-Gold. "Great," cried Zach. "At last we have some help to move this lot!" It took less than 10 minutes for the four dragons to unload the specific items. Everything was carried into the command centre cave where Dragon Brown had assigned a separate storage area and room for the children to work in. Brown inspected each of the items being carried and looked at times somewhat confused, for he was unable to see anything closely resembling a weapon. Still, he thought. "I'll give them the benefit of the doubt."

The three children waved an enthusiastic goodbye as the red truck disappeared from view heading towards the centre and highest point of the island, Volcano Peak. The three dragons had been ordered to evenly distribute the remainder of the cargo onto each of the 12 execution plinths that encircled the mouth of the volcano. The tips of each blackened sooty plinth protruded perilously towards the centre of the volcano's mouth. Any one or thing placed on them certainly would not survive for long, especially at times of eruptions. Fortunately the volcano had been quiet for some time with only wisps of rotten egg smelling smoke now seen disappearing into the starry sky.

Darkness had fallen as the last item, a pirate ship's spiked steering wheel was placed on the last, 12 o'clock positioned, stone slab. "I am sure glad that's over." Gold wiping his brow exhaled. He had not worked so hard for a long time and significantly out of breath was wheezing. "Let's get back as quickly as we can and hopefully not run into any of Black's Elite Guards, I don't think I can handle them right now," he said. "I agree," retorted Dragon Red. Vegas-Gold climbed onto the rear as the truck's engine was started and slowly, very noisily, in the stillness of the night, rolled back towards the city centre. In the distance, Dragon Gold could see a number of dragon flames being focussed on a single target. Little did he know that someone's misfortune would be his gain.

Earlier that afternoon, Joel had been lying on the rough wooden bench inside, what he considered to be the worst cell in the police station, when both Dragons Blue and Grey appeared. Each carried a 'Dragon Lamp' the flickering flames of which cast weird and sometimes scary shadows across the floor, walls and along the creviced ceiling of the cave. Dragon Grey was the first to growl, but in a sympathetic tone. "Well young boy you really have volunteered for quite a brave task, haven't you?" Joel was speechless, all he could do was think how ridiculous the comment was. He certainly could not recall having volunteered trial next Saturday." Blue led the way to Cerise's cell where Joel spent the next twenty minutes discussing and agreeing the plan George had previously given to him.

Meanwhile Grey had been waiting just a few minutes outside the Hall of Dragons when he heard the sound of wings and the thud as Dragon Black landed. Seeing Grey before him, Dragon Black called for his Elite Guards who quickly moved to their protective positions. "So what do I have the pleasure of a visit from you Grey?" Black in his customary fashion snarled as he entered the labyrinth of caves. Grey followed Black through the dimly lit corridor into the Great Hall where Black took his position on the tall plinth overseeing all beneath him.

Grey was not usually noted for his verbal skills, tending to be recognised more as a bit of a bumbling professor but recent events had made him more resolute. "Well Sir, I do have some excellent news for you." Without waiting for Black's approval to speak, Grey informed him of how Dragon Blue on hearing that there had been a sighting of a possible unauthorised visitor on the island, took immediate action and that after a successful search had made an arrest.

Black listened in silence, his brow furrowed as he became more and more suspicious of Grey's report. Grey went on to confirm that Blue had requested assistance with the interrogation and that unfortunately the prisoner was still held in the cell, but close to death. Dragon Black raising himself to full height spread out his large wings and spat a blast of bluish white flame into the air and roared. **"So how many of these visitors are there on the island, who are they, what are they and what are they doing here?"** Before Grey had time to respond there was an interruption as a senior guard entered clutching a pair of binoculars between pointed claws and saluted. "I am sorry to disturb you Sire, but these were found earlier today and we have been carrying out a cave by cave search for the whereabouts of its owner." Black snarled his eyes enflamed and stared at Grey. "So Grey, why are my guards searching for the so called perpetrator when Blue has supposedly captured them? Why were my guards not informed?"

Dragon Grey had already worked out his answers to obvious questions that Black would raise and immediately replied. "Sir, it was important that Dragon Blue established how many intruders there were. He and I have ascertained beyond any doubt there has only been one who has infiltrated our island. Unfortunately it has taken some time to interrogate him." Black lowered his head close to Grey's and menacingly asked. "And who and what is **him,** and how did he get here?" Grey stumbled for a second, his brain fighting for the answer to the one question he had not rehearsed. "I am not sure how he managed to arrive back on the island Sire but he poses no threat. Under extreme torture he has admitted that he and he alone found the island by chance. We have even ascertained he knows nothing of your return to the island." Black still eyes glaring snarled back at Grey. "And tell me Grey, who is he, who in your own word has come **back** to the island and knows nothing about my returning?" Grey swallowed hard. "Well Sire, it is one of the younger children who many years ago was shipwrecked. You may recall his name, Joel." Black let out a mighty roar. "Are you certain there is only one of them, I don't believe you? I want to see him. I will make him talk?" Grey interjected attempting in vain to slow down Black's increasing anger.

"Sire, the prisoner is very weak, I am afraid any attempt to re-interrogate him will result in his immediate and certain death and what good will that do you? I believe we should use him as a warning to everyone of your absolute authority?" Black, pulling his head away from Grey's returned to his upright stature and gruffed. "So, you're both sure he is alone. You are certain he had no idea I have returned and that his arrival is a complete coincidence?" Grey again gulped. "I know it seems tell you how we will destroy Black's flame but firstly we need to have a plan to capture Black after he has lost it." Grace enthusiastically continued. "The only time Black will be off guard is when he feels totally safe and that is when he has all his Elite Guards round him and is in a position where he can see every dragon when passing sentence. So, we plan to attack him this coming Saturday at the so called trial that he thinks will lead to the executions of seven dragons and Joel." Brown said nothing, listening in admiration wanting to hear more.

George picked up one of the packs of pyrotechnics. "These together with the other fireworks will be placed in such a position that when fired will at best throw Dragon Black off guard. We will create sufficient smoke to act as a screen for you and your dragon team to neutralise Black's Elite Guard." Grace pointed to the old fishing net and added. "Our plan is to have that net thrown over Black to restrain and prevent him from flying away." George moved across to where some stainless steel chain was curled up on the floor. "Our plan includes wrapping this chain around Black's tail to prevent him lashing out. If our actions are swift, Black's guards will be taken totally by surprise thus affording you the opportunity of dealing with them." Brown waited for the two to catch their breath. "You appear to me to be quite excited by your plan but you have not told me how you intend removing Black's flame and don't tell me you will use the chemical dart as we all know Black's hide is too tough. You cannot get close enough to him to administer it and even if the needle was strong and sharp enough, you have no delivery system."

Grace and George looked at each other and grinned. "We do have a delivery system," a smiling Grace retorted. George picked up one of the short clear but very thick plastic tubes and removing the chemical dart from a box it had been kept safely in during the journey, slipped it into the tube. "You see it fits exactly and glides along the inner part of the tube with ease."

Brown roared. "I suppose you expect one of the dragons to use that thing to blow the dart at Black?" "Don't be silly," retorted an indignant Grace. "There is no way a dragon could hold and take aim of any tube without Black or his guards witnessing the attack. Furthermore we know that Black's hide, his skin, is far too thick and too tough for the dart' tip to penetrate." "That is of course," added George. "If we were to aim anywhere other than his weak spot. Black's weak spot, his 'Achilles Heel', is his throat." Brown knowingly shook his head. "He might have softer skin under his throat but how would anyone get close enough to use the dart unseen." Grace laughed out loudly and pulled at the cylinder of compressed air. "This could be used to propel the dart but first we need to check out our theory using some makeshift darts." George pointed to the old rusty fire extinguisher. "We are also going to check out whether that still works and if it provides more pressure, but either way, we believe we have the means to propel the chemical dart, accurately, over a distance of at least 25 metres." Brown stroked his chin as he raised another question. "But how will your aim be controlled? Even if you were able to get within 25 meters of Black I am sure you would be seen and caught and anyway those cylinders are quite heavy and cumbersome for you."

George opened a box marked 'Ophthalmic' and revealed rows of tightly packed lenses and assorted mirrors. "These can be made to provide the sighting mechanism ensuring we do not have to be too close to Dragon Black." Grace seeing that Dragon Brown just could not see how their plan was to work explained further as she removed two lenses and a mirror from the box held by George. Grace placed the mirror on the edge of the compressed air bottle and faced it towards where George was standing. She then walked across to Dragon Brown and held the two lenses opposite each other in a line facing the tiny mirror. "Dragon Brown, lower your head and using just one eye squint through the lens I am holding through to the second one as I move them in line towards the mirror. Once you see the mirror let me know and I will then move the smaller lens closer to the larger one until you tell me you can see a clear image in the mirror." Squinting one eye, Brown lowered his head and followed Grace's instructions. Suddenly he let out a gasp as he could see an image of George, still holding the box clearly reflected in the mirror. "Well that is truly amazing," Brown bellowed.

George moved towards Grace and taking from her the lenses, returned them back to the box. "We will position the tube that will project the dart at a precise angle aimed to hit Black's throat. The mirrors and lenses will be set and used as our sighting mechanism." Grace could not contain her excitement and with great gusto added. "Just like telescopic sights of a rifle barrel and we will run the flexible tubing of our makeshift barrel to the hidden compressed air cylinder that will be used to propel the dart."

Brown shook his head, shrugged his shoulders and smiled. "Your plan to overthrow Black is outrageous and will require a great deal of luck as well as skill, but we have nothing to lose. If you're able to make good effect of the chemical dart, if you can fire it with total accuracy, if you believe Black's throat can be penetrated, if you think those explosives or fireworks as you call them will create a diversion and if you think one of us can get close enough to put a chain on Black's formidable tail, then you indeed have a strategy." Brown once again shrugged opened and closed his clipped wings and before returning back to his war table, encouragingly growled. "I do have confidence in all of you, but for my liking there are too many ifs."

CHAPTER 29

Black Tightens His Grip.

Having inspected the apparently very injured and weak Joel, Dragon Black together with his formidable Elite Guards, exited the Police station. Black was delighted with what he saw. He had congratulated Blue on his diligence and hard work. He had praised Dragon Grey for ensuring the interrogation had been such a success and he was well pleased that in a few days time he would witness the removal of seven dragons and an insignificant child, who in part had been the cause of such annoyance.

Still smiling, Black looked up towards the smoky volcano silhouetted against the darkening skies. It was well past curfew, yet ahead of him was a spectre of something approaching. Black's Elite Guards quickly closed round their leader affording him total protection. "Who goes there?" An Elite Guard yelled. Black did not wait for an answer. He was not going to take chances. Whoever it was should have immediately declared themselves. Rushing to the conclusion this was a hostile approach; Black took a great intake of breath and fired a blast of scorching red, white and bluish yellow flames in the direction of the unsuspecting oncoming object. The two Elite Guards acted in unison believing their master had spotted an attacking foe. They too opened their huge mouths and fired a swage of fiercely red hot flames towards their attacker. There was a tortuous and painful dragon scream, as the full force of three dragons fiery onslaught, connected with their target.

CHAPTER 30

An Extinguisher to the Rescue

Dragon Pink was recovering well. Her wings were tightly strapped but she was surprised at how good she was feeling. Earlier she had been told of the suffering dragons incurred as a result of the 'Wing Clipping Ceremony' yet she was in no pain. Pink rolled off her hospital slab and crouched on the floor just as Dragon Grey entered the recovery room. "Now, now Pink get back up onto your bed we don't want you injuring yourself, do we?" Grey was not noted for being a conversationalist and picking up a dragon chart either did not hear or want to hear Pink's questions relating to her operation, the children and what was happening. Grey mumbled under his breath. "Pink, you need rest and understand everything is under control, you have nothing..." Before Grey had chance to complete his assurances, Dragon Vegas-Gold's head appeared in the door way. "Dragon Grey you're needed we left a dragon body in your morgue last night. We need to provide you with details of how the death occurred and importantly who the poor soul was." Pink's eyes widened at the news but before she could utter a word Grey hurried out of the door, heading to where Dragons Red and Vegas-Gold had left the remains of Black's latest killing.

Towards the north George, observed by an impressed Dragon Brown, was in deep conversation with his two cousins. They had been given a working area in a small cave off the main command centre room where Dragon Umber was preparing breakfast of fresh fruit and crystal clear water.

"So how are we are going to fire the dart and where we will fire it from?" Zach asked. Grace was quick to reply. "Well we know that Dragon Black's throat is his weakest point. We know that we have to aim up towards and under his head, possibly when his head is held high and his mouth is wide open. More importantly we know that our aim has to be absolutely precise."

"That's absolutely right Grace," agreed George. He was showing Zach a number of complex drawings. "Here is a sketch showing where we should hide the tube. It must be hidden within the ground, at an exact angle in front of the high plinth, that Black will be perched upon when he presides over the trial." "And," Grace added. "We will run a connecting hose to the barrel from the compressed air cylinders. I have checked the cylinders' contents and believe they should provide more than enough pressure to propel the dart."

Zach looked intently at each of the sketches. Suddenly, pointing a finger at one he shouted. "Look we cannot be seen anywhere near the plinth and not in sight of any of Black's loyal dragons. So how will we be able to look along the sights and know when Black is in the right position to fire the dart, without being seen?" George grinned. "Good question but I have thought of that. What Grace and I have designed is a series of strategically positioned lenses and mirrors. These will be placed and fixed in positions that will reflect the exact aim we will require. The first mirror closest to where we will be hiding will be angled to reflect the line of sight through all the other lenses. The only thing that we must obtain is Joel's binoculars as these will be necessary for us to be able to see the image of the first mirror."

Zach scratched his head. "Wow it sounds great but complicated and what happens if a dragon gets in the way of any of the strategically placed lenses?" Grace laughed out aloud. "An excellent point Zach, but that's where Dragon Gold plays his part. He will be responsible for the layout of the court in order to accommodate so many prisoners on trial. We are to cordon off a route along which the prisoners will walk. They will be pre-briefed where the lenses are placed, where to stand and will leave the necessary gaps between them and Dragon Black." "OK but how are we going to capture him if we are unable to get anywhere near him?" Zach once more queried. George smiled and patted Zach on his shoulder in encouragement. "This is where you will play your part Zach. We need you to be out of sight but close to the plinth. As Black's tail settles during the trial you are to wrap the chains that will be hidden behind the plinth, round his tail and lock them, thus preventing him from flying off. Unfortunately, we have nothing to cut the stainless steel chain so it will allow him to fly into the air but not away from Volcano Peak."

Zach was quiet, considering his role that sounded somewhat dangerous. "But how do we prevent him from ordering his Elite Guard from attacking as soon as he realises that he has been hit by the dart?" Before George could say another word Grace hugged her brother. "Don't worry Zach; as soon as the dart is fired we will set off the pyrotechnics that we will also have concealed around the plinth. These will all be fired simultaneously and provide sufficient distraction for the prisoners to capture the Elite Guards." Dragon Brown who had been listening and nodding in agreement spoke for the first time. "My army of dragons will also aid the attack on the Elite Guards. In addition, Dragons Candy, Goldenrod, Tango, Mango and the others below who are now recovering and soon fit for action will be in waiting to overpower those who might aid Black. I think the plan is audacious, but more than feasible." George winked his left eye at Grace and smiled. "Dragon Brown, any plan that is aimed at taking down the most formidable dragon of all times is always going to be audacious, but what will make our plan work is the commitment and dedication of everyone and our ability to work as a co-ordinated team. Black does not have that benefit and I am sure as soon as his enforced supporters see our strength, they will either run or join with us, either way we will eliminate the evil dragon, hopefully once and for all time."

Brown roared with laughter, he could not help but admire the three little ones before him but wanted to know more. "When do you plan to set up your equipment? Surely it needs to be done after Black has flown past you on his routine surveillance flight of the island and you will need to have everything in place before his next patrol. George looked at his wrist watch. "You're right Dragon Brown so if we set off mid afternoon and work through the night we should have everything in place and well hidden for Black's next fly past. However we will need two of your dragons to assist us as the items are bulky and quite heavy." Brown smiled. "That is not a problem. Wenge and Wine will carry everything for you and will dig out any holes you require with their claws, I will go and arrange everything whilst you finish off in here." Brown turned smartly and galloped off at high speed to the main command centre room.

Zach, still concentrating hard on the diagrams of the dart tube, sighting arrangement, fireworks distribution points and where the all important steel anchor chain was to be placed, suddenly looked up at Grace. "I think we have a problem." "And what might that be?" retorted his sister. "Well look, the thick plastic tube is about a metre long and needs to be placed and angled up within 7-10 metres of the plinth that hopefully Black will be perched upon." "That's right," interjected George, "What's the problem?"

Zach took the pencil he had been making some calculations with and pointed to where there was an X on the diagram. "Well, if we're going to run a flexible hose from our hiding place, connected to those old diver's air bottles and expect the pressure to be sufficient to travel the whole length of the tube with sufficient pressure to propel the dart, is one thing but timing is another. The distance for the compressed air to travel will take a few seconds, in that time Black's head would have inevitably

CHAPTER 31

Preparing for Battle

"So Dragon Grey how long do you believe I should be kept in here, I am getting really bored you know?" Grey's steely eyes scanned Pink's bandages and noticed that they were quite loose. "Have you been fiddling with these?" He mumbled as he adjusted the dressing to her left wing. "Dragon Grey, I will ask you a direct question and I want a truthful answer." Grey took a step back, a bemused look on his face. "You see Dragon Grey, I do not believe you have actually clipped my wings, as I feel tender in one wing only and experience nothing like the pain other dragons have apparently suffered in the past."

Grey hesitated, his bemused look faded. He was concerned for not only Pink's safety but for the safety of all who knew that Pink's wings had not been clipped. What was he to say or do? Pink made his decision easier. "I think," she said. "That you have pretended to complete the operation. I think that my wings were bound so tightly so that I would not find out but being on my own all day I had nothing else to do but try to look at your handy work."

Grey moved across the room and closed the door and in a calm voice told Pink of the subterfuge that had taken place. "You mean that I will still be able to fly? How long will the muscles take to heal, do I have to wear the bandages?"

"For goodness sake Pink hold on, you are talking to fast and too loudly. You must not be found out hence the reason why we have kept you here." Pink stood up and with a warm affectionate smile whispered. "I agree, we of course need to keep things secret but instead of my wings being so tightly bound can I not start exercising them? Black is unlikely to return to see me and I will of course stay here, but I cannot just crouch round doing nothing."

Grey slowly nodded in agreement. "Well in one way I am pleased you now know the truth, but be careful. Your friends have made plans with Dragon Brown to capture Black when he presides over the trial of the prisoners and young Joel."

"WHAT, Who, Joel!" exclaimed Pink. "Where is he and why..........." Dragon Grey raising his paws beckoned Pink to calm down. "Look Pink, everything is under control but if you try to interfere with any of the plans now in place, you could well jeopardise the whole operation. Joel volunteered to be caught so that he may act as a link to George, Zach and Grace who are with Dragon Brown in the north. Joel is now closely working with Dragon Cerise and others held in the cells." Pink listened in amazement realising that much had been done and that this was not the time for her to interfere or be the cause of any upset but she was insistent on one important thing. "I want to be able to use the exercise room and strengthen my wings. I feel that my right one will heal more quickly than my left but I really want to aid my own recovery if at all possible." Grey smiled back at Pink who he had known since birth recognising that she was turning from a baby dragon into a young lady dragon with strength of character that her parents would have been proud of.

Grey opened the recovery room door, turned and in a soft voice whispered. "OK Pink, it's a deal. You stay out of sight and I will make the exercise support centre totally at your disposal, but remember you are supposed to be recovering from a very painful wing clipping procedure, no one must see you."

Back at Volcano Peak, Dragons Wenge and Wine were finishing off the completion of 6 strategically placed holes within the stony ground. These formed a rough circle around the central tall plinth where Black was soon to hold court. George placed the containers marked 'Thunder Shells' and 'Aerial Shells' in front of the plinth. Their tops were just level with the surface. Grace lightly covered them with shingle and dust, carefully blending them within the surroundings. Next, a battery of 20 'Roman Candles' and a modified set of 20 'Tubular Fountains' were buried either side of the plinth and to its rear in the last of the holes dug to contain the fireworks, were hidden, 10 'Mines' and 12 'Venus Exploding Rockets'. The two children worked furiously but nonetheless taking great care to perfectly and accurately position everything, they knew there would be no second chances. Failure was not an option.

"OK, Grace it's getting dark and we need to get the last jobs done as quickly as possible. I only wish Zach was here to help." Grace rubbed the dust from her hands. "Yes I agree but if we need those binoculars then Zach is probably the quickest and smallest to sneak in and out of the city before dawn." George said nothing; he was now in deep concentration, laying down the fuses made from thin, oily soaked string that was covered in gunpowder. Grace looked on and raised her eyebrows. "Will the fuses burn even though they will be covered up with dust George?"

"Well the ones I tested earlier worked. Let's just hope we don't have any rain before the trial, as that could cause a problem." Dragons Wenge and Wine had completed digging all the holes ordered and now stood silently watching the industrious two. George and Grace had started to work on the most difficult structure and complex layout of lens sights, the makeshift barrel to hold the dart and the cage to hold the cylinder of gas that would propel it.

Grace carefully positioned the lenses and mirrors alongside the roped corridor where the prisoners would be marched to stand trial and be sentenced. She placed subtle markings as indicators to ensure they would not be obstructed and camouflaged them to avoid detection. Meanwhile George was busy hammering into the ground several hardened steel spikes, the tops of which carried small eyelets. A thin metal wire would run through each eyelet from the gas cylinder's firing mechanism back to where George and Grace planned to be in hiding.

As the sun sank beyond the horizon the air became cool and with lowering cloud quite misty. "I am exhausted George how much longer is this going to take?" asked Grace as she checked and lined up the last optical lens. "Not long Grace, all we need to do is place the final two mirrors and sight everything so that we will be able to see whatever the tip of our barrel is pointing at." George pointed his hand towards the 45 degree angled mirror that Grace had placed a few metres from where they were going to be in hiding.

"Using the binoculars we should be able to see the image of our target appear through those other lenses and mirrors and once firmly situated within our sights we pull that lever." George pointed into the larger hole strategically positioned by a few boulders where the lines of fuses met. "The lever will give us good purchase to yank out the extinguishers safety pin, thus releasing the propellant and firing the dart."

Grace showed her concern. "Is there any way we could test the sight for accuracy? We would look pretty stupid if the dart missed its target because the sighting was out? George smiling asked Grace for her laser penlight and shone the bright red light towards the angled mirror closest to them. The pin sharp beam of light hit the mirror and reflected off towards the base of the plastic tube that could just be seen appearing out of the ground and hidden in part by a clump of recently planted course grass midday for his usual inspection. Do you want me to have everyone in position as planned?" Brown responded, observed by the three children as he confirmed that Black needed to be convinced that everything and everyone was in its place. "Tuscan-Red you, Wenge and Wine will need to assume the identities of Black's Guards and make the dragons who are supposed to be completing their hard labour sentence appear to be suffering. They however look fitter and stronger than ever and so it will be essential for you to look as though you are forcing them into deeper water to place heavier and larger boulders. You and your team must appear to be whipping your prisoners and they need to play their part by growling and moaning as though in pain. That should convince Black all is well and no need for him to land and carry out any inspection."

Grace had been watching the expression on Tuscan-Red's face as he took on board the importance of his task, but had a question of her own. "What if Black looks as though he is not going to fly past but intends landing, what contingency plan have we?" Brown pointed to his war table where the chess pieces were still laid out and pointed to 8 white pawns, 2 knights and a castle. "These," he said. "Represent our 8 masquerading prisoners, Wenge, Wine and you Tuscan-Red. That's 11 of my finest and although a tough call you all need to be ready as we".......Brown paused and changing his emphasis growled. "As I, dive from the top of the point with the aim of landing on top of the tyrant." "But the fall could kill you." Grace cried out. Brown just glared and barked loudly. "Look Grace if Black lands then we must take the fight to him and perhaps the strength in numbers and surprise may well over power him. His key strength is the ability to fly and if I manage to drop on him to weaken that ability then so be it. Whatever happens the time has come for us to make a stand."

Tuscan-Red saluted, smartly turned and exited to pass on his orders. George eyed Brown with great respect. They both knew that the intended fall would inflict more damage to Brown than it would to the armour plated body of Dragon Black. Brown continued issuing orders and with steely cold eyes viewed the three before him. "All of you get some rest, I fear tomorrow is going to be a very long day."

As the early morning sun rose, generating increasing warmth as the morning progressed; three children hidden from obvious view were checking their equipment at Volcano Peak. Zach had been asked by George to see if he could see the lenses, fuses or the hole in the ground holding the Extinguisher and makeshift gun barrel. It took Zach a little while but eventually he made out the feint lines of the fuse runs and with the help of light glistening off the chrome lens holders, the sighting mechanism. Grace, seeing that the reflection of light from the lense holders may betray their existence had an idea. "I recall there was a tar-like liquid substance in one of the jars we brought up. I think it would be a good idea to paint the edges to prevent them from glistening in the sun." "That's a good idea Grace; I'll go and get it." Volunteered Zach and before anyone could say yes or no, he was off. "Whew, I don't know where he gets his energy from do you?" Grace laughed. George watched as Zach disappeared from sight. "One thing you can say is that he is enthusiastic and always wants to please, he is a real asset." Grace with a proud smile on her face agreed wholeheartedly.

The sun was past its peak signifying that the time was fast approaching for Black's routine patrol. Tuscan-Red had fully briefed his dragon troops together with the eight dragons still pretending to be prisoners. The prisoners' bodies had been daubed with a red waterproof liquid that from a distance looked as though they had suffered terribly from whippings and beatings. In addition their skins had been rubbed with sticky volcanic ash making them appear very bedraggled and worn. To add a little more effect they had all gone through an exercise of face pulling to look forlorn and hurt.

The preparation was well thought out and within a couple of hours Brown's dragons acting as the 'Dragon Guards' saw the large shadow of Dragon Black as he appeared over the high cliffs above them. Black circled for a brief moment then flew a few hundred metres out to sea. Tuscan-Red raised his tail and flicked it towards the rear of Dragon Tango's neck. Tuscan-Red's aim was amazingly accurate falling short by just 5 millimetres from connecting. Tango let out a well rehearsed yell rearing his head up high as though in acute pain. Dragons Wine and Wenge let out blasts of their flame that from a distance gave the impression they were forcing their prisoners to move faster.

Dragons Tool-Box, Mango and Apple-Red, flames rippling over their rears stumbled as they appeared to be forced into deeper water where earlier large boulders had been placed and now could just be seen protruding from the murky water. Black silently approached diving lower as he eyed all beneath him. As he came closer for a better view, Tuscan-Red held his breath and lowering his head to avoid the gaze of Black again cracked his tail over the heads of the two dragons nearest to him. Black swooped lower and then in a climbing right hand turn, speedily soared high into the sky, to continue his patrol. He had a wry smile on his evil face as he thought how well his guards were doing. But, Black halted his climb. Something was wrong.

Tuscan-Red watched as Dragon Black flew off into the distance but just as he was about to relax, cold fear raced up his long spine. Black had turned he was coming back. Tuscan-Red quickly scanned the scene and took a gasp. Dragon Wenge's partridge pattern reddish brown tail could be clearly seen through the washed off dust that earlier had changed his appearance. Tuscan-Red realised that Black had probably noticed that one of his guards was of a different colour; he had no time to lose. Tuscan-Red shouted to Wenge to move well out of sight of the approaching Dragon Black. "Quickly, get to the cliff's edge and quickly roll on the ground." Wenge heard the shout as he realised his camouflage had been compromised and charged for the shore.

Black slowly descended, quizzically peering at the scene ahead of him. There were the eight prisoners showing severe wounds, cuts and abrasions. There was his officer in charge and there was........Black held his gaze on the one dragon who was whipping his tail towards the prisoners, but where was?

Black was just about to land when from the bottom of the cliff face cave spied his third Guard. Wenge took the initiative and seeing Dragon Black approach stood to attention and saluted and as he did so let out a small blast of flame signifying respect. Wenge out of sight had quickly covered his body with a mixture of sand and volcanic fine ash and now just looked as though he was somewhat tired and unkempt. Black responded to Wenge's salute and fired a huge blast of yellow and red flame high into the sky as he swooped past.

Black did not see anything out of place but still had the feeling that there was something. He circled once more and then to the relief of all behind him, disappeared into the distance.

Hidden from view overlooking the entire scene was a much relieved Dragon Brown and three children. "That was too close for comfort," whispered Grace. George with his customary nod agreed. Dragon Brown licked his dry lips; he had been ready to pounce but was more than relieved that everything had gone according to plan.

deep intake of breath as he came to what he considered the most important and probably most dangerous task.

"Private Zinwaldite, Dragon Red and I will attack from the rear to specifically overpower Black. He will be disorientated by the pyrotechnics and restrained by the tightened chain placed around his tail by young Zach." Brown looked up as Grace and Zach now entered the room. They also had overheard his briefing and knew the importance of showing their total support and agreement with the attack plan. Dragon Brown continued to bark out instructions and orders as an anxious Grace, quietly sighed.

"I think we had better leave for Volcano Peak and re-check everything, don't you?" Zach was the first to respond grabbing a rucksack containing water, some food and the all important box of matches he had removed earlier from Grace's bag. "Wow, it's a good job you brought these Grace, or we could have had problems lighting the fuses." Grace didn't reply, she had other, more important thoughts, racing through her head. Within a few hours they would be in the middle of a war zone, she now was solely focussed on the safety of her brothers.

George had been listening and noting down all of Brown's instructions decided the time had come for them to leave. "OK let's go. Dragon Brown we have a great deal to do if we are to be in position before the first of Black's guards arrive. Once the prisoners are in front of Dragon Black we will wait for Black's order to commit the rubbish that has been placed on the execution slabs, to be thrown into the volcano. That will create sufficient noise and distraction for Zach and Joel to move into operation. Then, Grace and I will wait for Dragon Onyx's customary ordering for silence. At that point, Black usually tosses his head back and lets out a blast of flame. That's when we will fire the dart." George then clarified. "Well, we will release the dart, but only if we are 100 % sure of hitting our target."

The three left the dragons finalising their tactics and headed for Volcano Peak. The tall plinth from where Dragon Black would perch looked formidable as the sun approached its mid point in the sky. The two roped off lines leading to the front of the plinth were checked for tightness so that no stray dragon foot would touch any of the fuse lines running along their sides. Zach checked each of the sight lenses and mirrors making sure they were clean and had not been moved. Grace checked the fireworks making sure they were thinly covered with dust to blend in with their surroundings. Some boxes were showing as their covering had been blown away by the occasional breeze that swirled round from the heat of the volcano's mouth.

George walked over towards the 6 o'clock positioned plinth protruding into the volcano's mouth recalling the death sentence passed on him by Dragon Black some two years earlier. The unbearable heat emanating from the gaping hole, together with wisps of hot bluish smoke, rose high into the air creating shimmering images as he peered across its wide expanse. George shuddered as he thought that nothing could survive being thrown or pushed into the fiery furnace below.

Grace, glancing at her watch, shouted across to George. "Is there anything else we need to do?" George nodded and walked towards the covered hole in the ground close to the rear of the plinth that would be Zach's hideout for the next few hours. "Yes, we need to check that there are no kinks in the chain that Zach will wrap round Black's tail. Make sure it is firmly fixed to those boulders and will not part and Zach, you need to take cover."

Grace patted Zach on his back in encouragement. "You have an important role to play in Dragon Black's capture, we are counting on you." Zach said nothing but winked and as he kicked some more dust concealing the chain lying in a curl close to the tall ceremonial plinth, hurried across to his hideout hole and jumped in. "Cover me up please, and both of you get to your hideout, we have little time left."

The streets of Draegonia were emptying fast as dragons made their way to Volcano Peak. Some moved in subdued silence, knowing they were to witness the trial and ultimate death of innocent dragons held on trumped-up charges.

Dragon Blue, together with his two officers, assisted by Dragons Red and Vegas-Gold, had finished placing thin rings to the left rear leg of each of the dragon prisoners. The rings had a round metal eye through which a thin chain was passed interlinking all dragons with the ends of the chain held by Dragon Blue's two officers. They were now positioned front and rear of the line. Joel, still looking as though he had been severely tortured and too ill to walk, was perched high up on Blue's back. The convoy of dragons was ready to make the arduous journey up to Volcano Peak and the eagerly waiting, Dragon Black.

Dragon Black, perched high up on his ceremonial granite like plinth, placed high on top of a smooth, almost round very tall rock, was eagerly waiting. From his vantage point he surveyed all beneath him. To his immediate left and right stood a total of eight of his loyal Elite Guards regaled in tabards carrying the motif of Dragon Black. The Elite Guards stood motionless, their blood-red eyes fixed on the gathering of Draegonian Dragons now being crammed into the spectators' area to Black's right. Immediately in front of Black, was the roped cordoned off channel where the prisoners were to be marched into to face their ordeal.

To Black's left running up a slight slope could be seen the edge of the Volcano's mouth and the 12 execution slabs containing items to be cast into the furnace below. Close to each slab were smaller boulders with iron rings where the condemned would be shackled. Lining either side of the cordoned route were equally spaced dragons wearing tabards, but of a slightly different colour, signifying their lower rank. These were the young dragons who recently had been forcibly conscripted into Black's growing army.

The air was now alive with grunts and growls from the dragon spectators who were all suffering in the heat of early afternoon sun. Black, moving his head from side to side studied all before him, spitting out repetitive violent blasts of red hot flames, high into the air adding to the stifling heat of the occasion. Black peered into the distance towards the city studying the rough track where the prisoners would soon appear. He snarled and growled his eyes red with hatred as he planned the demise of those he considered were threats and traitors. As he let out one more blast from his evil razor toothed mouth a sly grin could be seen.

His eyes had focussed on a little human who was tightly strapped on top of Dragon Blue who was closely following the convoy of prisoners. Black pointed a claw towards Dragon Onyx who held the position of Clerk to the Dragon Court. "Onyx," commanded Black. "Call for silence and order the fuelling of the furnace." The dragon spectators all turned their heads towards the 12 execution plinths as four Elite Guards, using long poles pushed the collection of washed up items into the volcano's voluptuous smoky mouth. Red and yellow flames shot high into the sky, the enormity of the heat generated forcing the Elite Guards to fall back. The congregation of dragons murmured and growled knowing that the actions were the prelude to the death sentence. Black smiled, he had awakened the volcano from its slumber.

Black growled at Onyx to establish order. Dragon Onyx, with an appearance and attitude of authority stood up from his previously crouched position and bellowed. **"Order, order, quiet**, the court is now in session."

Onyx waited for a hush to descend and then returned to his crouched position close to the wide eyed dragon spectators who gazed in some trepidation as each of the prisoners came into view. Six dragon prisoners, headed by Dragon Cerise entered the cordoned off corridor and stood two abreast directly in front of the plinth where Black's fearsome silhouette against the bright sun overshadowed them.

Vegas-Gold carefully lifted Joel from Blue's back and laid him down on the rough ground to the rear of the dragon prisoners, just out of Dragon Black's line of sight. Blue, earlier that morning had briefed his officers and now as planned, they were taking their positions to the rear of the prisoners. From Black's perspective it appeared that they were there to prevent any of the prisoners from escaping. In reality, they were strategically positioned to protect Joel, who now out of sight, was slowly pulling and removing the single chain linking all the imprisoned dragons together.

Black, oblivious to what was transpiring, looked across and nodded to Dragon Onyx. Onyx once again stood and called for order and read out the charges being brought against the six dragons and one small boy. The closing question Onyx was heard to demand was. "How do you plead?" The on looking spectacle of dragons murmured as they discussed amongst themselves the prisoners' fate. Dragon Onyx thumped his tail on the hard ground and once more shouted for order and silence. Black tossed his head back and roared in anger. Red, Yellow and Blue flames blasted from his wide open mouth and lowering his head down he glared at the prisoners before him. He again tossed his head back and bellowed. "They plead **GUILTY, GUILTY,** as indeed they are."

CHAPTER 34

Black's Revenge

George and Grace lifted the thin sheet of wood covering the hole where they were positioned eagerly waiting their chance to fire both the dart and ignite the fuses leading to the fireworks. George had been using the binoculars to focus on the hidden mirror that reflected the sights aimed along their makeshift barrel to where Dragon Black was perched. Grace followed the procession of chained dragons as they slowly moved along the roped corridor to take up their positions in front of an animated Dragon Black.

George was worried, he found it difficult to see Black's throat reflected in the sights and when it was, it was only for a split second. "Grace, I think this is going to be far more difficult than we envisaged, Black doesn't stay in one position for any time and when his throat does come into my sights I fear by the time I pull the lever and fire the extinguisher to propel the dart, he will have moved." Grace understood the problem. She had been watching events but offered encouragement. "Look George, the dragon prisoners have only just arrived I am sure you will get your opportunity just keep your eyes on the target and above all, when you do decide to pull the lever, let me know and I will light the fuse."

On the other side of the plinth just as Dragon Onyx was bellowing for the first time for silence, Zach had carefully slid back the covering of his dugout and pulled himself from its cramped hole. He slowly slid on his stomach towards the concealed chain. He quietly picked up the loose end and slid even more slowly to where Dragon Black's tail was trailed idly along the ground. Every so often Black's tail would ripple giving the appearance of the tracks of a small roller coaster. Zach passed the chain under a convenient gap and waited. Sure enough the tail of Black straightened out allowing Zach to reach across and return the chain's end to its lower links. Using an old sea chest padlock he connected the links, locking them tightly together. Zach rolled quickly away back towards his hide hole and with a big sigh of relief slumped in.

Zach's brave feat had been observed by Corporal Umber, Private Wenge, Tango, Apple-Red, Goldenrod and Mango. They had all taken up, well out of sight, strategic positions ready to defend Zach if required.

Dragon Brown, Private Zinnwaldite and Dragon Red were also hidden from view waiting for the all important signal to grab Black. None could do anymore, than just wait.

George continued to peer through the binoculars holding them with one hand his other firmly grasping the lever with the taught wire stretched and connected to the firing mechanism of the extinguisher. Grace held onto the box of matches ready to strike one held match poised to light the main fuse. This connected to individual lines leading to the individual explosive charges.

George heard Onyx shout "How do you plead?" Through the reflections within the mirror, George spied Black's throat coming into view. George whispered for only Grace to hear. "Ready" and squeezing the lever, started to pull it towards him, but abruptly stopped. Black's head had turned from view. Grace thinking that ready meant light the fuse struck a match that immediately went out and in her panic she dropped the box.

George heard another order for silence from Onyx and again missed an opportunity to fire the dart as Black quickly lowered his raised head towards the prisoners. Grace fumbled on the floor and grabbed the match box picking up a couple of matches that had fallen from it. She violently struck them on the side of the box and lit the fuse. George shouted "Not Yet Grace." But as he did so Black's head could be seen to rise up again and his throat come into full view within George's firing sights. George wasted no time and as he heard the words of "Guilty, Guilty" from an irate Dragon Black, yanked hard on the lever.

None of the dragons surrounding Black heard the fire extinguisher being fired. None saw the dart as it was propelled at great speed from the barrel aimed at Black's throat. None saw the tip of the dart penetrate the soft folds of his throat skin and none saw the slight flinch by Black who thought he had been stung. By what he had been stung or how he had been stung, Black had no idea. But what he did know and did see, initiated great anger.

Dragon Cerise was the first to realise the dart had not only been fired but had hit its target. She bellowed and fired a blast of flame at two of the nearest conscripts. The other dragon prisoners followed suit and quickly had all the conscripts under control fearing that any move they might make would be their last.

Black yelled out an order at the same time fired a blast of ferocious red hot flame catching Dragon Iceberg full on and turning him into a carbon replica of his forma self. The Elite Guards merged into a formidable line in front of Black and simultaneously fired blasts of flame at Cerise's team. Two more dragons fell down injured as they returned fire. Then there was a sound of six heavy battle hardened dragons entering the fray as Tuscan-Red, Private Wine, Wild Watermelon, Hot magenta, Toolbox and Candy attacked forcing the guards into three smaller, more manageable groups.

Black realising that this was a major attack and that his Elite Guard was not having things their own way spread out his enormous wings and soared into the air and as he did so fired yet another blast of his awesome fire power, severely wounding Dragon Tool-Box and Candy.

All of a sudden Black was yanked back. Something was fixed to his tail and before he had time to think he splattered back down onto his plinth. Black's anger was now full on. He could see that more dragons had appeared from behind him led by Dragon Brown who was now within his range to turn into charcoal. Black took a deep intake of breath and bellowed firing the largest, hottest, and most powerful flame he could possibly muster, aimed directly at Dragon Brown.

Brown saw Black's flame appear from his wide open mouth being projected towards him but as it did so the tail end of the flame became weaker and before the flame reached Brown, it went out. Black had 'Flame Out'.

The Elite Guard however had not lost theirs and they were inflicting considerable damage when all hell broke loose. Several huge explosions were heard sending shock waves all around. A terrified Dragon Black, realising he had lost his flame, once again flew into the air, forcing his might against the chain that was securely tethering him to the ground. Bright lights appeared either side of the plinth with a range of thunder claps exploding from a series of missiles shooting up from all around, some narrowly missing Dragon Black by only a few centimetres. Black strained and heaved. He knew that he was useless without an ability to shoot flame, his primary aim now was to fly to safety, but the chain locked to his tail was preventing this. One more heave, but it still did not break. Then the unthinkable happened. From the enveloping smoke beneath him a series of flares and powerful rockets shot up and as they did so exploded with tremendous force all around him.

Black was taken fully by surprise and toppled backwoods, the chain holding his tail now wrapping itself around his right wing.

Black was completely out of control, fell and as he passed through the thickening smoke, saw the red hot bubbling molten rock of the furnace beneath. He was heading for the centre of the Volcano. The few Elite Guards remaining paused from their fruitless task. They grimaced as the weight and speed of Black's fall made the chain go taught, pulling him towards the edge of the Volcano, before the weakest link finally snapped, sending him to his death.

Black's surviving four Elite Guards looked on in total amazement as their leader plummeted to oblivion. They immediately surrendered and were taken into custody by Dragons Brown, Red, and Blue. The fight was over, the smoke from the pyrotechnics began to clear and in the carnage surrounding them several dragons loyal to Black could be seen sprawled across the open ground.

Brown joined by Dragon Gold, lined up his troops and congratulated each of them on a job well done. The air was hot lifting the last remnants of smoke high into the air revealing four very grubby but relieved smiling children. Brown, still facing his dragon troops called for attention, turned and saluted them. Grace blushed, George smiled, and Joel looked down in embarrassment whilst Zach puffed out his chest. All four listened intently to Dragon Brown's warm accolades. "We have a great deal to thank our visitors for. It is they who gave us encouragement and put their own lives at risk to overthrow Dragon Black. They demonstrated the importance of team work, looking after each other, friendship and loyalty. Without their effort, commitment and belief I am sure we would not have had sufficient confidence to stand up to Dragon Black. I am sure that without their ingenuity we would never have had the means to tackle him, we salute you." Dragon Gold pulled from a fold in his skin and placed round his neck the gold chain of office. "As Mayor of Draegonia I award you freedom of the city." The impromptu ceremony was witnessed by dragons arriving from all directions that some minutes earlier had fled to safety. There were smiles, happy grunts and growls as the realisation hit that Black was no more.

Clearing up the war zone took considerable time with Dragon Red's truck making frequent trips to and from Dragonia's Hospital carrying the wounded. Those who had died (including the Elite Guard) were given a ceremonial volcanic cremation with full honours.

As dusk approached and Volcano Peak returned to some normality Dragon Red's truck made the last journey of the day transporting four very exhausted children back to the city. Crossing the bumpy rough terrain George and Grace had but one thought, now that Black was gone their work complete, how were they to return back home to tell their parents the story of Blacks' Revenge.

CHAPTER 35

The End

The following day, Dragon Blue was the first to rise. His first task was to feed the four Elite Guard dragons now held in the cells awaiting a proper trial to be held in the Great Hall, the traditional place for administering justice. Blue considered that those of the four who had not committed any real crimes other than defending Dragon Black in the course of their duty, would perhaps be given somewhat lenient sentences, where as the two who he saw assist Black charcoal the deceased Dragon Russet, would receive the justice they deserved.

Still in deep thought Blue did not hear the clatter of four pairs of feet as George, Grace, Joel and Zach entered the office. They had rested overnight in Dragon Blue's spare room and having not eaten for many hours were eager for breakfast. Zach picked up a coconut shell and filled it with water, Grace and George grabbed some fruit and started eating whilst Joel deliberated unable to make his mind up as to what he would have. Joel was just about to ask for some chocolate covered cornflakes (he was back to form knowing that there were none) when Dragon Grey entered.

"Good morning Blue and a very good morning to you four," he said. I am pleased to report that all the injured dragons delivered to me yesterday will make full recoveries but that the severest of burns will probably take a couple of months to fully heal. I understand from Vegas-Gold and Dragon Red that the battle at Volcano Peak was very fierce." Blue nodded and gruffed in response, not wishing to be reminded of the carnage and loss of life. Before Grey had chance to ask more, Grace sprang up. "How is Dragon Pink, are her wings improving, is she in any pain?" Grey answered with a warm smile. "I am very pleased to tell you that Dragon Pink is making a remarkable recovery. Her wounds from the operation have healed well and her exercising regime is making her wing muscles stronger than before." The three boys listened without saying a word; they were too busy finishing their breakfast. "Can we see her then?" Grace asked. Grey let out a huge dragon laugh. "Of course you can, but I suggest you visit her later this morning after she has completed her exercises." Blue became a little irritated. "Look Grey, it's a delight to chat with you but I have four charge sheets to write up, a report of events for the Dragon Council and four little ones to take care of, so perhaps you would let me get on?" Grey said no more, turned and with a slight scowl on his face departed. "You were a little rude Dragon Blue," sighed Grace. "Dragon Grey has been very helpful and supportive and I think should be treated with a little more respect." Blue rolled his eyes, looked up to the cave's cavernous roof and just nodded in agreement, he knew she was right.

Having finished their breakfast George and his cousins settled down to discuss a very important issue and probably their greatest challenge. How were they to get off the island and return home? "So, any ideas?" George asked. "We could use the life raft," cried out Joel. "How about making a raft?" offered Zach. "Oh don't be so foolish you two," an exasperated Grace sighed. "A raft or even the dingy would not get us far and in any event we have no idea which ocean or sea in the world we are in." "OK, OK you lot," interjected George. "We have a problem so let's list all the things, no matter how stupid or strange they might sound, to see if any might work." Blue was not listening; he had much to do and headed for the cells, leaving the four with the dilemma, of how they were to return home.

Dragon Pink was finishing off her two hour exercise. The bandages had been removed from her and the tiny scars where incisions had been made were almost healed. Her wings seemed to have more strength in them and the rest and exercise had certainly done her a great deal of good. The time, she thought, had come for her to get some fresh air and as no one was about to argue with her, she set off towards the hospital exit.

Entering the hospital courtyard she met Dragon White who explained the events of the previous day and the reasons why so many dragons were visiting the hospital. "Grey has not told me any of this White, are you really telling me that Black has met his just end?" White explained in detail how the attack had progressed, those who were unfortunately killed and that the four children were safe. "I am so pleased," Pink cried, fluttering her wings. As she did so her body lifted slowly into the air. "Well done Pink you obviously have not lost the ability to fly, all you need now is a bit of training to be more proficient." Pink gave White a slight grin and chuckled. "It's a good job Dragon Black is not here anymore to see how he was duped."

"You're up and looking well Dragon Pink!" "Thank you Grace," she replied. "We saw you fly a few feet from the ground. Is your strength fully returned, can you fly long distances?" George enquired. "Yes," shouted out Joel. "Are you strong enough to get us back home?" "That was my suggestion," an indignant Zach added. Pink blushed in embarrassment but it made little difference to her already pink complexion. "I am so sorry, but I tried flying before the operation without much success. My sense of direction is awful and I do tend to lose control ending up crashing into things." The four, together with Dragon White found it difficult to suppress their laughter.

Grace could see Pink's feelings were obviously being hurt told everyone to stop laughing and turning to Pink gave her a cuddle. "Don't worry Pink, you just get yourself fit and when the time is right you will be able to fly without any difficulty In the meantime we will return to the Dragon Blue to consider other ways to return home."

Pink and White watched as the four disappeared from view. "Pink," asked White. "Have you any magical aids to return the children? You helped to get them here; you must have something to get them back to their families!" Pink, thought long and hard and then with a glint in her eye told Dragon White that she had an idea. She explained that whilst she had no potion or spell that could directly return the children home, she did have an idea that would require White's help and that she needed to return immediately to her own cave. "So let's go," cried White. "There's nothing here to stop you and I will inform Dragon Grey of your decision to check yourself out." Pink required no more encouragement and closely followed by a quizzical Dragon White, headed for her pink cave.

It was early evening that the four received a message delivered via the weird but efficient telecommunications system linking most caves. Dragon Blue informed them that they were urgently needed to be at Pink's cave where she was waiting for them. Grace and George held the view that something terrible may have had happened. Joel jokingly suggested that her wings had fallen off. Whereas Zach believed she had perhaps found a way for them to leave the island.

The four arrived outside the pink door of the pink cave of Dragon Pink. They did not have to knock as she had been looking out for them and opening the entrance door, invited them in. "OK Dragon Pink, what's the urgency? Are you ill?" "No Grace," she replied. "But I do have a solution to your problem however we have little time for my plan to work." The four looked at each other in disbelief. Did they hear correctly? Did Pink say she had a plan? Pink could see the looks of surprise called out to Dragon White who appeared from a corridor that led to the many smaller caves.

"Dragon White has been assisting me to find a way to use one of the many magical potions and spells handed down to me by my ancestors. We unfortunately could not find a second wish spell or a spell to carry you back home but we did find something helpful." Dragon White moving closer to the four children offered an explanation. "You see there is one way to get you back home but it relies on the ability of a dragon that can fly. Pink is the only dragon but her wings are only just strong enough to lift her off the ground and certainly not powerful enough to carry four grown up children like you."

"But we know that," said George. "Yes," cried Grace. "We are fully aware that Pink is still too young to fly very far and certainly not so soon after her operation carried out to fool Dragon Black." Pink held up her paw in a bid for silence. "But there is a way," she said. I have the Draegonia Wizard Book of Chants and found two spells that could be used. However, they have to be used at the time of the full moon and tonight will be the last opportunity for some time." Pink could see from the expressions of the four that they wanted to hear more. "The spells and potions will do two things. The first, for a period of three to four days, will make my wings stronger. The second spell." Pink stopped talking and for the first time looked very concerned. "The second potion and spell allows me to make you four smaller. You will be one fifth of your size making it possible for me to carry you. However, the spell of reduction is not designed for human beings and I just do not know how long it would last. If it reversed whilst we were in flight I would not be able to support your weight and you can guess what the consequences could be."

Joel piped up first. "But how long could it last? Suppose we do get back, will we remain at 20% of our normal size for very long?" George scratched his head. "Do you have any idea of any time scale say the shortest time to the longest that the spell would work for?" Pink was just about to answer when Zach clapped his hands together and laughed out aloud. "Just think Grace you would be less than 33 centimetres tall." "I don't find that funny Zach," a bemused Grace replied. George was thinking of all the ramifications and finally brought the chatter to an abrupt stop. "Look, we know that we are unlikely to get off the island by any other means than fly. We also know Pink is the only dragon who in the future would be strong enough to carry us home but that could be months away, or even years. I say we go for it on the basis the reduction spell is not permanent, shall we put our trust in Dragon Pink?" Grace said nothing; she was thinking how she would look being smaller than her next door neighbour's dog! Zach and Joel enthusiastically raised their hands in support and agreement. White moved towards the door and faced the children. "What Pink has not told you is the potion has to be drunk two hours before midnight and the spell has to be carried out beneath the ceremonial plinth at Volcano Peak and we are really short of time."

"Well that' settles it," shouted out George. Pink and you White, go now to Volcano Peak where after we collect a few of our belongings from the police station we will join you." There was no time to lose and as two dragons scampered towards the Volcano, four children sped off to say their goodbyes to Dragon Blue.

The dormant but smoky Volcano which had devoured the body of Dragon Black seemed to be making gurgling noises. The odd thin flame interspersed with whitish smoke could clearly be seen emanating from its cavernous mouth as though it was enjoying a well-earned meal. In the shadow of the plinth cast by the brilliance of the full moon stood two dragons shortly to be joined by four somewhat nervous children carrying back packs and bags. "I am sorry," said Pink."But you won't be able to take those, the spell will only make you and what you're wearing smaller, not anything you may be carrying." "Umph, that was a waste of time carrying all this then," moaned Joel kicking his bag some feet away from him. "Oh don't be such a grump box," responded an exasperated Grace. Pink could see the four were worried and made allowances for their unusual irritability. It was important for them not to be enthused about being made small. "Please drink this." Pink handed each of them a small mauve and pink twisted bottle containing a bright luminous liquid. Zach took a smell and screwed up his face. Joel was just about to say he was not going to drink it when he caught the stern gaze of his sister and thought better of it. All four swallowed their individual potions and waited. "Nothing has happened," yelled Zach. Pink just grinned and stood in front of the four. In her paws held tightly by her claws was a 'Dragon Swaft." This was the equivalent to a magician's wand but shaped in the form of a wooden thin flat rod made up of several layers. Pink waved the Swaft over the four and under her breath chanted.

"When the time is right and the moon is full
When potions digested and are tummies full
Let all within the spell who stand up to be tall
See for themselves to have become very small."

Earlier Pink had taken her potion and cast the spell to make her wings stronger. As she now completed the reduction chant, she felt a tingle in wing tips. "Goodness," growled Dragon White. "Your wings are growing Pink." Sure enough Pink's wings became bulkier, wider and slightly more muscular. The four children just stared as the events unfolded. They too began to feel peculiar and one by one started to shrink and as they did so they were heard to speak in very high pitched voices. Joel pulled from his pocket the one and only item he thought would be essential for the trip back. It was the compass retrieved from his sister's hold hall. "Well done, screeched Grace in a voice that resembled one of the 'Chip Monks'. "That was shrewd thinking." "Look at you," laughed Zach, pointing towards a miniature George. George said nothing but beckoned Dragon White to lift them up and place all four of them on the back of Dragon Pink. White gently lifted and placed the four close to the neck of Pink where a small harness had been conveniently fitted for them to hold on to. Joel looked at the small compass tightly clutched in his sweaty hand and also in a high pitched voice shouted out to Pink. "We need to head east and once we find land determine exactly where we are before setting a final course for home.

White, tear in her eyes waved as Pink and her tiny cargo soared into the stillness of the moonlit sky. As she watched them all disappear into the distance she heard a muffled groaning sound which seemed to be coming from the volcano. No, it was no more than the gurgling of molten lava beneath. But there it was again an echoing groan interspersed with the odd sounding grunt and groan. Then, silence.

White waited a few seconds in the silence broken by the sound of an owl as it passed overhead. Still unsure of what she thought she had heard White slowly turned away from gazing at the sparkles of light and wispy threads of smoke and trotted back towards the City of Draegonia.

Out of earshot, halfway down the hot and rugged cavernous volcano hole, a narrow ledge jutted out over the molten lava that lay deep below. Behind the ledge set into the jet black, glistening rock face was a large indentation, hewn out over the centuries, through violent volcanic activity.

Hidden within the shadows created by flames forced up from the orange and yellow molten glare below, was some painful movement, coupled with groans of agony.......................

Was it the Ghost of Dragon Black? Could he have survived? Or was it a trick of light and sound?

What we do know is that even now, maybe it's not.......

THE END.

Postscript

As youngsters leave their early childhood years and enter their teens, their attitudes and outlook often changes. Teenagers by default become more confident, willing to take on challenges that many observers may see as beyond them. Young adults (that is what they are growing into) however, become stronger both in character and confidence, especially when given responsibility, an aim and the authority to make decisions.

The four children decide to return to Draegonia displaying courage and loyalty. A natural leader evolves not purely on age or experience but by the authority invested upon him by way of a wish card. During the adventure, team effort and individual skills combine to develop a plan. The children however demonstrate that no plan succeeds unless there is a clear goal to focus upon. All plans require flexible strategies if they are to adapt to changing circumstances or needs.

Different societies or groups often require understanding and appreciation that their views differ from yours. The four have learnt to listen, not jump to conclusions and be more understanding not only with each other but also those outside their group.

Courage and determination of course is not enough and clearly having absorbed all they have learnt at school, the four are able to adapt, build and create solutions and material aids to assist their friends.

Lessons they have learnt from Book 2.

1) Education is not a chore but a necessity for later life.
2) Listening to others is a skill to develop as opposed to forcing your own point of view.
3) Evil never wins in the long term and should always be opposed.
4) Other civilisations have much we can learn from as they themselves learn from us.
5) Planning is only effective if you have a strategy to make it work and an overall goal to aim for.
6) Working as part of a team is more effective than trying to do everything on your own.
7) Explaining and discussing and being willing to be flexible is a communication skill.
8) Respecting others is not just about your elders but also respecting <u>each</u> other.
9) No one expects any more than you doing your best.

Always try, try and keep trying. Achievement of what seemed impossible is simply developing a new skill through repetition. And remember, there is always someone who will be willing to help you.

Glossary

Dragons of Draegonia - Dragon Black's Revenge

Dragon Black

The scariest self appointed leader and most feared dragon of all time. Black is the largest and most powerful of all dragons, uses his long steel like tail, both as a lethal weapon and symbol of his unquestioning authority. Black sports two enormous powerful wings and is the only dragon that has been able to fly. His threatening appearance is further enhanced by two fiery red piercing eyes. Dragon Black is one dragon never to be crossed. Having been banished from Draegonia (Book 1 The Adventure Begins) he seeks to regain his ability to spit flame, planning to wreak havoc once more on the inhabitants of the Island of Draegonia.

Dragon Gold

Dragon Gold is Mayor and part time Judge of Draegonia. Gold is a little pompous, full of his own self importance, a worrier, cautious, honest and absolutely fair. He used to waddle due to a rather fat stomach and little exercise but through a series of worrying events becomes fitter and more agile and assumes the role as one of the leaders of Draegonia's resistance movement.

Dragon Blue

Dragon Blue is head of the Draegonia Dragon Police Force. He too is a little on the plump side, stern faced and fastidious when administering and implementing the full letter of the law. Dragon Blue is totally loyal, a stickler for accuracy tending to want everything orderly and well documented. He rarely takes chances but will consider taking calculated risks if the end justifies the means.

Dragon Red

Head of Draegonia's Fire Service. Dragon Red is very fit and has a good sense of humour. Red does not put fires out but starts them for those dragons that may have lost their flames.

Dragon Brown

Brown was appointed Commander in Chief of the Draegonia Army. He is One of the oldest of dragons. He is strong both in strength and character but can be abrupt and austere. Brown is astute, quick witted and highly respected.

Dragon Green

An envious, jealous dragon, who because of his deceit, lies and devious efforts to command respect, ended up in some hot lava. (Book 1 Chapter 17)

Dragon Yellow

Dragon Yellow, as with most of his relations, is both yellow in colour and nature. He tends to be easily frightened and because of nerves tends to rush and bump into things, especially when he has concerns or his anxiety level is raised.

Dragon White

White is a large female dragon responsible for the environment of South Island. She has a very large mouth and cleans the beach by turning drift wood into ashes with one burst of her ferocious flames. She has a warm smile and helpful nature.

Dragon Cream

Sister to Dragon White who patrols the northern side of the Island also keeping it clear of washed up debris. Like her sister she also has the ability to shoot flames up to ten metres turning everything to dust and ashes in its path. Unfortunately because North Island tends to be colder, wetter and difficult to work she has developed arthritis and is often seen with a look of pain on her round creamy white face.

Dragon Rainbow

Head Waiter of the exclusive Draegonia Rainbow Restaurant. Rainbow is a connoisseur of 'Dragon Wine' and all types of food. Originally from the South of France, Rainbow Dragon communicates with a very strong French accent.

Dragon Pink

Pink is the smallest and youngest of all dragons. She is the friendliest and kindest of all and is the only dragon (apart from Dragon Black) that has not had her wings clipped. She however has been too young to fly but approaching the age of 'Wing Clip'. Dragon Pink has important ancestry and is a direct descendent of a Wizard Dragon and known only to a very few dragons, she has some magical properties.

Dragon Onyx

Onyx is Clerk to the Draegonian Court. He has a distinctive and very loud autocratic voice and a head that never stays still for a moment. When his head rolls one way his eyes tend to go in the opposite direction.

Dragon Smokey-Blue

Smokey-Blue is Draegonia's Chief Technical Dragon. A scientist typified by his large monocle necessary for his weak right eye. Although very intelligent has a habit of staring but not finishing sentences, assuming those around him, have understood his point, without any further explanation.

Dragon Mauve

A self opinionated legal prosecutor who talks in legalise. He has long thin dragon paws that he uses to direct his audience's attention.

Dragon Purple

Dragon Purple is the court's appointed legal defender. He is a slick, smooth talking dragon able to twist witness statements to his advantage. Being shorter than Dragon Mauve he tends to roll back and forth on his hind legs, occasionally standing on the tips of his feet, to gain extra height.

Dragon Grey

Grey is Draegonia's Chief Physician. Dragons rarely become ill thus the Draegonia Hospital is mainly used as a dragon maternity unit and research centre. Grey's main duties are as 'Personal Physician' to Dragon Black and senior surgeon overseeing the 'Wing Clipping Ceremony'. Dragon Black's enforced law called for all dragons on reaching the age of five to have their wings clipped thus preventing dragons from leaving the island. Dragon Grey, had in the past, tried unsuccessfully to rescind the law but did manage to increase the age of clipping from five to Seven Dragon Years. Grey is a very fit dragon, priding himself on good eating habits and exercise. He does appear boring, has little conversational skills and sometimes can be a bit of a bumbler but nonetheless he is very clever.

Twin Lilac Dragons

Brother and sister, the Lilac Twins are Draegonia's environmental engineers commonly known as the refuse disposal duo. They are always seen together with each one finishing the others sentence when they speak. They are the 'Jedward's' of Draegonia and even sport a similar head style.

Dragon Indigo

Indigo is a hard working young dragon holding down two jobs within the Hall of Dragons. He is both the security officer at night and during the day works in administrations. He is full of his own self importance.

Dragon Tuscan Red

A rich red coloured dragon who has been number two to Dragon Brown. Appointed as sergeant Tuscan Red is brave, intelligent and diligent. He is totally reliable and would give his own life to protect Dragon Brown.

Dragon Umber

A deep dark red coloured dragon who is very light on his feet. Appointed as corporal in Dragon Brown's army, Dragon Umber tends to be at the forefront of any action. He is a good strategist, planner and motivator of dragons reporting to him.

Dragon Wenge

Wenge is a Private in the Draegonian army. Wenge has the ability of firing flames further than most dragons. He is powerfully built and moves very quietly for his size.

Dragon Wine

Wine is a member of the family of red coloured dragons. Wine is distinctive for being taller and thinner than most other dragons. His build however make him one of the fastest moving dragons and he holds a' Dragon Gold Medal' for the fastest sprint time.

Dragon Zinnwaldite

Zinnwaldite is a dragon born into one of the elite very wealthy dragon families. Tends to talk in a rather posh dragon accent but decided to join as a private in the Draegonian Army for some fun and adventure. Not interested in any position of seniority and content to do whatever is asked of him. His best friend is Dragon Wenge who has been training him to improve his flame spitting performance. Dragon Zinnwaldite has one other important skill, the ability to see objects clearly, at great distances, especially in the dark.

Dragon Iceberg

Like his colour, Iceberg is cold and unyielding. He has deep blue eyes that stand out of an almost translucent white face, his vivid white torso incongruous to the Island's lush colours of deep greens, blues, yellows and golden browns.

Dragon Dandelion

Dandelion is one of the younger male, yellowish coloured dragons, who related to Dragon Yellow has similar characteristics. He is nervous, hesitant and very unwilling to take chances although easily persuaded. Dandelion's best friend is Dragon Vegas-Gold.

Dragon Vegas-Gold

Vegas-Gold is a lively, very fit, strong dragon who displays great determination. Quick thinking, he has courage of his convictions. He, like his good friend Dragon Dandelion is a 'Conscientious Objector', unwilling to fight or kill.

Dragon Chameleon

Usually seen sporting a reddish orange skin, Dragon Chameleon is the only dragon that has the ability to alter his skin colour, enabling him to blend in with his surroundings, at will.

Dragon Byzantine

A very wealthy, rich purple coloured dragon, who resides in one of the larger dwellings within the caves of Draegonia. He is a dragon of few growls (words) but when he does speak he commands great respect. Byzantine is one dragon that Black fears could rouse the support of others against him.

Dragon Cerise

An unusual pinkish red dragon, Dragon Cerise is one of the very few female dragons who Dragon Brown respects. She has a warm exterior and considered by other dragons to be attractive. Beneath her pleasantries however lies a tough fighting dragon whose ancestors were some of the most famous fighters of all time.

Dragon Ecru

An aristocratic unusual yellowish-brown coloured dragon who has shades of light and dark grey streaks highlighting his muscular body. Dragon Ecru, like all other dragons on Draegonia cannot fly, but he holds the record for the fastest sprint over five miles and able to jump higher than any other dragon.

Dragon Sea-Green

The cousin of Dragon Green (deceased), Dragon Sea-Green has a deep greenish blue hue about him. Running through the family of green dragons is the envious characteristic and unfortunately a characteristic that Sea-Green portrays from time to time. But when given responsibility tends to rise to the occasion.

Dragon Apple-Red

A bright very fit, young, impetuous, glistening red coloured dragon. Apple-Red tends to get himself into difficult situations because he fails to properly listen.

Dragon Candy

Candy is a strong female dragon who like her very best friend Dragon Cerise, does not shy away from confrontation. The two dragons together are a formidable pair.

Dragon Tool-Box

A strong, robust, middle aged, bronze red dragon who has a reputation for being able to obtain anything. Known as a wheeler dealer, Tool-Box is ready to defend himself and his friends at any time.

Dragon Tango

Tango is a small, stubby, dark orange coloured dragon who wanted to join the Draegonia Army one hundred 'Dragon Years' ago but was rejected because he was too young.

Dragon Mango

A swarve smooth talking, eloquent dragon of a yellowish orange hue over a salmon pink thick smooth skin. His appearance however, hides a ferocious temper, when aroused.

Dragon Krugerrand

Krugerrand a cousin to Dragon Gold has a rich, deep dark golden coloured skin and is one of the families of South African dragons who dwell in caves situated on the opposite side of the mountain to the city.

Dragon Russet

Dragon Russet's skin is of a brown colour with a reddish-orange tinge. His family, threatened by Dragon Black, forced him much against his will, into Black's army as officer in charge of one of the prisoner guard units. Russet follows orders inflicting pain under duress for underneath his harsh looking exterior; he is in fact caring and has the greatest respect for Dragon Brown.

Dragon Time

The Island of Draegonia is shrouded in a magical mist. All within the mist live their lives under Dragon Time where time, outside the island's protective shield almost stands still in comparison.

Flame Out

'Flame Out' is a condition known only to dragons. Dragons that lose their ability to spit flames and fire and are unable to reignite them, face severe consequences. *WITHOUT DRAGON FLAMES ALL DRAGONS DIE.*

The History of Pyrotechnics/Fireworks

Classical fireworks originated in China more than 2000 years ago, when a simple experiment mixed saltpeter (Potassium nitrate $KNO3$), sulphur and charcoal.

When heated and dried they formed a black, flaky powder, which the Chinese called 'huo yao' ("fire chemical"), known today as gun powder.

The Chinese were fascinated by this mysterious fire chemical and began experimenting with various materials to hold the powder. Eventually they discovered that a hollow bamboo shoot filled with the fire chemical allowed for a build-up of gas pressure inside. A loud bang would be heard when the shoot was thrown onto a fire. The shoot is now known as the simple fire cracker.

The Chinese believed gun powder had mystical powers that could ward off evil spirits, and was used for weddings and other religious rituals. It was also used for warfare applications including fire arrows and 'ground rats' that scared soldiers and their horses.

Marco Polo took the knowledge from China to the Middle East and European Crusaders took it from there to England. Englishman Roger Bacon realised it was the saltpeter compound that caused the explosion but, realising its destructive potential, wrote his findings in a code which was not deciphered for hundreds of years.

It was European chemists who in 1560 mixed the ratio of saltpeter, charcoal and sulphur that is still used today. The use of fireworks for displays progressed in medieval times with steel and charcoal creating yellows and oranges. Reds, greens and blues followed in the 19th century.